Readers love
B.G. THOMAS

The Real Thing

"…they do say that good things come in small packages. And I think that this story is a *great* thing!"

—Rainbow Book Reviews

"This is a feel good read that I really enjoyed."

—Gay Book Reviews

Do You Trust Me?

"…I am so incredibly happy I picked up this story and recommend it highly for anyone who is looking for a contemporary story with a serious message, a life story and a romance to top it off."

—Love Bytes

"I *highly* recommend this book. It will make you run the gamut of emotions and by the time you finish, you'll feel so happy."

—Joyfully Jay

Winter Heart

"The treasure in this story is Wyatt. I got an unfiltered look into his heart and what I saw is unforgettably beautiful."

—Alpha Book Club

By B.G. Thomas

All Alone in a Sea of Romance
All Snug
Anything Could Happen
The Beary Best Holiday Party
Ever
Bianca's Plan
Blue
The Boy Who Came In From the
Cold
Christmas Cole
Christmas Wish
Derek
Do You Trust Me?
Desert Crossing
Grumble Monkey and the
Department Store Elf
Hound Dog and Bean
How Could Love Be Wrong?
It Had to Be You
Just Guys
With Noah Willoughby: Mele
Kilikimaka
A More Perfect Union (Multiple
Author Anthology)
New Lease
The Real Thing
Red
A Secret Valentine
Soul of the Mummy
Editor: A Taste of Honey
(Dreamspinner Anthology)
Until I Found You

GOTHIKA
Bones (Multiple Author
Anthology)
Spirit (Multiple Author
Anthology)
Contact (Multiple Author
Anthology)

SEASONS OF LOVE
Spring Affair
Summer Lover
Autumn Changes
Winter Heart

Published by DREAMSPINNER PRESS
www.dreamspinnerpress.com

BLUE

B.G. THOMAS

Published by
DREAMSPINNER PRESS

5032 Capital Circle SW, Suite 2, PMB# 279, Tallahassee, FL 32305-7886 USA
www.dreamspinnerpress.com

Blue
© 2017 B.G. Thomas.
The Poem "Big Joy Kyrie" by James Broughton used with permission of Joel Singer, heir to the estate of James Broughton.

Cover Photograph
© 2017 Suntown Photography.
Cover Design
© 2017 Paul Richmond.
http://www.paulrichmondstudio.com
Cover content is for illustrative purposes only and any person depicted on the cover is a model.

ISBN: 978-1-63533-629-0
Digital ISBN: 978-1-63533-630-6
Library of Congress Control Number: 2017902894
Published May 2017
v. 1.0

Printed in the United States of America

This paper meets the requirements of
ANSI/NISO Z39.48-1992 (Permanence of Paper).

Acknowledgments

SPECIAL THANKS to F.E. Feeley Jr. for writing a song for me!

And of course to Noah Willoughby, Chris Scully, C.L. Miles, and Angelia Sparrow for your unbelievable help with research.

Thanks to Andi Byassee, which really goes without saying. I don't know what I would do if I didn't have her at my back. Especially with *Blue*.

Thanks also to Brian Holliday. I mean it, man. Thank you.

Tippy! Thank you so much! You saved me, man. Wow!

And most especially to Lynn. Who saved this book.

CHAPTER ONE

IT WAS a chilly evening. Someone had stolen Blue McCoy's electric blanket, but of course there was no power in the abandoned house on Wyandotte Street. Not lately anyway. So it wasn't like it would have kept him warmer than any other blanket. Luckily he'd hidden an old quilt in the attic. The room he'd claimed had a little door in the ceiling of the closet. The blanket was full of cigarette burns and a couple of ugly stains, but it gave him something to fight the chill.

That and Chewie.

Chewie was a labradoodle, a big, happy brown furry ball of joy—maybe even purebred—that Blue had met the week before. The stray had been matted and dirty and obviously hungry—Blue could see that even with his thick fur—and he had lured the dog to him with half his McDonald's Chicken McNuggets.

Which cost nearly five dollars for only ten, and that wasn't even the meal deal. He would have gone to Wendy's, which was much better—four nuggets for ninety-nine cents—but now that he no longer had a skateboard, it was a hell of a walk, even though it was also a hell of a savings.

Blue went to bed that night still hungry. He supposed Chewie did too. The labradoodle was far skinnier than he was. But there were people way worse off than them. Hell yes!

Tonight, cuddling with the dog helped. They kept each other warm.

Blue had named the dog after the famous sidekick from the *Star Wars* movies, of course. Movies his family had never tired of watching.

Back when things were magic.

That was a long time ago.

Not that his life was bad. He knew he had it better than a lot of people.

He kept finding jobs. Crazy, silly ones that didn't last long, but they paid for the necessities in life.

Selling Christmas trees. He'd been surprisingly good at that one. He'd found that out when he'd done it for charity one weekend. He'd even scored a date with a real cute guy, but it hadn't panned out. He had a knack for selling those trees and found a place that very Monday that paid him.

Dog walker. He'd loved that. He could manage seven dogs at once, even as slim as he was. Dogs liked him. Maybe they sensed a kindred soul in him. He didn't know. All he knew was that he loved dogs, loved other people's cats, loved animals in general. Their love was unconditional. Marilyn Monroe had said it so well. "Dogs never bite me. Just humans." That was sure the truth. She was also rumored to have said "Give a girl the right shoes and she can conquer the world." Wise woman. Just look at what Lady Gaga had done with hers! Especially those gold ones she wore with the short-sleeved red, black, and gold Alexander McQueen at the 2010 VMAs! So *hawt*. Or those green armadillo shoes from the "Bad Romance" video. God. How he'd wanted to see what they'd look like on his own feet. They might even make him as tall as a normal person. But Vans were probably the best he'd ever have. Of course, his were secondhand....

Another crazy job he did now and then was note taker for college students. There were actually kids who would hire him to go to class for them and take notes. Crazy, but oh so cool. He had neat handwriting, which they liked, and he learned shit besides. Lots of shit. Cool shit. Blue knew lots of shit.

Jelly doughnut filler—*that* had been fun.

Dressing up as the Statue of Liberty and standing out on Thirty-Ninth Street in front of a tax place. That one could be rough because some of the days were very cold, and standing so close to the street meant that the wind wasn't broken by buildings and could cut through his thin jacket almost as if it weren't there. But who else could say they'd gotten paid, cash under the table—and wasn't that ironic, considering—for dressing up like Lady Liberty?

He'd picked apples. He'd hitchhiked for three days to do that, and it had been easy to get the job. Everyone cried and boo-hooed that Mexicans were "taking jobs from Americans," but the truth was that most people didn't *want* to do stuff like that. The hours were long, it was monotonous, and the average person would consider it very boring. But Blue liked it. Picking apples allowed him to turn his brain off. His brain could go so fast—so *very* fast. And if he started talking when his brain was going quintuple (or milluple?) speed, then sometimes he couldn't stop. The words would start pouring out of him, and they just wouldn't end. They'd go on and on and on and on and on and on. And then he would suddenly realize what he was doing and be so embarrassed.

But it filled the silence.

The silences.

He picked up a lot of Spanish while picking apples. Even his coworkers were surprised how much he learned.

People thought he was stupid. But he wasn't.

It bothered him that people thought he was some kind of moron, but what was he to do? And sometimes it helped. He learned to let people think he was an airhead. People—especially older men who thought he was pretty—liked airheaded boys. Not that he was a boy. He was twenty-three!

Blue didn't look for handouts, though. He worked; that's what he did. Unlike a lot of people he knew, he found some kind of job.

And he moved through the days, one by one.

He peeled potatoes and washed dishes by the billions.

Painted fire hydrants—recently in South Hyde Park—a *hideous* orange and black.

He'd been a call center rep—he'd liked that job, but they said he talked to the people *too* much. He wasn't supposed to ask them about their kids or if they'd seen the new *Star Wars* movie, and if they liked it or thought it was just a retread of *A New Hope*. His boss didn't even like it when he asked what kind of dogs they had. (And why wouldn't he? The calls he took were for people ordering dog food!) And she certainly didn't like it if he gave them advice on how to get their husbands to pay attention to them. They fired him, and it was just as well, because he didn't have a car and getting there every day had been a bitch.

And of course, there were always the men who wanted… things. "Favors."

Of the… intimate kind.

It had shocked him the first time. When he realized what was happening. "Spend the night with me and I'll feed you and give you a place to spend the night that has air conditioning"—or heat, depending on the time of the year. That was nice!

The next morning Blue had felt a bit sick, though.

But then he thought, *Why not?* It wasn't like he was a whore or anything. He wasn't *charging*. And maybe, just maybe, one of them would want him for something besides his body or his… talent.

Part of the deal, after all, was that he got to spend the night. Sometimes it was even a classy hotel instead of some cheap no-tell motel, and that usually meant at least a continental breakfast of croissants and rolls and muffins and bagels and fruit. At the worst he could expect coffee and those blueberry muffins in the sealed plastic bags (and there usually wasn't anyone watching, so he could pop quite a few of them in his backpack for later and to share with his housemates). If he was really lucky, he could order room service after the guy left to go home to his girlfriend or wife or—surprisingly—husband. Men who had lives where they couldn't be gay (or at least thought they couldn't). Or maybe spouses who wouldn't understand them or, for whatever reason, were unable to give those men what they needed.

Mom said those men used him.

"Like Kleenex! They blow their loads and use you to wipe it up and throw you away!"

Maybe.

Maybe not.

He and the men both got something out of it. He a nice place to stay and maybe a few bucks—not that he charged! He was right up-front about that. Always. "I'm not a hustler!" But if some guy wanted to slip him a little money, it meant he would eat. At least he had the looks that a lot of men seemed to want. He looked young. Much younger than he was. And oh, weren't they relieved when they found out he was legal? So yes, he used it. Used his looks and acted young as well. Let them think he was an airhead. And he survived. Thanked God too that life on the streets hadn't aged him.

The truth was that Blue felt sorry for them. Felt sorry for the men who needed *him*! Usually—although not always—they were men who couldn't face who or what they were. Men who had chosen "safety" in a heterosexual lifestyle and then now and again couldn't stand the loneliness of it one second longer and sought out people like him. Even if it was just for one night.

There was this one regular—afterward the guy would always go into the bathroom and get on his knees and beg his God for forgiveness—who Blue finally had to stop seeing because those prayers made him cry. He couldn't convince the man that God loved everyone. God loved all his children. All the children of the world.

Red and yellow, black and white....

That's what they sang at Blue's grandparents' church. The songs were the only things he'd liked about their church. "This Little Light of Mine" (… I'm gonna let it shine…), "Jesus Loves Me" (… this I know, for the Bible tells me so…), "Zacchaeus" (… was a wee little man, a wee little man was he…), "Kumbaya" (… kumbaya, my Lord, kumbaya…).

Songs he'd liked before everything went *really* bad.

There was another good thing about those hotels. Blue was able to snitch some towels, sheets, little bottles of shampoo, conditioner, and lotion. Stuff like that. He didn't feel guilty about it—well, a little bit about the sheets—because most of those men could afford the extra charges on their credit cards.

What would it be like to have a credit card? Blue wondered. He figured a credit card was something the likes of him would never have.

Blue was not unhappy. He liked his life. It was usually pretty cool. Sure there was some bad stuff. The incident last summer at camp (that had been pretty damned bad). Or the time he'd almost gotten arrested and what he'd had to do for that cop (there had been handcuffs and a trunk involved) to keep himself out of jail. And of course there was what had happened what felt like a thousand years ago when he lost his other half. Nothing would ever be that bad.

But Blue knew how to look for blessings.

Like tonight. It wasn't as cold as it was last night.

And if it was, he knew he could always go to one of the other rooms in the house. Ruby had made it clear that he wanted Blue.

Gavel and Sly said he was always welcome to sleep in between them. He had the night before. That had been a regular three dog night. After they had sex, Chewie had even been welcomed onto the mattress to help keep them warm. So a four dog night.

But tonight Blue didn't want that. He wanted to be alone.

Well, alone except for Chewie.

Hey! He *had* a place to be alone. So many people slept on a park bench or in an alley or under a bridge. He was blessed to have a roof over his head. And he liked the room he had claimed.

He liked the Grateful Dead poster on the wall. He'd found it at a garage sale for a buck, and it was more than he could afford right then, but he remembered his dad had liked them and he wanted it.

He liked the poster for some group called Electric I that had been on the wall already. Blue hadn't been sure who they were, but then Sly had played him some of their music on his iPod—

Hey girl, with your eyes so blue
With your hair let down, can I git wich-u
Can I hold your hand and be your man?
Can I be your boy
Friend?

—and while they weren't the Beatles (who could be?) or even the Backstreet Boys (very cute, especially the oldest one, Kevin Richardson), they weren't bad, not bad at all.

Blue liked the big table he'd made out of an old door and cinder blocks. It held all his stuff: his books and QuikTrip mug and CDs and candles.

He liked his candles. He had a ton of them, and he especially liked the ones that he'd cast from real men's penises. It didn't take much to convince a guy to let him cast his cock to make a candle. Men liked it when a big deal was made over their dicks. And it gave him something to remember them by. It showed that it had really happened. Someone had wanted him for at least a night. Someone had been willing to take the time to let him take a mold of their hard-on. *And* he had the added fun of making sure they stayed hard while the plaster of paris set.

It was sexy. And fun. And silly.

Silly was good.

If only he could get some famous people to let him cast their cocks! Maybe he'd get famous someday because of them. Some lady named Cynthia Plaster Caster—although her real name was Cynthia Albritton—had gotten famous casting cocks way back in the sixties. Rock stars and their road managers. Even Jimi Hendrix. Today she had a museum in New York. And not just Hendrix, who was famous to Blue as the guy whose "'scuse me while I kiss the sky" lyrics sounded like "'scuse me while I kiss this guy." Lots more. A list of names Blue recognized even though he didn't know who most of them *were*. Zal Yanovsky from the Lovin' Spoonful, Ricky Fataar of the Beach Boys (who hadn't heard of them?), Jello Biafra from the Dead Kennedys. And Frank Cook, Richard Cole, Bob Pridden, Danay West, Eddie Brigati, Harvey Mandel, Lee Mallory….

That list went on and on (a list he couldn't help but remember because that's just the way his brain worked). And it was kinda cool to look at all those candles and even cooler to look at his own candles and marvel at how many men let *him* make molds of their dicks. The candles really were… well, gorgeous.

If he had the chance to cast famous cocks, it would be—and as he lay there on the piss-stained mattress it gave him a hard-on to think of them—Justin Timberlake and Adam Levine (oh fuck!) and Bruno Mars and Nick Jonas and Austin Mahone (*ggiiiirl!*) and Jared Leto (*oh!!!*) and Zac Efron (those eyes, those abs, and if there *was* a God, then those pics on the Internet of Zac jacking off were real) and Michael Bublé (whose voice made Blue's skin tingle) and Justin Bieber (a bit of a douche, but he had a *huge* dick) and Adam Lambert and Connor Jacobus of the Districts and Tobias Jesso Jr. and Keith Urban and LennyKravitzandUsherBillieJoeArmstrongZaynMalik—

Chewie began to lick Blue's face in huge, desperate, sloppy doggy kisses, and—*whoa!*—it brought him back to the here and now.

Blue had done it again.

His brain had started going faster and faster, thoughts piling on thoughts, overlapping, going into overdrive so that he didn't know what was coming next. Even without people around for him to try to impress….

Or maybe, as he'd begun to suspect (realize?), it happened so he could fill in the silences.

Maybe he didn't want to be alone tonight after all.

He got up and slipped into his jeans, and Chewie looked at him with big puppy-dog-eyed concern, and Blue said, "Come on, little man, let's go," and the labradoodle was up and at the door, tail wagging in anticipation. Blue put on his purple Converse high-tops (just to be sure; he didn't want anyone taking them) and went to Ruby's room, but he wasn't there. So he tried Gavel and Sly's room, but shit, they already had someone—they were all arms and legs and thrusting butts. Sly grinningly told him to join the party, but Blue wasn't looking for an orgy tonight, only bodies to help keep him warm and feeling less alone. They only had a full-sized mattress anyway, and there wouldn't be room for him after everyone was done.

Blue shook his head, mouthed a "Thank you," and flashed them the "hang loose" sign, and then he took Chewie for a walk. The labradoodle approved of this decision and happily peed on half of Kansas City. Blue bummed a cigarette off a guy walking his own dog—a big shaggy red something—and he and Chewie walked on for a half hour after that, and then it really was just too cold.

He took Chewie home. They climbed into bed, spooned very close, and Blue hoped the weather forecast was right and that warm weather would greet him when he got up. He fell asleep fast and dreamed of better times in much sweeter places.

CHAPTER TWO

JOHN WILLIAMS had first seen the angel six months before on a late autumn day when the leaves were a fiery riot of orange and red and yellow. In fact, he almost hit him. He was backing out of his driveway in his Lexus, and suddenly something, some*one*, rushed behind him—

Damn kids not looking where they were going. Think they're immortal!

—and he slammed on his brakes—

Thank God for the rearview camera!

—and jumped out to see if whoever-the-hell was okay and maybe rip them a new one and….

He froze, electrified.

For one split second, John didn't even know if the kid was male or female. Young, definitely young. John's son was probably older, although they looked nothing alike. Hair so blond it shone white in the morning sunlight, and eyes so deep and such a lovely brown John could fall into them. Mesmerizing, just like an angel would be. Slim, narrow waisted, wearing a hoodie that hid his torso, short, but with the longest legs and a full crotch and—*oh!*—this *was* a man. Quite a young man, to be sure, but very much male.

"Sorry, dude!" the kid exclaimed. "I wasn't paying attention. My bad—totally."

John gulped and tried not to stare, and his upper lip broke out into a sweat.

Move. Do something. Say something. Anything.

"No, no… I.…"

You're acting like an idiot!

"I should've been watching closer," he sputtered.

There. Something.

"Man!" The kid smiled, and John's heart seemed to stop at how dazzling the smile was: beautiful white teeth and sweet dimples and....

Whoa. He's a guy. *Get yourself together!*

"Thank God you were watching! Otherwise I'd be *paste* right now. A big smear in your driveway. A gone kitty. Roadkill, man! Thanks for making sure I'm still breathing."

And John was aware that the young man *was* breathing. Alive. So alive! He couldn't take his eyes off him.

Him. The kid *was* a him.

Not that John wasn't aware that he was sometimes attracted to men, but for God's sake, this kid was hardly a man. Was he even legal? Was he even eighteen? *Get your tongue back in your mouth!*

Then, quite suddenly, the kid leapt forward and threw his arms around John's neck and gave him a kiss on the cheek. An electric jolt flashed through John at the young man's touch. He smelled like mint gum and youthful sweat, and John was immediately aroused, his cock surging to life in his suit slacks, and he blushed, and dammit, what if the kid noticed?

He folded his hands in front of him the second the kid stepped back, but that only served to make him look down, and John hoped, hoped, hoped he was covering things down there. But....

The kid looked back up, and his smile grew ever bigger. Those brown eyes flashed, and he said, "See you 'round. I'm late, I'm late, for a very important date." Then he turned and dashed down the sidewalk after a skateboard John hadn't seen and hopped onto the thing and, with a knowing grin cast over his shoulder, winked, and away he went.

"God. He kissed me."

John looked around desperately—had anyone seen?—and toward the house. Remembered Vivian was gone. Gone for a month today (happy anniversary), and the desperate shock of that impossibility came back *again*, but then....

Then he felt the kiss on his cheek, and it was....

John didn't know what it was.

He reached up to touch the spot and froze, finding that he didn't want to do anything to make the ghostlike tingle that still rested there go away.

A boy kissed me.

It was one of the most erotic moments of his entire life.

John stood there for he didn't know how long, and when he finally realized it and told himself once more to *Get it together* and got back in his car, he wiped his mouth with the handkerchief in his suit pocket, backed out of the driveway—*carefully this time, for God's sake!*—and headed to work.

THAT NIGHT—

(the one-month anniversary of Vivian leaving him)

—he ate a small steak he made on the grill on the island in his kitchen (he was just getting a grasp on cooking for one) along with some leftover rice and a third of a premade salad he'd gotten with pizza the other day from Papa Murphy's. He had a glass or two (or three) of wine and watched some television (sort of—he marveled that with so much to watch on Netflix, he couldn't find anything he could stay focused on), and then, without warning, the angel came to mind.

That hair—it was hard to tell in morning sunlight if it was natural—and those brown eyes and that smile and those dimples and those flashing white teeth and the amply stuffed crotch of his well-worn jeans and....

No!

John shook his head and gulped half the contents of his glass.

It was a good wine. He was sure Vivian would love it and thought he should see if she wanted some, and then he remembered, *again*, that she wasn't here anymore. The shock hit once more—it wasn't grief exactly, just a stunning disorientation—and the only good thing he could say about these returning slaps of reality was that, in this case at least, it had gotten him to stop thinking about the kid for a moment.

For a moment.

The angel.

Then the beautiful young man (emphasis on "young") returned to his mind's eye, and he *saw* him jump on that skateboard, saw him look at John over his shoulder and—*God!*—that bottom. Perfect. It put Vivian's to shame, and he had always admitted his soon-to-be-ex-wife's bottom was perfection.

But the kid's!

John closed his eyes, not to try to envision it but to make that image go away.

When was the last time he'd looked at a guy's ass?

At the gym a few months ago.

There had been a client of the bank who came from out of town, and he had asked if John knew where he could work out. John had invited him to be his guest at the Gold's where he was a member and hadn't realized the young man was flirting with him until they went to the locker room afterward. The kid—well, at least this one was more than a kid; late twenties anyway—had announced he needed a steam and a shower and bent over with exaggerated slowness as he peeled off his gym shorts to reveal a beautiful, round, smooth butt.

Later, John had started to tell Viv about what had happened and then couldn't. She would only shake her head and ask him how naïve he really was. Not mean. Just surprised at him, as always. He frequently surprised her, but never in an exciting or romantic way. She would sigh and ask him if the hotel his client was staying at had a gym, and then he would have to admit that it probably did. That the way the guy was undressing—slowly, ever so slowly, unveiling that smooth, muscular ass, lifting one foot and resting it on the bench so that he was practically showing John his asshole—there was nothing else it could have been but an attempt at seduction. John had seen part of his smooth balls hanging down before he forced himself to look away.

How does he know?

Not that John was attracted to the client. He wasn't. The guy was too polished, his nigh-on perfection manufactured rather than natural. But how did the young man know that sometimes John was attracted to men? Had John done something? Implied something with a look or a lingering handshake? He didn't think so, but then he realized that the client had let *his* hand remain ever so subtly in John's. And hadn't he stroked John's palm with a finger as he let go?

John had never slept with a man in his life. Not in college (although he'd had more than a few advances directed his way) or even the normal rutting fumblings with high school friends in the showers after wrestling practice or during a sleepover. (Like the evening when two of his buddies decided it was time to watch porn and jerk off, and he'd gone upstairs to his friend's room and made himself a place to sleep on the floor with a quilt from the end of the bed and his arm for a pillow. The only thing that had been said the next day was a whispered, "Hope we didn't freak you out. We're not gay or anything, man." And John had waved it off and quickly asked if they were going to be watching the Royals game that night, and of course the answer had been yes.)

All the dodging hadn't been because John didn't want to be sexual with those boys. The problem was he *did*. He really did. The very idea made sweat break out across his upper lip, and he knew—*he knew*—that if he had sex with a guy even once, that would be it. It would be like those people who tried crack cocaine or meth just once. He would be addicted forever and never have a chance at a normal, incognito life.

That was what John wanted more than anything. Not anonymity per se, but just to be a quiet part of things. Normal. Like everyone else. The only reason he had the Lexus LS 600h L (and wasn't that a stupid name for a car?) was that Vivian had insisted. She'd wanted him to get the Bentley Bentayga, but it came with a price tag of $230,000 to $300,000, and he couldn't do it—couldn't justify a good two years' income while living in a world that had diseases to cure and starving children and people sleeping in the park not a mile from where they lived. It jarred him to the very marrow of his bones that a half-dozen houses or more could be bought for that kind of money in certain parts of the city.

14

"Honey, there will always be homeless," Vivian had said. That reminded him of the line from *A Christmas Carol* about shelters and surplus population, and he told her so, and she had frozen at that and left the room. He'd felt like shit, because she wasn't a bad person, hadn't deserved the comment. Viv had simply grown up with money and didn't understand what it was like *not* to have it. Couldn't, really. She'd just had so much that she had nothing to compare her life to. Living with him had been the poorest she'd ever been, and they were more comfortable than he'd ever dreamed of being.

What did she ever see in me? he wondered for about the billionth time.

"You were safe, I guess," she said, standing in the foyer with her suitcases, their cockapoo, Moxie, on his leash.

She's taking the dog?

"I love you, John. I do. But I can't take this anymore. I am dying of boredom." Then she winced and ducked her head and apologized again. "I feel like a total shit saying that. But it's true. I'm forty now, and dammit, there are things I want to do and see while I'm still young enough to enjoy them. I don't want to be like my mother, stuck and thinking that what is done is done."

Stuck.

That hurt. Hurt like a knife, if not a sword, because he didn't think he was boring.

Boring.

But how could he be surprised? She'd been saying these things bit by bit, more and more, for years now. He just hadn't been paying attention. Not really.

"I want to go to Carnival in Rio de Janeiro!" she was wont to say. "Or Barcelona." Over the years she had all but begged him to take her to St. Tropez or Amsterdam or Berlin or Mykonos or Paris. "I want to go snorkeling somewhere that just might be dangerous." Or "I want to get a tattoo, even if it's someplace only you would see."

On that day, that last day, she'd said, "We never *traveled*, John. And we have the money. We can afford it. So *I'm* going. I'm going to take my friend Lillian, who can't afford anything. Someplace with a live volcano

15

or voodoo priests or lions running about in the brush. You remember that scene in *Out of Africa* I love so much? Where Meryl Streep encounters that lion, and if Robert Redford hadn't been there, she might have gotten eaten up? I wanted something like that to happen, but with *you* rescuing me instead. But you never wanted anything like that, did you? To save me from a lion. Never wanted to be my Denys Finch Hatton."

That had hurt too, because they had traveled. They'd gone to the Virgin Islands on their honeymoon, and then only a few years ago—maybe five?—they'd gone to the Grand Canyon, and what could be more beautiful than that?

A pained expression came into her lovely, incredibly dark eyes (he had always loved her eyes), and she said, "See? I'm hurting you, and I don't want to. I'm leaving so I will stop hurting you and so I can do what I want to do while I still can."

"Tell me where you want to go," he'd quietly replied, frozen, shocked, feeling more helpless than he ever had in his life.

"Bora Bora!" she cried. "Bali. Indonesia. India—to where those ruins are with all those people having sex carved into the buildings. I want to spend the night in a pyramid. Or go to Dracula's castle for Halloween. I want to parachute. Or visit the fleshpots of Bangkok. I want to experience a three-way!"

He'd stiffened at that, and she'd shaken her head. She'd suggested it more than once recently and told him she didn't care if it was with another man or another woman. "Isn't that a man's number one fantasy? To watch his wife with another woman?"

But God, *no*, he didn't want to see her with another woman! The idea frankly made his stomach cramp. And another man? What might happen then? Either him standing there watching, left out, or him and the other man each taking a side of his wife and maybe accidentally touching or.... Or something much more involved than anything accidental at all?

And when Viv would whisper the possible scenarios to him, he would feel the color drain from his face even as hers became flushed with excitement. Her kissing another woman, bare breast to bare breast, grinding against each other and then placing him in the middle.

16

Or him and another man, one fucking her from the front and the other from behind. Or… and she would get out of breath saying, "Or you fucking him while he fucks me. Christ, that would be hot. You, John. Fucking a *man*."

None of that sounded good to him. He didn't want to see her with another woman. And what if they took a man to their bed and… and he liked it? Liked it too much?

He knew he very well could. Would.

On that final day, when he'd just stood there listening to her apologize, hardly saying a word himself because he didn't know what to say, she'd kissed him and said good-bye, took Moxie—*she took the dog!*—and climbed into her Tesla S P8FD and was gone.

Just gone.

He didn't hear from her for two weeks and then not directly. His father-in-law called and explained that John shouldn't try to contact her. In fact he insisted. Told John that when she was ready, she would call him.

She didn't.

And now he was alone, alone, alone.

Sitting by himself in the dark with only the light of the TV, John thought of all these things. And seeing that thinking was doing nothing to help, that it only brought confusion and hurt and loneliness, he decided to go to bed. He had an early day tomorrow, what with the following Monday being a bank holiday.

But even after what had turned into four glasses of wine, he simply stared by turns at the insides of his eyelids and the bedroom ceiling (with lots of looking at the seemingly unmoving red numbers of his alarm clock).

He'd done a lot of that in the last six months, even after he'd moved out of the master suite he'd shared with Vivian and made the guest room "his" bedroom. Granted, the full-sized bed there was only as comfortable as it was because he was the only one in it. John was a big man at just over six foot, and wide in the shoulders. A football player's build, they called it—a real one, not just a euphemism for being overweight (although he did have a bit of padding on his stomach).

He'd played football in high school—tight end—twenty years ago, and he hadn't been bad at all. Good enough to get a scholarship for college, although it was clear he'd never be a professional. He'd thought of going out and getting a new king-size bed, but that seemed like so much work, and he just wasn't up for it. Picking out a bed all alone seemed like the ultimate "The End."

Then, abruptly, the angel boy appeared in his mind's eye again, and John almost instantly began to grow hard.

Hell, no.

But cursing to a God he really didn't believe in did nothing to distract or dissuade his cock, and soon it was painfully erect.

Picturing the boy's dimples, wondering what those jeans hid on such a slim kid, and yes, remembering that ass were what clinched it. So he did the only thing he could. He took his hard-on in hand, and although he tried to envision Vivian, soon he was thinking about the angel's sweet, high, round ass instead, and a moment or so after that, he cried out in release and drenched his chest and belly like a teenager.

He didn't even have time to punish himself for it, for he was asleep almost instantly afterward.

And dreaming of angels on skateboards.

CHAPTER THREE

BLUE STOPPED by Mom's house to see if she wanted some help with her garden. He hadn't seen her in weeks, not since it had snowed last and he'd shoveled her driveway and sidewalk for twenty bucks. That evening she'd insisted he spend the night on the couch.

"That place is too fuckin' cold for you without electricity."

"It's not so bad," Blue had argued. "The next-door neighbors went to Florida for two months, and we hooked up a couple of those big orange power cords to their outdoor outlet."

She'd furrowed her brows at him. "Who paid for those power cords? Those things are pretty frigging expensive."

"Sly got them cheap at a garage sale last year," he'd explained.

"You sure one of ya didn't steal them?" She was leaning forward then, the blanket she'd been crocheting for the last hundred years or so in her lap.

Blue had laughed at that. "Wouldn't stealing those huge things be kinda hard?"

She lifted a brow and then leaned back on her couch. "I guess if you don't have a dress. I put a lot of things up my dress in bad times. I put a frozen goose in there once for Christmas dinner. I got frostbite between my thighs."

Blue had looked at her agog and exploded into laughter so hard he'd almost peed his pants. In fact, he did a little bit. But just a squirt.

She'd rolled them a rockin' jay then. She grew marijuana in her backyard, behind her biggest flowers and shrubs. She kept the plants tight and trimmed and hidden, and it was good shit. A product of keeping them so small, all the THC—sticky and quite lovely—gathered heavy in the big buds. She didn't sell it and shared it only with those she cared about. She grew it for her fibromyalgia, claimed that was the only reason, and while Blue believed the first part, he doubted the latter.

Mom rolled a joint like a champ, and it took them an hour to finish it, because if they had smoked it any faster, it would have put him in a coma—it was that good. Another reason he didn't go home, even though it was only a few blocks away. He was too fucked up to move.

"You might not have stolen those cords," she said and took a hit. "But you are stealing electricity."

"At least we won't get frostbite on our thighs," he shot back.

She nodded. "Touché," she said in that way someone does when they're holding in a hit, and then she blew out a cloud of smoke so big it reminded Blue of one of the dragons from *Game of Thrones*. That image had sent him into new peals of laughter.

But today he saw there really wasn't any gardening to do. It was still early in the year, and right now all that was growing were daffodils, hyacinth, the beginnings of tulips, and the end of the crocuses. There were hardly any weeds yet. But the leaves needed raking. She left them where they fell in the fall for mulch, but now seemed to be the time to get rid of them.

Besides, Mom hadn't met Chewie.

Her tulips were the reason they'd met in the first place. He'd been walking down the sidewalk, hands deep in his back pockets, and quite suddenly they'd hit him with their blazing colors, and he'd stopped in his tracks. He learned later they were called parrot tulips, but all he knew that day was that they were gorgeous. Each petal was ruffled and rippled, and there were so many wonderful colors. He'd been delighted.

Like a child being led by the tune from the Pied Piper's flute, he followed them up the driveway, around the side of the house, and out back—which was actually surrounded by a white picket fence— and he saw a yard full of daffodils of every shape, size, color, and description (and more tulips), and he simply couldn't stop what he did next. He opened the gate, walked through, and, laughing, kicked off his shoes, pulled off his socks, and went tiptoeing—dancing— through the tulips. Laughing! He couldn't stop. He was reaching to pick one, knowing he shouldn't, when her voice rang out loud and clear—

"What the *fuck* are you doing?"

—and yes, he had peed his pants (a little).

He had frozen in place, and his eyes had flown wide. His mouth had fallen open, but *nothing* came out.

On a very small back porch was a woman, probably about seventy years old, with a wild mane of *very* curly black-and-gray hair, standing with her hands on her slim hips, a blazing fire in her dark eyes. Eyes that could turn people into stone. Maybe that's why he couldn't move. Medusa's eyes.

Put your right foot down.

But he couldn't.

"Well, are you just going to stand there like a *frigging* lawn flamingo, or are you going to answer my *god*damned *question*?"

Somehow he was finally able to put his foot on the ground.

And then? "I am *soooooo* sorry," he managed. "I knew I shouldn't have. I knew it! But they were so pretty. I mean... so *gorgeous*. The petals. They... they look like feathers, and there are so many colors!" He'd looked down at them—cataloging. "Orange and red and yellow and green and pink and white and lavender and black and burgundy, and I've never seen anything like them, and suddenly I just started thinking about that song my mom used to play on her little record player, the one about tiptoeing through the tulips, and I took my shoes and socksoffandjumpedrightinthere—"

"Whoa!" the woman shouted and made the time-out symbol. "Jesus H. Christ on a Popsicle stick!" She shook her head, then motioned to him. "Come here, kid."

Somehow she had unfrozen him as easily as she had frozen him in the first place. His face blazed hot with embarrassment.

"Come *here*," she said again and pointed at one of the rattan chairs on that itty-bitty back porch.

When Blue didn't move, her brows came together again, a big furrow, and his heart jumped. Then she shrugged and said, "Suit yourself," and sat down herself, quite elegantly, like a queen on her throne.

A moment later he went to her and folded himself lotus style into the second chair. His was painted a dark teal, and hers was more of a deep blue.

"You smoke?" she asked.

He smiled. "I'm proud to say that I've never had a single puff of a cigarette in my life."

"Well, good for you." She nodded. "I mean that. It's a nasty fricking habit. But I wasn't talking about tobacco."

"Oh!" His smile turned into a tremendous grin. "*Girl*! Now *that* I smoke."

"Somehow I thought a little bleached blond like you would," she said, staring out at her tulips and drawing out a perfect joint from her blouse pocket.

Blue's mouth fell open. "I-I don't b-bleach my hair!"

"I-I d-don't b-b-bleach m-my hair," she mocked.

The mockery hurt for about a second, and then he saw the bemused look on her face. She was teasing him.

"Honey." She pointed at his head. "That color doesn't come in nature except on albinos and very old people. And your roots are dark blond."

While she lit the joint with a lighter that seemed to have appeared in her hand by magic, Blue's eyes went wide in horror. He reached for his scalp, pressed and dug as if his fingertips had eyes and could see the blasphemy of a hair color gone bad.

"Relax," she said, blowing out an incredible cloud of smoke and handing him the joint.

Blue took the jay and hit it, and the pot went down smooth and fine as a shot of frigid cold Patrón, but when he released it, he started coughing, hard, and blushed that the old woman could take her smoke so much better than him.

She eyed him, a twinkle in her eyes, and retrieved the joint. She shrugged. "You don't get off until you cough," she said. "Or so I've heard."

He could only stare. Who *was* this woman?

"Now me?" She shrugged again. "*I* have adamantine lungs."

When he didn't say anything, she said, "Adamantine means—"

"Rigidly firm," he supplied. "Unyielding. Resembling a diamond in hardness or luster."

She looked at him in surprise.

"It was the metal used by the gods to chain Prometheus to the rocks for stealing fire from heaven. It was also the inspiration for adamantium, the fictional metal that was used to make Wolverine's skeleton and claws and—"

She held up her hand—*Halt!*—and when he halted, she passed the joint. "You're an interesting cookie."

"Really?" For some reason that made him quite happy. This lady was fascinating, and for her to say that *he* was interesting was pretty fripping cool.

They sat quietly, passing the jay, neither talking. Blue wanted to say something. God, he wanted to. But he was afraid if he did he wouldn't be able to stop, caught up in one of his avalanches of words, his diarrhea of the mouth.

But then the joint was way too small for him to keep passing. He couldn't believe how long she nursed it, down to a mind-bogglingly miniscule snippet of paper and marijuana. It wasn't even like she had long nails! Were her fingers made of asbestos?

She finally broke the silence. "Okay, what saved you in *my* book was the tiptoeing. You really like my flowers. And you were being careful. Even if you were about to pick one."

"Oh yes!" he cried, sitting up and then almost falling forward from the effect of the pot.

"What would you think of helping me out around here?" She waved an arm expansively in the direction of—well, *everything*. "Mowing my front yard. It's a small one. I only have an old-fashioned push mower. Never needed more. I'd need you to do some weeding, planting bulbs and annuals in the spring and bulbs in the fall. Raking. Mulching. I just can't keep up with it anymore. I'll pay you."

His eyes flew wide. *Pay me?* To do something fun? "*Sure!*"

That's how it began.

Somewhere along the line, he started calling her Mom.

"You know I'm old enough to be your *grand*mother, right?"

Yes. He knew that. But the last thing he wanted to do was think of her as his grandmother. The *very* last thing.

Mom was better.

And after a while, he even started pretending she was his mom. He even told people he had a mom.

It was nice.

Today he wanted to see her. But when he knocked on the door, there was no answer, and he went to the rickety old garage and peeked in through the little windows. Her car wasn't there.

Where could she be?

He called her, and she answered on the third ring. "Blue, whaddya want?"

"I'm sitting on my chair," he said. The teal one. He had one foot on the ground and the other over his knee, and then habit took over and the other foot came up to join the first. "Wondering where you are."

"Outta town, sugar dumpling."

"Where?" he asked.

"Wouldn't *you* like to know?"

It stung.

"Branson, hon."

Branson? Mom was in Branson? "*Branson?*"

"What can I say? I got invited. Harry invited me. There are massages. Hot stones. Pedicures even."

"Pedicures?" He stuck out a lip.

"Stop pouting."

She knew. How did she always know?

"I got a dog," he replied, hoping to surprise her.

"You did?" He couldn't tell if he'd gotten her or not.

"A labradoodle. I named him Chewie."

"Like the Wookiee?"

He nodded. Funny that people did that when they were on the phone and the other person couldn't see.

Hearing his name, Chewie came over and laid his shaggy head in Blue's lap. Blue smiled. How could he help it? What with those big brown eyes looking up at him. He scratched behind Chewie's ears.

And oh, the depth of those eyes....

"Do you have any dog food? *Good* dog food?"

No.

"Look under the fern pot. There's fifty bucks."

Fifty bucks?

"I want you to go to Four-Footed Friends and get him something good."

Those big brown eyes!

"And you know where the key is. There is some leftover lasagna in the refrigerator that'll make you cum in your pants."

Blue burst into laughter.

"Kidness? I gotta go. The hot rocks are calling."

He sighed. "Okay, Mom."

"I'll be home in a day or two."

"Okay, Mom," he said again and laughed.

"Okay, then. Later 'gator."

"While 'dile."

They hung up.

And he tried to be happy for her.

He was just so fucking lonely.

CHAPTER FOUR

BLUE WAS walking down Main with Chewie when it happened. Without warning, the labradoodle dashed out into the street, and before Blue could even open his mouth to call out his dog's name, it was over.

A car hit him.

Blue screamed louder than Chewie was howling, ran into the traffic, and was barely missed by a truck himself.

"Chewie! Oh my God, Chewie!" By the time he reached his dog, he was crying, and then he screamed again. Like a girl. Like a girl running from a slasher in a horror movie. He was so hysterical he nearly fainted.

The driver was out of the car himself now and a total mess. "Oh, dear Christ, I'm so sorry! He just ran out into the street! I couldn't stop!"

Blue was crying, and Chewie was crying and shuddering, and in his mind's eye Blue could see his dog—lifeless.

But. No.

Chewie *couldn't* die. They had been on their way to get him some dog food! He. Could. Not. Die.

Blue looked around. A lot of cars had stopped now, and people were out of their vehicles. The world was blurry through his constant tears, his nose was already clogged with snot, and he didn't know—what—to—do.

Then it hit him. He had been on the way to Four-Footed Friends! And heedless of what might happen, he carefully started to pick the trembling dog up—and was immediately bitten. Blue barely felt it, and ignoring growled warnings, he managed to get the dog into his arms—a labradoodle wasn't a small dog—and then ran across the street and down Westport Road. The shelter was only a half block or so away.

He couldn't open the door. His arms were too full. There was a doorknob, and not the handle kind. He couldn't shift Chewie without hurting him more.

Snot running down his face, Blue began to kick at it, hysteria returning, and thankfully on the fourth kick, the door opened to reveal a large woman with shoulder-length graying hair.

"What the—" Her eyes went wide. She took everything in immediately and declared, "Get him in here. Right away. Back. Follow me."

Chewie was panting deeply and shaking and whimpering, and Blue began to cry again. "Don't die, Chewie. Please, please, please don't die."

He followed the woman through the lobby, past a counter where a startled black-and-white cat arched its back at them, and into the back. She guided him to a room with an examination table, and after Blue placed Chewie carefully upon it, she began to cautiously look him over.

"What happened?" she asked. She withdrew her hand as Chewie weakly snapped at her when she touched his left rear leg. Then before Blue could answer: "Car?"

"Y-yes," Blue sobbed. "He just ran out in the street!" And then the only reason he didn't faint dead away was that Chewie looked up into his face with big pleading eyes.

"Is there any reason you didn't have him on a leash?" she asked, and Blue flinched with *hideous* guilt and looked up at her and saw… no blame.

"I found him. He's my new friend. I've been taking care of him. Mom gave me money, and we were on our way here to get food and stuff." He pulled the fifty-dollar bill from his pocket, wrinkled and damp, and held it out to her as proof.

She nodded. "Can you hold him?" she asked.

"Yes," he answered, trembling himself.

"This is going to hurt, but I need you to be strong for him, okay?"

"Y-yes," he said, and then the world started to go gray.

"Young man!"

The world snapped back into focus.

"Chewie needs you." Her expression was as serious as a heart attack.

27

That's what Blue had needed to hear, for now at least, and he leaned in and gathered Chewie's upper body carefully into his arms with his muzzle tight against his shoulder so the dog couldn't bite him.

Blue couldn't see what the lady did next, but Chewie cried mournfully, and Blue gathered all his reserves not to start bawling like a child. He had to be strong for his dog!

"Yes, it's his leg. It's broken in at least one place and—"

"Elaine! What's going on?"

They both turned to see a slim young man with a mane of blond dreadlocks, and Blue was flooded with relief. He knew this man. Intimately. This was his friend H.D. Or as he was usually called… "Oh, Hound Dog," Blue cried. "My dog got hit by a car!"

"Blue," said H.D. "Let me see."

Blue couldn't move.

"Come on, babe." H.D. nodded, and there was something about his blue eyes that helped with the pain and fear in Blue's heart. Hesitantly, carefully, he slipped away from Chewie, gently letting his head rest on the metal table. He hated that his sweet doggie face was against that cold metal, and before H.D. could move, Blue pulled his shirt off over his head and turned it into a bundle to pillow his dog's head.

"Let me in now?" H.D. asked.

Blue nodded reluctantly and stepped away. At least far enough to let H.D. step in.

Chewie bared his teeth, and H.D. made soothing noises. Assuring sounds that he was here only to take care of him. The labradoodle dropped his head down and began to pant. H.D. laid hands on him, and Chewie showed those teeth for only a second more. His panting began to slow down. H.D. glanced at Elaine, who ever so slightly shook her head.

"No!" Blue wailed. "Please! Oh, *please*."

They both turned to him. Elaine smiled, even though Blue thought it looked rather forced. "Don't worry. No animal left behind. Not if we can help it. H.D., call Dr. Lee."

Hound Dog smiled and held up his cell. "Got it," he said and began to punch a number into his phone.

"It's Saturday," she said, and Blue heard the caution in her voice. "He'll come. You know he will."

"Elaine," Blue said, looking back down over his dog. He reached out tentatively, and Chewie lifted his head and licked Blue's hand before dropping it back down weakly a few seconds later. Blue sighed. "Can't you give him something for the pain?" He laid a hand on Chewie's side.

She shook her head. "I don't want to do that, honey. It might interfere with the anesthesia Dr. Lee's going to have to give him. That's something interesting about dogs. By now a natural numbness has set in. He's going to be okay. Dr. Lee is amazing. He'll wave his wand and help Chewie… as long as there are no internal injuries, and I don't think that's the case."

"Then what's that look on your face?" he asked. He knew he saw something.

She sighed. "It's a good thing you brought him here. I bet most shelters would have put him down. This is going to be expensive. But if we're lucky, Dr. Lee will do it pro bono. If not…. God, Blue. That's your name? Blue?"

"Yes," he whispered.

"Christ. We'll do what we can do."

"I'll find some way to pay," he cried. "I will. I'll do whatever I have to. Chewie is my responsibility. You don't take on a dog if you aren't willing to be there for them, for better or for worse!"

"If only most people felt that way," she said. She stepped forward and opened her arms, and he all but fell into them. Never taking his hand off Chewie, he rested his head on her shoulder, and she hugged him and rocked him like a baby.

Then H.D. was saying that Dr. Lee was on his way—*Oh thank you, thank you, thank you*—and the three of them stayed there with Chewie until Dr. Lee—what a sweet-looking man; he *had* to be good!—arrived. Then Hound Dog took Blue back out to the lobby. Elaine came out for an instant and gave Blue his shirt and assured him Chewie didn't need it. H.D. sat down with him. Slung an arm around his shoulder and told him all would be fine. Told him that Dr. Lee was the *best*.

They sat there for an hour, and Blue managed not to cry—mostly. He rambled on about one subject after another, and H.D. let him. He was just worried, and his thoughts led him to blather on like a drunken monkey—the latest *Star Wars* movie, his disappointment that Thai Place in Westport had closed, if in a crossover movie war the *Walking Dead* zombies would win or the pod people from *Invasion of the Body Snatchers*, why were the honeybees disappearing, and did H.D. think feet could be sexy? And God, he was just *sooooo* tired. He had too little energy for his rambling words to be swept up into one of those tornadoes.

But then Hound Dog got a call, and he needed to leave right away. Another shelter was going to put an old Labrador down now unless he could come get it. "You want to go with?"

Blue shook his head. He couldn't.

"It'll help get your mind off—"

"I couldn't possibly get my mind off Chewie," he said. "I don't want to."

"I don't like the idea of leaving you here alone," H.D. said.

"I'll be okay," Blue said. He'd made it through a lot of tough shit in his life.

H.D. nodded. Smiled weakly. "I know you will. And Chewie will too."

"You think?"

"I think," H.D. said. "I know."

Blue put on a brave smile and then made it his mantra.

Chewie will be okay, and so will I. Chewie will be okay, and so will I. Chewie will be okay, and so will I....

CHAPTER FIVE

THE OUTSIDE of Four-Footed Friends was pretty innocuous. A simple cinder-block building in a rather boring tan color with the name of the shelter painted in dark brown and a set of paw prints—quite enormous ones—along the far left. John supposed that even that was fancier than the average shelter.

Would they have the kind of dog he wanted? Did he know what he wanted? A cockapoo would be nice, caramel-colored like Moxie.

Why did she have to take the dog?

From what he'd heard through the grapevine, she was traveling, just like she'd claimed she wanted to do. So why take the dog? Surely she hadn't taken Moxie to Cancún, which was where rumor put her. That or Cabo San Lucas. That was what Lillian told him when he'd bumped into her at the Sun Fresh last week. She'd acted like a criminal wracked with guilt during a police interrogation, although all he'd done was ask her how she was. He wasn't even talking about Vivian. Lillian talked and talked, the whole time looking like she was either going to cry or expected him to yell at her, about how Viv had indeed taken her on a trip—to New Orleans—and then a week after they got back, Vivian had headed off to Mexico. She wouldn't say, at first, where Vivian was staying in the meantime—had winced when she said she couldn't—but John figured it was with her parents. It was only at the end that she'd slipped.

Fuck it.

It was obvious there was nothing he could do. Viv was on a mission and could not be stopped.

John opened the door, the bell above it tinkling happily.

What he saw, though, didn't reflect that cheer.

And who he saw shocked him to the core.

31

Sitting on a stack of dog food in a window, bathed in light, head bowed, was John's angel.

It couldn't be.

John stood there, staring, unable to move for what seemed forever.

It's him.

Can't be.

That hair. So white. It's got to be.

The only thing he was wearing was jeans and some kind of sneakers. He was kneading something made of cloth in his hands—a dark red shirt perhaps—and his skin was beautiful....

John's face heated up. Blushing. He was blushing. God. His heart was racing.

He clenched his jaw. *Get ahold of yourself.*

He waited for the youth to look up, recognize him maybe, but his head remained down. John couldn't even see his face. There was no way of knowing if this was really the young man he'd seen all those months ago.

And so what if it was? So what? Because what then?

John shifted his weight. A floorboard creaked.

The young man looked up, and it was him.

The pure shock and surprise and unexpectedness of it all was so… unreal. The way the white light enveloped the kid (angel), illuminating the flawless bare skin of his lightly built chest, the dust specks floating in the air, the pure silence of the room, made him seem truly otherworldly. No wonder John had thought the kid looked like an angel.

And John didn't even believe in angels.

The kid trembled, and it was only then John saw he'd been crying. His eyes were red, his face wet.

John's heart leapt, and as if someone had taken over his body, his lips, he asked, "Are you okay?"

There was a long pause—millennial, it seemed—and then the kid said, "No. I'm not."

And burst into fresh tears.

Again as if John had no control of himself, he moved to the kid's side and squatted down before him. He pulled out his handkerchief from his suit pocket and held it out, thinking to place it in the young man's hands but somehow afraid to touch him.

The kid shook his head. "I c-can't. I'll... I-I'd s-snot it u-up."

"That's what it's for," John heard himself saying and passed it to the youth. A shock passed through him as their fingers touched—the boy's fingers wet, his skin soft.

"A-are y-you su-su-sure?" the kid asked, and then he snuffled with a rattling sound.

John nodded. He'd carried the damned things for years, and how often had he actually used one? To blow his nose? Why, he could carry the same one day after day without touching it. Viv had hated washing them even when, for all intents and purposes, they were clean.

"Why would you use one of those? Stick a snotty rag back in your pocket?" She'd shudder and carry it to the laundry room pinched between two fingers.

His father had insisted that a man always carry a handkerchief.

"Please," he said now to the kid. "That's what they're for." And then: "I've always wanted to do that. It's like something from a movie, you know?" He blushed then. In the movies it was always a man offering his kerchief to a lady.

The kid smiled a weak smile, took it and wiped his face, looked at him with big questioning eyes, and when John nodded, he did blow his nose.

It was a great rattling sound, long and deep, and the pure humanness of it instantly shattered the illusion that this young man was something unearthly or unreal. He was all too human. Surely angels didn't have snot.

Somehow that wasn't at all gross. Just real. So damned real. John shivered and felt goose bumps, and how ridiculous that something so "impolite," so personal, so physical as blowing your nose would make John react so.

But God. Even red-eyed and snotty (the kid quickly, as if seeing something in John's expression, wiped the last vestiges away) and disheveled and young (so young!), he still stunned John, almost rocked him back on his haunches with his beauty.

His skin was perfect (not a single defect, not a mark), and his eyes were not just brown but… honey? Russet? *Russet* brown. (It was hard to tell with his crying, but they were still stunning.) His nose was a boy's nose, upturned (button; that was called a button nose), and his cheeks were smooth and round, and his lips were full and dark pink (like *roses*—God, like his nipples), and even that groove between nose and mouth was—

What? What, John? What is this? You're looking at a boy*!*

—sexy.

The realization heated up his face again, and the kid had to see he was blushing, and—

Who gives a shit! He's crying. What's wrong, sweet boy?

John came back to reality again, and he took a deep breath and asked it aloud: "What's wrong? Are you okay?"

It hit him then.

You're in an animal shelter. His pet is dead. Poor boy. His—

"My dog, Chewie, got hit by a car, and it's my fault!"

And then the boy dropped his face into his palms and began to sob again.

John instinctively wanted to pull the youth into his arms and comfort him. But good God, him? John Williams? Hold someone in public while they cried? And a boy? A boy he didn't even know? He didn't know the kid's *name*. And what would anyone think if—

The decision was taken away from him when the kid surged forward, threw his arms around John, buried his face in John's shoulder, tightened his hold, and *cried*. Great wracking sobs.

Without thinking, John put his arms around him and held him. God. He was holding someone. When had he done that last? When was the last time he'd held his own son? When Alistair was ten? Younger? Williams men didn't hug. That's what John's father had always said. Certainly not in public. It was weak.

(What might the world be like today, though, if maybe he'd ignored the man and hugged his son a little more?)

He'd hugged his wife.

When?

When he told her he loved her (when had he said that last?), or when they danced (when was that? The day they got married?), and of course, when they made love (a year ago?).

Then John couldn't help it.

He pulled the youth tightly to him, their bodies locking together, and a shock went through him at how... how *real* it was. How human. How alive. He couldn't remember ever feeling this way, and *that* in turn made him feel like shit because this poor boy was in pain. Crying as if he were destroyed, and John had no idea what to say.

He knew this much: it would be utterly insulting to say "There, there," or "It'll be all right," or as his father would have said, "You can always get another dog."

Or cat? Had this boy lost a cat? No. He'd said that Chewie—from *Star Wars*?—was a dog.

"Excuse me, please" came a woman's voice. "Blue?"

The kid froze in his arms and loosened his hold only by the slightest bit.

"I want you to know that Chewie came through, and he's resting, and—"

"Oh, thank God!" The kid sprang from John's arms, practically leapt over him (he did swing a leg over John's head), and as John fell back on his ass, he saw the kid launch himself into a heavyset woman's arms instead. "Oh, thank you!" he sobbed. "Oh my God, thank you!"

"There, there," said the woman. She stroked his back, and John realized it wasn't placating or condescending at all, but it would have sounded that way had *he* said it. Why the hell was that?

The kid was crying again. What had she called him? Blue? Surely not. What kind of name was that?

She meant that he was blue. She'd meant it sweet and comforting and—

"Blue, it's okay. He's going to be okay. Chewie is going to be fine, although the break was bad. In three places. He's pretty young, and his bones are soft. Dr. Lee had to wrap one bone in wire and...."

Blue started crying again—she really was calling him Blue—and God, how could anyone have that many tears? John couldn't remember the last time he'd cried. Not when Viv left. Not when his son had—rather indifferently—moved to Santa Fe, New Mexico, to become an artist (and who actually *did* that in real life?). Certainly not when his father died a little over a year ago. Even Alistair hadn't cried about that, but then, when was the last time he'd seen his son cry?

John's heart hurt at the thought, but what could he do about it? It wasn't like he hadn't reached out to his boy.

Well… maybe not often. Somewhere along the way he'd just sort of given up.

The woman had Blue at arm's length now and was looking at him very seriously. "He's going to need a lot of care, and in the first few days, help even getting outside to use the bathroom. Can you carry him? He's not light and—"

"I… I can carry him, Elaine," said Blue. "I carried him here, didn't I? I'm a lot… lot stronger than I look." He was nodding very vigorously at that last, and then he held up his arm and made a muscle, and it was lovely and surprisingly large for such a slight kid. His whole arm—and look, even his hand—was lovely.

Lovely? You really think the kid's arm is lovely?

Blue. His name is Blue.

And yes. God, yes. Lovely.

The woman—apparently her name was Elaine; was he ever going to catch up here?—turned to him. "Are you Blue's father?" she asked.

Father? He blushed fiercely then. He had no idea why. It wasn't like he'd done anything wrong. But why *wouldn't* she think he was Blue's father? Blue had to be younger than Alistair. And when she walked in, he'd been holding Blue, and that made him blush harder—feel guilty, even—and he didn't know why!

Of course you do.

Holding him like that. A boy. What's wrong with you?

I was comforting him.

Blue had grabbed *him*. What was he supposed to do?

John climbed up off the floor. "No. I never met him before today."

Blue shook his head while Elaine raised a curious eyebrow. "No. I don't even know his name," Blue said. "He just held me." He turned and aimed drenched eyes and soaked eyelashes—all stuck together—at John and smiled rapturously.

"John Williams," he said, introducing himself and trying to decide if this was a decorous time to offer his hand.

"Like the composer?" Blue asked, and it took John by surprise. As famous as that man was, John had only been asked the question a half-dozen times in his whole life. He loved the composer's music. Had followed him since he was a little kid. Who *didn't* love the music of *Star Wars* and *Superman* and *Raiders of the Lost Ark* and *E.T.* and *Jurassic Park*?

"Yes," he said with a slight smile. "Just like that."

Elaine did offer her hand to shake, and he took it and then was startled when Blue stepped into him and laid his head back onto his shoulder.

"Elaine Arehart," she said and explained she was the co-owner of Four-Footed Friends and that Chewie was a labradoodle that belonged to Blue and had just had an operation. "I think he's going to be fine."

John, who wasn't sure why she was sharing all this with him, or just what a labradoodle was, told her he was happy to hear it.

"*Probably* will," she replied. "If he's properly fed and brought back in for a few checkups. He was pretty malnourished."

"Food!" Blue cried and stepped away from John and dug into the pocket of his tight (very tight) jeans. John couldn't believe how tight. Blue was slim but well-shaped in the legs, and his ass—it was like… well, he didn't know what it was like except full and incredibly round. Blue pulled his hand back out after that struggle of getting it in and held out a very wrinkled bill of some kind. John wasn't sure which denomination.

Elaine nodded. "Good."

"When can I take him home?" Blue wanted to know, and the answer was not for a couple of days.

"We want to keep him for observation."

That made Blue's eyes get all big again, and she assured him it was best for Chewie.

It was only then that she asked what John was doing there. "Sorry about that," she offered. "With all the drama...."

"No, I understand," John said. And he told her the impulsive reason he'd come, but suddenly he wasn't sure if now was the time to look at dogs.

"Do you know what kind of dog you might be interested in?"

"A cockapoo?" he blurted, even after thinking now wasn't the time after all.

Elaine pursed her lips. "We don't have one right now. Got a shepherd and a border collie and an—"

It was right then that Blue staggered and would have fallen to the floor if John hadn't been there to catch him. He helped him sit back down on a pile of bagged dog food, and Elaine squatted and asked him if he was okay.

"Do you want some water?"

"I—I think I need more than water."

"I think I've got a little juice. Or coffee. I can make some *great* coffee."

"Juice," he muttered.

She stood and went off to get it, and John sat down next to him and, without thinking about it, put an arm around his shoulder. Blue snuggled closer, and another one of those shocks went through John. Electricity and—he trembled—a surprising... rightness.

I can't believe this.

Elaine came back and handed Blue a small bottle of some kind of juice. And then this... *knowing* look came into her eyes and she asked, "When was the last time you had something to eat, Blue?"

He shrugged. "I had some lasagna yesterday," he replied.

"And today?"

Blue shrugged again. Frowned. "Nothing?"

Nothing? John asked himself. It had to be three in the afternoon. And then before he even knew what he'd done, John said, "Why don't I take you to dinner?"

Blue pulled away just enough to look up at him with those beautiful russet-brown eyes. "I couldn't do that...."

"Why not?"

"Yes," Elaine said. "Why not? Chewie is going to be out for a while, and we're closing at six."

Blue looked back and forth between them, an obvious war of decision going on in the eyes that had become such a fascination (obsession) to John.

"I'd feel so guilty," Blue said. "Leaving Chewie alone and letting you"—he looked up at John again—"feed me?"

A protectiveness he couldn't begin to explain rushed through John at the words, a feeling he couldn't remember having since Alistair was about eight years old. *I don't know this kid!* But he saw a depth of sadness in Blue's expression, heard a questioning, a need, and he gave Blue a little squeeze and told him it was okay.

"And Chewie probably won't be awake for some time," he told Blue.

"You mean I won't be able to talk to him today at all?" he asked, and John thought the boy might cry again.

"Probably not," Elaine told him.

Blue took a shuddering breath.

"Can I see him for a second?"

Elaine smiled. It was a lovely thing. "Of course," she said, and the three of them went to the back. Chewie was in a kennel, deeply asleep, with an IV bag helping, presumably, to keep him there. Or give him fluids. Whatever. John didn't know. Both probably.

Blue talked to his dog for a few moments, and for some reason it made John's heart swell, and that protective feeling grew even stronger.

Then Blue looked back up at Elaine. "You sure I can't come see him one more time before you close?"

"Honey," Elaine said and reached out to clasp his upper arm. "He will be out of it."

"I don't care. I know that he'll know I'm here for him."

She let out a long sigh, dropped her shoulders in obvious defeat, and then actually gave a half laugh. "I'll wait for you. But don't make me wait too long! Mara has a movie she really wants to see tonight. Something with Cate Blanchett. She's been wanting to see it for months, so don't get me killed."

"I promise!" He turned to John. "We can be back by then, can't we?"

John nodded. Sure. Of course. "I'll make sure."

Blue smiled, and even though his eyes were damp from tears, John thought it might just be the most beautiful smile he had ever seen.

"I just wish more people cared for our four-footed friends the way you do," Elaine remarked. "Maybe there wouldn't be so many homeless animals."

Finally Blue said he was ready, although John thought he could easily have waited another hour with the youth. Or two. (Three.) Blue hugged Elaine and then looked at John with an I'm-in-your-hands expression, and John felt that protectiveness grow even more. Without forethought, he put his arm around Blue's shoulders—the top of his head came to John's chest—and led him outside to his car.

CHAPTER SIX

BLUE'S EYES grew wide at the sight of the car, and then… then… he turned and looked up at the big hunky man and *remembered*.

Remembered where he had seen the guy before.

And the car.

The guy had almost hit him with this very car several months ago. Blue had been flying along on his skateboard—a thing of the past now; he'd sold it for grocery money—and he'd been lost in his head, singing a song probably. He'd been on the sidewalk, where he admittedly shouldn't have been, and the big copper-colored luxury tank had come down a steep driveway and almost rolled right over him.

The car had stopped on a dime, but the driver had burst out of it like a jack-in-the-box, and Blue had steeled himself to be screamed at. To his surprise, the man—big and broad shouldered, with a businessman's very short hairstyle and piercing hazel eyes—had just frozen and then fumbled over his words and stared at him in a way that made Blue hard almost instantly. The big dude, a good head taller than him at least, really didn't say anything after that, and then Blue had gotten this overwhelming desire to touch him and he'd thrown his arms around him and….

I kissed him. I kissed his cheek.

Blue's own cheeks heated at the memory, and he didn't know if was embarrassment or something much more primal.

"I remember you," he whispered. There was a flash in the man's eyes, and then John was blushing, and damn, Blue loved it when a big ol' hunky man blushed. It was so fucking sweet. So sexy.

"Yeah—ah, yes," the man said.

John.

John Williams was his name, and wasn't that a fucking sexy name? Strong. Secure. None of those silly names like Chaz or Sly or even

Blue—although he did like his name, more or less. And everything about John was so… man. Tall and shouldery, and—Blue shivered—he was wearing a suit. On a Saturday afternoon. Was there ever anything as sexy and assured as a man in a suit? He wasn't wearing a tie. No undershirt either, and his shirt was unbuttoned just enough to show a hint of hair.

"It was the day," John said, "that I stupidly almost—"

"The day I stupidly almost got myself run over."

John nodded once. "I should have been paying attention."

"You paid attention enough," Blue said, and he would have said more, but the dizziness hit him again, dammit. It had been a way-too-much day, what with sweet, sweet Chewie being hit by that car, and Blue being sure he was dead, and then he wasn't and then he was running with his dog to Four-Footed Friends and then the operation and then this big kind man—so many big men *weren't* kind, it seemed—was holding him and letting him cry.

As Blue felt the world go light, John leapt forward and helped him to the car—it was such a beautiful car, some part of him noticed—and all but lifted Blue inside, where he settled into the mind-bogglingly comfortable seat. He wasn't sure if he'd ever seen anything like this. It was as if he were in some kind of leather-upholstered spaceship.

Then John let himself in on the driver's side and asked Blue to put on his seat belt, and Blue almost said, as he always did, "I don't wear seat belts," which he mostly got away with. But now—he had no idea why—he didn't want to argue with John or put up a fuss or anything.

So Blue clicked it on. For a moment there it'd looked like John was going to help him—like he was a kid or something—and it gave him a shiver of delightful goose bumps. Then John asked him where he wanted to eat, and the truth was he didn't know. And didn't care. Blue was quite suddenly ravenous and would have eaten anything.

A pang of pain hit him from nowhere, and Blue looked out the window at the big tan building—Four-Footed Friends painted along its length—and thought of Chewie and the way his dog had *screamed* when the car hit him.

"Think of him resting," John said, as if he were reading Blue's mind.

Blue trembled and looked at him, at that masculine face and that strong jaw and those kind eyes, and he felt that maybe everything would be okay.

"He's not in pain now, and Elaine said he's going to be okay. I can tell that woman is a no-bullshit kind of lady. Can't you?"

Oh, those eyes. So caring. His little smile so sure. What a wonderful man. Mysteriously reassured and feeling a tiny bit better, Blue nodded. "Okay," he said and closed his eyes and imagined it. Imagined Chewie resting. No. Sleeping. But not in that kennel. At home. In their bed.

He opened his eyes to find John looking at him, and Blue felt a little bit better still. Then John asked him again where he wanted to eat.

Blue shook his head. "I don't know."

John looked out the windshield for a long moment, then bit his lower lip and nodded. "Okay," he said, and they were off.

Blue settled in. Pretended he really was in a spaceship of some kind. Something from *Star Wars* maybe. Not an X-Wing…. "What is this thing called, anyway?"

"Thing?" John asked.

"This car," Blue said.

"Oh. A Lexus." John pursed his lips. "An LS 600h L."

Blue burst into laughter. He couldn't help it. It felt good to laugh. "A… what? LX 600?"

"LS 600h L," John corrected.

"That's the name of the *car*?" What kind of name was that?

John rolled his eyes. "I know, right? What happened to a car being called a Saturn or a Sentra or Taurus or Mustang or Focus or—"

"It's like a robot from *Star Wars*!" Blue cried. "C-3PO, R2-D2, BB-8, and now… LS-600!" And then he clapped his hand over his mouth and realized he'd done it again. No filter. Something entered his head and then flew right out his mouth and—God!—this guy was taking him out to eat and Blue was making fun of his car.

To Blue's relief John laughed, and it was all rumbly and manly. "I'm never going to think of this car as a Lexus again."

"Is that okay?" Blue asked.

John smiled at him. "It's fine. I'm just happy you're laughing."

JOHN WASN'T sure where to take him. Anyplace fast? Because the kid needed something to eat, and soon.

Blue. His name was Blue. Could that really be his name? He'd have to ask, but not now. Food! Maybe Chubby's on Broadway for a big burger or something? McCoy's in Westport? They had a good variety. Jerusalem Cafe was wonderful, but maybe Blue didn't like Middle Eastern food? Freebirds made huge burritos to order. He loved Minsky's Pizza. Everyone liked pizza, right? Or right nearby there was Temujin's Mongolian Grill, where Blue could pick out exactly what he wanted, and they cooked it up right there in front of you. He could have as much as he wanted, and he looked *hungry*.

And Temujin's was quiet.

Quiet was good.

"Do you like food with an Asian feel?" he asked.

Blue nodded but didn't say anything. Was that good or bad? Did he need to think of another place?

In the end, John thought, *What the hell*, and that's where they went. It wasn't far, which was a plus, and again, there was the quiet aspect. No loud music. They could talk, if that was what they were going to do, although John was at a total loss what they would talk about. What was he doing? He was taking a *boy* to dinner.

A boy he'd been dreaming about.

It shocked him to think it, and he had to be careful not to hit the brakes. John dared a glance toward Blue, and he....

Why, it looked like he'd drifted off to sleep.

And why not? He'd been through quite a lot.

The West Thirty-Ninth Street neighborhood wasn't one you drove through swiftly, not normally anyway. The street wasn't wide—one lane going either direction—and there were a lot of lights. They seemed to be stopping at every one. It gave John time to look at the kid, and every time he did, his heart skipped a beat.

It's a guy, John. A guy. *A* young *guy. A* very *young guy!*

Blue's head was tilted to the right against the window. His hair was so ridiculously white, it couldn't possibly be natural. Even oblivious John saw that it wasn't that well done. Blue's eyebrows were quite thick, more than one might expect on such a face, but John couldn't think of them as a flaw. How would he describe Blue's face? Certainly not feminine. But not masculine. Elfin, maybe. There was that nose, of course. A button nose. He had a long neck, clearly revealed from the way his head was turned, and John wondered how the skin there would taste.

His eyes widened at the thought, and he jerked his face back to the windshield and forced himself to stare forward. Taste? What would Blue's skin *taste* like?

What are you? A damned vampire or something?

John managed to keep his face pointed forward for about a block. But then he had to turn and look again.

Blue was wearing a burgundy sleeveless shirt, and John could see now it hadn't come that way. The sleeves had been removed. It really wasn't that warm yet. Was Blue cold in that? His left arm had fallen in such a way that John could see hair showing at his pits, and damn, it looked just as white-blond as his head. Could that really be his natural color, or had the kid found a way to bleach his pits? There wasn't a lot of it from what he could see, but then, the kid's arms weren't up over his head either.

His imagination flashed him a view of what that might look like—Blue lying on a bed asleep, arms over his head—and he could only wonder why he was conjuring such images. Why a bed?

John shook his head, looked forward, and then once more his eyes drifted back as if he had no will to stop them. He noted again just how tight Blue's jeans were. And well worn. And showing a surprising large…. What to call it?

Bulge. You know what it's called.

And God, just how big was Blue's…?

Forward! Look forward, goddammit!

45

But by then he knew he couldn't fight it. He was going to look. He was going to fill his mind's eye, drink the kid in, memorize as many details as possible, and save them all for later, and then he would masturbate to very real pictures instead of the ethereal ones he'd used now and again for months.

John didn't know what he was doing. Not exactly. Heart pounding, he realized that these were very homosexual feelings. He couldn't deny it. But until today, until this moment, he'd never allowed himself to think such thoughts. He'd only ever allowed himself to think of men in the most peripheral or superficial way. Because he knew, he knew, dammit, that if he ever tasted that forbidden fruit—

or the skin of someone's (Blue's) neck

—he could very well be lost.

Lost because he didn't want to be different. He had nothing against gay men. Nothing at all. And it was certainly easier to be a gay man today than it was a decade ago. Even a few years ago. Gays could marry now. Who would have ever thought that would happen so fast? John never thought it would happen in his lifetime.

But able to get married or not, by the most liberal of statistics, homosexuals made up only 10 percent of the population, and he felt it was likely that the reality was much closer to 2 percent. So said an online article he'd read lately. Not that he spent that much time reading about those things….

Liar.

The point was he didn't want to be part of that 1.8 percent. He didn't want to be that one gay guy in the room, one of the few gays at work, the only guy with another man at the neighborhood block party. He just wanted to fucking blend in. And since he liked making love to women—or at least Vivian—why be anything else? Sometimes he shuddered to think what it must be like to live a gay life.

John wasn't sure when he'd looked back at Blue again. Looked at his purple sneakers—Converse sneakers, he thought they were called— and saw they were quite old. There was a hole worn at the left little toe and… skin. John saw skin. A tiny fraction of toenail. Blue wasn't wearing socks.

John's cock shifted in the confines of his slacks, and two things happened.

The first was a quick flash of Vivian shaking her head because he was wearing slacks on a Saturday afternoon. But he'd worked that morning and left at two and somehow found himself in front of an animal shelter instead of going home and doing something like changing into jeans and mowing the lawn.

The second thing was that the vision of his wife drifted away like a puff of smoke.

And he found himself wondering why it was that a peek at Blue's toe had made him get hard—and he *was* hard now, fully erect— and none of the ogling he'd done of Blue's every inch before had done that. Did he have a foot fetish? He'd certainly never paid that much attention to Vivian's feet, no matter what new (and probably expensive) pair of shoes she'd purchased. Never really paid them much attention at all.

But he knew right then that he wanted this young *man*. He had no true idea precisely what he'd do *with* Blue. He supposed there was the obvious, but he didn't know if he could suck a cock any more than he could leap off a building and take flight.

And he knew that *wanting* Blue could be just as dangerous as actually leaping from a building.

Because John knew that if he so much as *touched* Blue—more than he already had, touched him in an intentional way—he would want to go on touching for the rest of his life. And he thought Blue would let him. He remembered the way Blue had looked at him over his shoulder before he'd disappeared down John's street on a skateboard. Surely the boy was gay.

John's cock throbbed, and if Blue looked, he would see, would know. If he'd been wearing jeans like Viv said he should on a Saturday afternoon, the denseness of the fabric might have hidden it. But the light flannel wool of the slacks? No. He might as well be naked.

Please don't look, Blue. Please.

What should he do? They were almost there. Think of squirrel guts; wasn't that it? Maggoty squirrel guts. Hadn't he read that in a book once? Or was it a movie?

The street was before him. He turned left onto Bell without even having to slow down, because suddenly there were no other cars and no lights turning red. Now, when it would be convenient. He had to get rid of this infuriating hard-on before it was too late. His one hope was how notoriously difficult it was to find a parking space here, and... an Oldsmobile pulled out right in front of him, vacating a space directly in front of Temujin's. It wasn't a handicapped space either.

Shit.

He pulled into the empty spot as easy as could be.

Think of something sad.

But what?

His wife leaving.

And he suddenly heard her say, "For Christ's sake, John. Even your *name* is boring. I know that's mean. I *know* it. It's really mean to say, and I'm a bitch to say it, but it's true. Do you know that John is the *second* most common name in this country? What were your parents thinking?"

"It was my father's name" he'd stopped saying years ago. *"And my grandfather's."*

"Then there's Williams. The third most common last name. You don't even have a middle name, dull or otherwise, to spice it up."

And his erection was gone. Just in time.

Blue sat upright then.

"Are we there?" he asked.

"Here," John said. "We're here."

It DIDN'T look like so much from the outside, Blue thought. But gosh, Temujin's Mongolian Grill was cool *inside*.

It was kinda dark for one thing, and Blue found he liked eating in the dark. Not the pitch dark, of course. Then you couldn't see. He'd paid the price for eating Chinese food by nothing but the light from a television once. He'd had some General Tso's chicken, popped one of those little flaming hot peppers into his mouth without realizing it, and just about choked himself to death. It had taken damn near a ton of water before he was okay. Spicy food was not his forte, at least not the really spicy stuff. Of course, that hadn't stopped him from eating by the light of a TV after that. When he had that rare chance. There was just something so... unappetizing about eating by the glare of fluorescent lights. The food got a funny color. Now sunlight was okay. Picnic tables and picnic food and all that? But of course, that was natural lighting and—

"Any preference where you want to sit?"

Blue snapped to and realized someone was talking to *him*. He saw that John and a waiter were both looking at him. They were asking him where he wanted to sit? He shrugged. Looked around. Saw a couple dozen tables situated around the room and booths against two walls. The backs of each booth were high, offering plenty of privacy from the adjacent ones. And for some reason he wanted privacy for the two of them. John seemed so... not stuffy. If John were stuffy, he wouldn't have held Blue when he launched himself into John's arms. Shy, then? Was that it? Something was going on with John. Privacy would be a good thing. "How about a booth?" Blue asked.

"Whatever you're most comfortable with," John said. He even waited for Blue to sit first.

Wow.

He stood right there waiting for Blue to sit down.

Wow again.

Blue sat.

John's sweetness didn't make everything all right, but all the attention and kindness this stranger was showing Blue did make things a little better.

He could believe that Chewie would get better.

He had to.

But simply telling himself that Chewie would be okay reminded him of why Chewie wasn't okay in the first place.

Why, oh why, hadn't he put Chewie on a leash? A piece of rope would have done. Anything. And dammit, the tears were coming back.

John reached across the table and placed his big hand next to Blue's. It looked to be almost twice as big as Blue's, a real man's hand, and then he said, "Chewie is going to be all right, Blue."

"Do you promise?" Blue asked, fighting the tears.

There was pain in the big man's eyes. John swallowed and nodded, but then more pain darkened his gaze.

"May I get you two gentlemen something to drink?" said a new waitress, one who had quite abruptly appeared at their side. "We have the standards. Tea, soda—Coke products if that's all right."

Blue looked at her straightaway. "Do you mind if I have something with a little more… punch? I could sure use it."

"Is your son old enough to drink?" the waitress asked, focusing on John. She was very thin, Asian—or at least part—and had a mop of black hair hiding one of her heavily mascara-lined eyes.

"He's not—"

"I'm twenty-three," Blue said, sensing that this whole father/son thing was bothering John. Bothering him a lot. "I *just* turned twenty-three two weeks ago."

CHAPTER SEVEN

THE RELIEF of those words—"*I'm twenty-three*"—was so immense
John almost moaned, but he bit it off at the last second (because how
strange would that have been?).

Twenty-three? Really?

"I'm so sorry," the waitress said and tossed her head so that
her other eye was visible—for about three seconds. "But I'll need
to see ID."

"Sure," Blue said and then fumbled around before standing up
and grimacing as he struggled to get his hand in his back pocket.

That tight. His jeans were that tight.

Then Blue pulled his hand out with a flourish, revealed several
cards, and fanned them out before him. "Male Box VIP card," he said,
fingering them, "library card—"

Library card? Why did that surprise John? He smiled.

"—Disney World card—"

Blue had been to Disney World?

"—bus pass, and... ID!"

Blue held it out—the kind distributed by the department of
motor vehicles—and showed it to One Eye.

She applied that eye to good use and then handed it back. "What
can I get you both?"

Blue sat down, and John felt a little less like some kind of pervert.
But geez, Blue was still his son's age. What would Alistair think if he
saw him sitting here with Blue? What would Vivian think?

They're not here came an inner voice. *Alistair hasn't called you
in months. Viv is in Cancún. Or Cabo San Lucas. Or reveling in the
fleshpots of Bangkok.* And John couldn't help but wonder if it was
the devil on his left shoulder or the angel on his right that whispered
to him.

51

Whichever, he needed something a little strong too. He nodded at the waitress. "Gin martini, very clean, *very* cold, two olives. Blue?"

"Well… uh… I… I've never had a martini. Not one that isn't all fruity or chocolaty. Or faggy." He giggled, and for some reason John felt it in his balls, even though Blue had said faggy right in front of their waitress.

"You can have whatever you want."

"Maybe I should try what you're having?"

"They're not for everyone," he warned. "Not at all fruity or chocolaty."

"Or faggy?" Blue asked, and dammit, John couldn't help but blush.

John shrugged, not sure in this case what the answer to the question was.

"How about a screwdriver?" Blue said. "Heavy on the screw."

He winked at John, who gulped at the open flirtatiousness.

"Double tall?" One Eye asked.

Blue nodded. "But I don't want no *steen-keen'* extra orange juice," he said in a horrible Mexican accent, then laughed, and damned if that didn't make John's balls tingle again.

"So what do you eat here?" Blue asked.

John looked off to his right. "The grill," he said and pointed. "You get a bowl and fill it with the vegetables and meat that you want and then give it to the guy behind the counter, and he cooks it up for you in just a couple of minutes."

"Oh!" Blue's eyes went wide. "That sounds cool!"

John found himself grinning. "It is pretty cool," he said. Viv had hated it, but Alistair hadn't. He'd brought his son here for his birthday for years.

You bring this guy who could be your son to the place your son likes to eat? What the hell is that about?

He felt his face heat up and hoped Blue couldn't tell in the low lighting.

He hadn't brought Blue here for that reason, had he? No. Of course not.

But oh, the nice memories of being here with Alistair. He couldn't help but feel a little sigh in his heart. He and Alistair hadn't done much "hanging out" the last few years his son was still living in Kansas City. When they did, it was for things like his birthday. They were special nights, even if they felt guarded. Like there was some wall between them. And in a way there was. There had always been. But John had never had any idea how to climb over it. How to reach Alistair. Be close to him. They were just so damned different. The thoughts made John feel sad, and he clenched his jaw and cast them away. *No feeling sad. Take care of this young man. The one actually in front of you. That's all you can do.*

Their drinks arrived, and Blue all but gulped half his down, then wiped his mouth with the back of his hand. He ducked his head. "Sorry," he said. "It's just been a fuck of a day."

"It's okay," John said and sipped what turned out to be a perfect martini. He needed it, and it had an almost immediate calming effect. He gazed at Blue, so sweet and so alive and going through so damned much.

John was struck by how human *he* felt at that moment. He'd felt… numb for so long. Long before Vivian had left. As if he'd been sort of sleepwalking through life. Turning old long before his time. He was only forty-five, after all. And fit. He worked out. Why had he been feeling that way?

But now? Sitting across the table from this young man—and he knew now that Blue was a man, not a boy, despite the way he looked—he was feeling… alive somehow, even though the circumstances were rather sad.

"We had a dog when I was a kid," John said. "A beagle. I loved that dog so much." A smile crept to his mouth. Where was this coming from? He didn't talk a lot about himself. He didn't feel as if anyone cared. But Blue seemed to be interested. Did he dare go on?

John threw caution to the wind. "Then one day Buddy just vanished, and I… I was devastated." An ancient pain welled up in him. "I think my old man got rid of him. He hated that dog. I've hoped my whole life Dad didn't hurt him." Then John had to clench his jaw. What the hell had made him tell Blue that?

Blue's eyes got huge, and he reached across the table and laid a hand on one of John's. John tried not to flinch. He hoped that Blue didn't notice. Their hands were right out there where anyone could see. And he'd already told the waitress that they weren't father and son, so there wasn't even that excuse. Anyone who saw… they'd think he and Blue were boyfriends. Or something worse because Blue was so much younger. More beautiful. So sexy. Would they think that he was some pathetic old man buying companionship?

Alistair's face swam into his mind's eye, and he couldn't help but wonder what his son was doing. Painting? Sculpting? Something with clay? Was he working? Was he living in a goddamned abandoned house?

What good did it do to wonder? And once more John let himself slip into a kind of numbness regarding his son. His son who didn't seem to want anything to do with him.

Because I'm boring? A banker instead of someone living life on the edge? Is that what Alistair thinks?

"Oh God," said Blue, bringing John back. "I hope your dad didn't do anything to him. What kind of person would hurt a dog?"

What kind of a person indeed? But John didn't dwell on that for even a minute. He was too busy staring at Blue's hand on his own. He almost trembled. It was so warm. And small as it was, it *was* a man's hand. And it *was* right there where anyone could see. And he was getting hard again. And it was time to get up and get food!

He noticed Blue eyeing his martini. "Did you want to try it?" John asked, surprising himself again. It wasn't something he did. The first time Vivian had suggested they share a large drink at the movies, about three thousand years ago, he'd looked at her in near shock. "What about the germs?" he'd asked.

"We've had our tongues in each other's mouths," she'd answered, rolling her eyes. "I think the germs thing is taken care of."

He'd had to give her that. Yet sharing drinks and straws and such had continued to bother him.

Until now, apparently.

"Sure," Blue said cautiously, and John pushed it across the table, careful of its fullness. Blue leaned in, touched his (lovely) lips to the rim of the glass, and sipped carefully, and John couldn't help but wonder what those lips would feel like on his.

John bit the insides of his cheeks and wondered again what the fuck was going on with him. He wasn't going to kiss Blue! He wasn't. Not a twenty-three-year-old. He wasn't going to kiss a man if he was forty-three (or forty-five) or a hundred and three.

Blue looked up from the rim of the martini glass and grimaced. "Yuck." Then he laughed and covered his face and said he was sorry, but "It's *gross!*"

John chuckled. "It's not for everyone. But I really love the piney taste. It's made from juniper berries."

"Well, I think they need to make it from *any* other kind of berries," Blue exclaimed. "Blueberries or strawberries"—he held up his glass—"or *orange* berries." He smirked, and even smirking that mouth was so beautiful that John knew right then and there if Blue *were* to try to kiss him, he wouldn't fight it for a second. And oh, a memory rushed in of that kiss on his cheek in his driveway the day they'd first met.

His cock throbbed, and once more he wished for those fabled jeans.

Think of something else. You don't want to stand up and have the front of your slacks pointing the way!

Squirrel guts. Maggoty *squirrel guts.*

"You gonna show me how to do this?" Blue asked.

John looked at him blankly for a second. *What? Do what?* For one instant all he could think of was kissing, and why would Blue need John to show him how to kiss? Then Blue cocked a thumb in the direction of the buffet of raw foods. John rolled mental eyes, laughed, hoped his cock wasn't showing, and said, "Sure. Come on."

He stood up and glanced down at himself as surreptitiously as he could, and yes, he was showing, but just a bit. As long as *Blue* didn't look, he thought in another minute or so all would be well.

Blue glanced down.

His thick brows shot up.

Then he looked up, and John thought he would die of embarrassment. But then the devil on his left shoulder said, *Fuck it, John. Go eat.*

So John pretended he didn't have a clue why Blue was looking at him that way, feigned indifference as much as he could, took a plunge he'd rarely taken (plunges were to be avoided whenever possible), and motioned for Blue to follow him. On the way across the room, he realized once again that he was wearing a suit and wished deeply he'd stopped at the house and changed. Blue must think he was incredibly lame. And God, he didn't want that. Didn't want the beautiful young man to think of him the way Vivian did. But what could he do? He *was* boring, wasn't he?

Fuck it.

So he took Blue to the buffet tables with the plastic sneeze guards, showed him the huge variety of vegetables and meats and sauces, and then couldn't help but smile at the pure delight the young man took in creating his meal. Blue made him feel twenty years younger. Who knew anyone could get so excited about picking out veggies and which meat he wanted?

"I can't decide!" exclaimed Blue, pointing at the cut-up pieces of chicken and pork and beef, fish, crab, shrimp, and more.

John shrugged. "Pick several. I just wouldn't put seafood with any of the other meats. The seafood gets done much faster than everything else and then gets rubbery while the rest finishes cooking."

Blue looked at him as if he were some wise guru, nodded, and then chose some beef, chicken, *and* pork.

And then watched with a delighted smile as the cook spilled his selections on the huge round solid griddle and begin to move it this way and that with long wooden sticks.

"We can get some appetizers over here while they do that," John offered, but Blue shook his head.

"I want to watch!"

So watch they did, and when the cook handed over their food, Blue thanked the man several times, and John thought that if the big counter hadn't separated them, Blue would have hugged him.

And somehow, that was really wonderful.

BLUE ATE his food quickly, voraciously even, speaking very little, which for him was a miracle. He couldn't help it. He'd learned that he should eat when he had the chance, and sometimes that meant *fast*. You never knew when someone might try to take your food from you.

At John's urging, he had gotten some appetizers from a counter against the wall—crab rangoon and egg rolls. But also some Mongolian ones—buuz, a type of dumpling, and khuushuur, a meat-filled pastry.

All of it was delicious. He'd had no idea how hungry he was!

It had been with some shame that Blue had first haunted the alleys behind restaurants, waiting for trash to be dumped. But he'd learned that people often left whole meals uneaten for some stupid reason, and so the employees would just throw it out. Of course, getting food from the trash was tricky. You wanted to make sure you didn't get something that would make you sick or had already been chewed or was covered in cigarette ashes (although these days, with restaurants not allowing smoking inside, that wasn't the problem it used to be when he was younger). It was best when he was right there, waiting for the trash to be taken out. It was freshest that way.

Anything could have happened to send the food to the trash. Why, he'd had steaks, virtually untouched baked potatoes, pork chops that were fatty or only a little bit burned, tons of fries, and enough vegetables to feed a host of vegetarians. Didn't anyone eat their broccoli these days? And sure, asparagus made your pee stink, but it was *delish* going down and…

John was looking at him.

It wasn't in a sexy way.

…maybe he should have stopped before licking his bowl.

"I'm sorry. That was weird, wasn't it?" Was that weird? Licking his bowl? "You think I'm weird, don't you?" Because in the end everyone did. Why else didn't anyone stick around long enough to share some cellophane-sealed blueberry muffins? And now here was this really nice (sexy) man thinking he was a weirdo! Damn.

John shrugged. "What do I know from weird? That's what my wife says."

Married. Of course he was. Married. John didn't care if he was weird. That explained it all. *Aaarrgghhh!* "Where *is* your wife?" Blue asked, trying not to clench his teeth. "Won't she be wondering where you are?"

"She left me." John's eyes went dark.

Blue froze. *Oh shit.*

"I think she's in Cancún," John said quietly. "No one will tell me for sure."

"Gosh," Blue said, wide-eyed. He put the bowl down. "I'm so sorry."

John pursed his lips. "I…." He shook his head. "Nothing," he whispered.

"No," Blue said. "What? Tell me."

And then, just when Blue thought that maybe John wasn't going to answer: "She says I'm boring. She says even my *name* is boring. She said she wanted to do something interesting with her life while she was still young enough to do it."

Blue swallowed hard. *Gosh, gosh,* and *gosh.*

What did he say?

"I'm sorry, John."

The big man sighed. He looked so defeated. When he'd been so strong all afternoon.

"I wish I knew what to say."

"It's okay," John said. He frowned.

He didn't look okay. "You don't look okay," Blue said.

John shrugged. "It is what it is."

Blue sighed and reached out and touched John's hand again, and this time John didn't flinch. But still…. Blue had misjudged everything. He had no idea what was going on. It looked like John was the real thing. A man just being nice to him. On a really horrible day. And here he was embarrassing the man by touching him in public. He

58

already knew John was self-conscious about the two of them—what people thought. Blue started to pull away, but John used his thumb to hold Blue's hand right where it was.

"Blue? *I* was happy. I was never bored. I liked my life. I love my job."

"What do ya do, John?"

"I'm a banker."

A banker?

John sighed. "See? You think the same thing, don't you? That I'm boring."

Boring? How was being a banker boring? It sounded so... sophisticated. "Oh, John. I can't balance a checkbook. You're a banker? I mean, *wow*!"

John stopped. He put down a meat pastry that he was about to take a bite of.

"I mean," Blue continued, "I hope I can get famous one day for my candles, and you're a banker? Really? Like... like what do you do?"

John blinked.

"I'm the president of Heartland United Bank."

"The *president*?" Blue exclaimed.

John visibly swallowed. "Yes."

"Wow."

"I mean... it's just—"

"Just *shit*, man!" Blue threw his free hand up in the air. "A fripping bank president? I mean, who gets to be a bank president? You must be really smart!"

John looked down at his nearly finished martini. And golly! Was he blushing? It was hard to tell by candlelight. Then he looked back up. He had such sexy eyes, and he was smiling, even if it was only a little bit.

"I'm pretty proud of it, Blue."

"You *should* be!" And he meant it. Blue would never be a bank teller, let alone a president. Imagine!

Now John's smile grew, even if it was only a little bit more. "Thank you, Blue. It wasn't easy."

Blue nodded.

"Now I feel guilty, though."

Guilty? Why would John feel guilty? He didn't want that!

"This was supposed to be about you," John said—and now he looked like a scolded puppy.

Blue smiled. Or tried to.

"I was trying to help," John added.

Blue sighed, and by gosh if he didn't feel a little of today's weight lift from his shoulders. "You are helping, John. You are."

"I'm glad. God, Blue. You're so beau—"

Now Blue could see John was definitely blushing. So "beau"? Now what did that mean? What had he been about to say?

"What do *you* do, Blue?" John asked, and Blue knew a conversation changer when he heard one.

"Do?"

"For a living?"

Blue rolled his eyes. "Man, what *don't* I do?" And he told him about walking dogs and dressing up as the Statue of Liberty (and how cold it could be on Thirty-Ninth Street in March—*heh*, just blocks from here!) and filling doughnuts or selling Christmas trees and… and John didn't look bored at all. Tears threatened again. John was *listening* to him as if picking apples were the most interesting job in the world.

"I can't imagine being brave enough to hitchhike west and take a job in an orchard," John said with a faraway look in his eyes. "Just to up and *do* something like that. To *see* the country. To meet people who have no agendas, no divorces to settle or college educations to set up for their kids. Not that I don't like doing that. I do. I like helping set up those accounts and knowing that one day some kid is going to get a college education. But to say fuck it and hit the road?" He shook his head. "You're pretty brave, Blue. A little guy like you? What if someone had tried to take advantage of you? Hurt you?"

And they had. The latest—last summer—being one of the worst ever. But for the most part? "For the most part people are nice," he said. "I had a backpack stolen once, but then I found it a mile down the road, and almost everything that had been in it lying on the ground along the way. They didn't seem to want what I thought was valuable. They didn't even want my copy of *Stranger in a Strange Land*."

John's eyes went wide. "I *love* that book!" He was actually grinning. "Or should I say I *grok* that book!"

That made Blue grin all the wider. John knew what grok meant!

"I ran an ice cream bicycle once," Blue said with a laugh.

"A what?" John leaned in, eyes flashing in curiosity.

Blue nodded enthusiastically. "It was more like an adult tricycle, actually. But backward, with the two wheels in front. That was where this big metal box rested—with dry ice and the ice cream inside. And I wheeled it around, and they were lying when they said it was easy to go uphill. At first it was a bitch to sell so much as a Popsicle, but then I figured out where to go. There was an old folk's place I'd take it to and sell a shitload. And I would go to places where kids were doing stuff like baseball practice. I never really made any money out of it—my percentage was stupid small. But it sure gave me good legs!" He jumped up and flexed his calf (it was easy to see because his jeans were so tight) and then blushed when he realized he was doing this right in the middle of a restaurant. But—he bit the insides of his cheeks to prevent a smile of Cheshirean proportions—John had looked. *Really* looked.

Blue didn't know if John was just being nice or if he liked Blue's legs. John was confusing the living shit out of him. He couldn't read the man at all. So many mixed signals. But then he had just nearly lost his beloved Chewie, and that could fuck you up good!

"You're pretty damned muscular for such a little guy," John said. He looked away, once more studying his martini.

For some reason that pleased Blue immensely. The praise, not the staring at the now nearly empty glass. But even that was cute, wasn't it? How nice that a big older daddy-type guy could be so cute.

"What you said about my car?" John said.

Car? Car? Blue's mind went into overdrive. What had he said about John's car? Something good? Something rude? God, he hoped it wasn't rude. What with having no filter, he could never be sure.

"About it sounding like a *Star Wars* droid name? Damn. That was so perfect. So funny!"

Blue grinned and nodded enthusiastically. "Yes! Cars used to have such cool names. I mean, who doesn't want to drive a Javelin or a Roadmaster or a Dodge Magnum—" Blue waggled his eyebrows suggestively. "—or a Rampage or a Viper or a—"

"An Eagle Talon!" John interjected.

Yes! Someone who was actually joining the conversation instead of just staring at Blue like he had a learning disability. "Or a Hudson Hornet," Blue added. "Or a—"

"Or an Interceptor!" John added.

Yes! Or "A Diablo!"

"A Defender," John said, "Although in actuality that is nothing more than a jeep."

Blue burst into giggles, and oh, he needed it. Wait! Should he be laughing like this when Chewie could have died? "A Marauder," John cried. "Or a Raider or a Cutlass...."

Wow. Someone who *knew* things. Who helped fill the empty silences. Blue wanted to cry again, but it was almost—*almost*—good tears. "And we can't forget the Toronado," Blue said. "And then there's the Prowler. Or the Phantom. Or the Cobra!"

"And we skipped the Firebird," John said, breaking in. "How did we do that? Geez, Blue. You know a lot of cars."

The giddy feeling was beyond belief. Blue couldn't remember this happening with anyone since he was a little kid. Then he took the plunge, daring John to think he was *really* weird. Blue threw his hands in the air. "As cool as R2-D2 and C-3PO are, robot names just don't work for a car. I have no wild desire to drive an AZ-3 or an EV-9D9 or a 2-1B or a R4-P17, and certainly not a Mouse Droid!"

John laughed in that wonderful rumbling way of his. "God yes! I will never forget when Chewbacca growled at the Mouse Droid, and it ran off like its pants were on fire."

Blue realized something then. Something quite wonderful. He closed his mouth slowly. Talking about cars and *Star Wars* droids, he had almost gone into one of his nonstop surges of *blahblahblahblah*. But then John had joined and brought Blue to a contented stop.

"You know, John," Blue said happily, "*I* don't think you're boring at all."

"I…." John swallowed hard. Blue saw his Adam's apple bob. "Really?"

"Really," Blue said.

John sighed. "You don't know me."

"I'd like to *get* to know you." *Oops!* That had popped right out. No filter. Oh well. Blue smiled.

"Me?" John's dark eyes sparked. "Why?"

"Because you're nice. You let a silly little faggot cry on your shoulder. You're buying me dinner. You're…." John was buying him dinner, wasn't he? "I mean, you are, right?"

John gave a little laugh. "Yes, Blue. And if you're hungry, and I'm starting to think you're very hungry—"

"Shit, John. You don't know, girlfriend! All I had to eat yesterday was some leftover lasagna. Well, I could have taken almost anything in her fridge, but Mom told me I could have the *lasagna*, and I don't want to take advantage of her. She trusts me, you know? I don't know why she trusts me, but she does. And once you fudge up your trust with someone, it's done. Gone. *Finito*. So I didn't take anything else. Well, except a slim little Fudgsicle. Which was better than the day a week ago when all I had was five Chicken McNuggets. I could have had ten, but I shared them with Chewie. Did you know it costs almost six bucks to get chicken nuggets at McDonald's these days? Now if I'd had a way to get to Wendy's…."

"You know you're allowed to have seconds, right?" John asked, and he cocked a thumb toward the food bar and grill.

"I what?" Damn! He'd done it again. Gone into one of his blathers. But somehow John—sweet John—had deactivated it. Without making Blue feel bad or stupid. And—wait. Blue's eyes went wide. "Seconds?"

John smiled, and Blue's heart skipped a beat. Oh, that smile.

"And thirds and fourths if you want it."

"Really? Do you think we could sneak something for Chewie?"

John's right eyebrow shot up and then lowered very slowly. He shrugged. "I've got pockets in the suit jacket. I've never known what they were for. Why not?"

Blue grinned and felt his heart skip another beat. Damn, John was such a nice guy.

Then a thought bubbled up from some dark depth of Blue's mind.

Sex.

Oh shit.

Was all this just John wanting sex? Another case of a married man—or separated or whatever he was—who liked sex with boys? And while Blue wasn't a boy anymore, he looked like one, and that had gotten him many a meal.

Was that what this was? So confusing. He hated not being able to read John.

One minute Blue had been on top of the world, but now?

He looked around the room. The drinks. Seconds on food. Sneaking something for Chewie?

Of course that was what it was.

Sex. It was always sex, wasn't it?

He sighed.

"Okay," he said. And he went to get his fill.

CHAPTER EIGHT

THEY HAD dessert. John insisted. Who knew when this boy—young man—would eat well again? John had the purple yam ice cream, and Blue tried the green tea flavor. He surprised John by offering him a taste. When he held out his spoon with the pretty light green blob of ice cream, John's lifetime fear of—what? Germs?—sharing utensils hit him, and…. And he looked into Blue's face and thought, *Oh fuck it*, and let Blue slide the spoon into his mouth. It was one of the most intimate things John had ever done. It made his heart do something strange and his cock shift in his slacks. *Again!*

So he shared a taste of his yam ice cream and barely even thought about it when he put the next spoonful in his own mouth. Hey! Despite Vivian getting him to share his Coke at the movies, this was new for him. Vivian was right. They'd made out. What germs should he have been afraid of? Still, that was Vivian—he didn't know Blue! But then he watched as Blue licked his own spoon with the tip of his pink tongue and quite suddenly wondered what that tongue would taste like.

What was Blue doing to him?

They finished, and John took Blue straight back to Four-Footed Friends to see Chewie, but just as Elaine had predicted, the dog was still out, resting peacefully.

"Take me home," Blue said, yet another tear slipping down one of his cheeks.

"I'll need the address," John said.

Blue looked at him with an unexpected expression—startled?—and after a blink or two, he gave John his address and then mumbled something that sounded like "I thought you were taking me to…."

To what? John wasn't sure what Blue meant.

Home was a shock for John.

He saw the old house immediately for what it was—an abandoned house. Blue was a squatter. Of course. John felt stupid. Now it made sense. And what a place: weathered and gray, some windows broken, shutters cockeyed, some gone, the gutter on one side of the house hanging down from one end, the first step up to the porch missing.

God. Blue lives here?

(And dammit, he still hadn't asked if Blue was his real name.)

John put the car in park and saw that Blue was studying him. Was looking at him thoughtfully, as if examining him or getting ready to ask a question. Blue opened his mouth—*here it comes*—but then shut it, and then he thanked John. Without warning, he leaned in and gave John a light, quick kiss. But this one was directly on the mouth.

John was rendered speechless—not that he spoke reams to begin with—but.... But his blood! John could feel it *zinging* through his veins, hot and cold by turns.

"Thank you, John," Blue said, so close John could feel the heat of his breath, smell the scent of orange juice and vodka and ginger and green tea ice cream.

John trembled and felt an almost overwhelming temptation to place his hand on the back of the young man's neck and pull him forward into another kiss—this one not nearly as chaste.

"Thank you so much," Blue said. "Thank you for everything."

Blue pulled back, and they locked eyes, and dammit, John couldn't read what he saw. Was… was that hurt? *Did I do something wrong?* Was it confusion? Damn! He couldn't read this young man, and that was what he was good at. What he used so well in business. He felt he was missing something important—very important!—and in the next few seconds, it was going to be too late.

Blue slumped, then sighed, opened his car door, and jumped out—all in one swift, fluid motion. "Good night," Blue said and then turned, leapt over a half-crumbled cement step up to the property's yard level, and dashed up the walkway to the house. He made a second leap over the missing wooden porch step. Blue stopped for one instant, peered over his shoulder, and—

John was electrified as he thought of that first time Blue had looked at him the same way.

—gave him a simple childlike wave and disappeared into the house.

John sat there for what felt like a decade, although when he finally glanced at the digital clock on the dashboard, he saw it had not been more than a moment or two. He found himself touching his lips *very* carefully, perhaps to see if his lips felt somehow different.

I didn't ask him if Blue is his real name!

But that was followed by something almost profound.

What difference does it make if that's his "real" name? That's what he calls himself. That's what matters.

But....

Why that for a name? Why Blue?

Blue as in bright blue and beautiful and lovely? Or blue as in sad?

John wanted to believe the former.

And for one long moment he considered—was tempted, was near *seduced* into—getting out of his car, running up to that house, knocking on the door, and asking.

But then the moment was gone.

I can't do that.

It would be crazy.

John Williams didn't do shit like that.

All that was followed by one more thought as he pulled his car away from Blue's house. It wasn't decorum or modesty or even shyness that kept him from knocking on that door. His wife—*ex*-wife now in every way except on paper—was right.

Boring.

I'm boring.

I'm too fucking scared to knock on a door.

Because if he did, everything in his life would change. And he didn't like change. He didn't like waking up in a hotel room, even in the Virgin Islands or the bottom of the Grand Canyon. He wanted *his* coffee and his back deck and always knowing where his bedroom slippers were. Always.

Blue had hitchhiked west all alone and picked apples in an orchard and learned Spanish with Mexican workers. Imagine doing something like that.

Boring. Vivian is right. I'm boring.

But I don't have to be.

I could take a chance.

I could go knock on that door.

A door that right now seemed as far away as a three-day hitchhike.

And God! The idea was near *terrifying*.

Because he knew as he looked back toward Blue's house that if he did knock on the door, it was very likely that an incredible change would take place in his life. He was just too afraid, and that made him feel very sad.

No.

Worse.

Lonely.

Perhaps more lonely than he'd ever felt in his life.

BLUE STEPPED into the foyer, remembering to avoid that six-foot-by-six-foot area to the right of the door where the floor was rotted out from the rain that came down from the leaky section of roof above. No one had fallen through yet, but someone very well could. It was getting gloomy, the corners and ceiling filling with shadows, so he knew he should light some of his candles that he always kept handy—normal candles, mostly bought from the Dollar Store, and not his penis ones. Those he rarely lit at all.

He went upstairs, struck by how Chewie-less the house felt already. No happy bark. No doggie toenails clip-clipping on the floor. No shaggy, incredibly soft head nudging under his hand for a scratch behind the ear or a pat on the head. And Blue hadn't even climbed into his empty bed yet.

Goddamn, it hurt.

It hurt knowing he was responsible, no matter what Hound Dog or Elaine or even John said.

John.

The thought of the big man came with its own hurt.

I thought he liked me. And then I thought he only wanted me for sex. And when that wasn't the case.... When that wasn't the case, he didn't know what was worse. Because right now he could use that big (wonderful) man in his bed.

Being wanted was important to Blue. Even if all anyone—men— wanted from him was sex. His mouth, his ass. Rarely his company.

That was something, at least.

Because the people in his life who had really mattered to him hadn't seemed to want him at all, had they? They'd gone away.

Tonight, company might have been exactly what John wanted. Yet John just dropped him off and left.

Neither company nor sex. Not being wanted for his company Blue was used to. But to be rejected sexually as well? Sex was where things always ended. It felt so strange that this evening had ended without it.

It all made Blue feel so... untethered. Like he might simply float away.

Or fade away.

It wasn't like he hadn't felt that way before.

God! He needed company. He ran up the stairs while he could still see well enough to do so, calling for "Ruby?" and then "Gavel? Sly? Anybody home?"

But there was no response, and when he checked their bedrooms, no one there.

In fact, Gavel and Sly's room looked stripped.

He stepped in and checked, and... damn... everything was pretty much gone.

They were gone.

They'd packed up and left. Moved. Vamoosed. Hit the road. Yet two more people who had simply gone away.

Blue was alone.

No Chewie.

No Ruby.

No Gavel or Sly.

And no John.

There was a sudden and very loud crack of thunder, so loud it shook the house, and he jumped and nearly peed himself.

And quite suddenly Blue felt more alone than he could remember feeling in a very long time.

THE INSIDE of John's car had never felt as big and empty as it had when Blue left. It was a ridiculous feeling, but nevertheless, it was how John felt. Blue, as small as he was, had *filled* the car with his presence. Now all there was in this preposterously large car was boring old John Williams.

Worse than boring.

I'm an asshole.

An asshole because he had so enjoyed being with Blue despite the fact that the kid was worried desperately about his dog. Enjoyed holding Blue despite the fact that he'd been crying, grieving. Enjoyed that kiss despite… despite what?

Despite it all.

I got a hard-on while he was feeling pain. What kind of a creep does that?

He was startled when the first *plunk-plunk-plunk* of heavy raindrops hit the windshield and then actually let out a strangled shout when a crack of thunder as loud as any he could remember in a long time shook the Lexus. A half block away a car alarm went off—*Wee-ah-wee-ah! Whoop-whoop-whoop!*—and then another, followed, of course, by the barking of dogs near and far.

John switched on his radio, and as if it were preordained, the words poured from the speakers. "…severe storm warnings lasting until one o'clock, with rain possibly turning to snow as temperatures drop down into the lower thirties—" John snapped it off as quickly as he'd turned it on and—

Shit! Blue's in that old house in this weather?

70

—he didn't even know he'd made the decision until he'd turned the car right at the first street, right again at the next, drove what he hoped were enough blocks—

That house didn't even look like it has power. Of course it doesn't. It's abandoned!

—and turned right and right again.

He'd made a perfect choice of where to turn, as the house was only a half block down. He was out of his car with no thought to the rain, which was growing heavier by the minute, managed the broken cement step and the missing wooden porch step, and without waiting even to knock, opened the door and stepped inside the house. He didn't even think about what he was doing until that moment. How crazy this was. What would Blue think of him busting in here without so much as knocking?

The foyer was dark, lit only by a few candles, and to the right was a huge room—even darker—probably a living room. When he stepped that way, ready to call out Blue's name, the floor sagged alarmingly, sending John's heart into his throat and his feet a good two inches into the hardwood (or in this case, *soft* wood!). John stepped back as quickly as he could and found sure footing again. He looked up, saw where the ceiling had fallen through and rain was already dripping heavily.

Shit! Blue lives *here?*

Small candles lit the way to the staircase on the back wall, thank goodness. This place was a frigging deathtrap.

Fuck, how crazy this was. He had to find Blue! Find him and at least for one night get him out of this wretched place.

BLUE LAY on his mattress, blanket pulled up around his ears, miserable.

Not so much from the cold, although he could *feel* it getting colder. It was the lack of Chewie, for one. Of friends. Of company.

He'd spent the whole afternoon with John, counting meeting him and making a fool of himself at Four-Footed Friends. But John hadn't seemed to feel he was foolish. Hadn't *seemed* to. John had been so kind.

Seemed genuinely interested in him, although he still wasn't sure if John was gay or not. He was married, although that seemed to be only technical at this point. His wife had left him.

It seemed like there had been something. The way John looked at him. Really *looked* at him. It made Blue's skin tingle and his heart skip. He couldn't figure the man out! Was he just a sweet man, or was he sexually interested in Blue?

But who cared if he was gay or not? John had paid attention to him. Better, he hadn't taken him to some hotel the minute after they found out Chewie was okay and then bent him over a bed. He'd taken Blue *home*. Hadn't used him like some piece of Kleenex, like Mom said men did.

All that made Blue feel even lonelier. He'd had some real human contact, and he didn't get a lot of that. He put people off for some reason—well, he knew why—and that made for a lonely existence.

It was the whole airheaded thing. It attracted people to him long enough to help him out—although that often came with a price—but they soon got bored with him. Wanted to get away. Was that what had happened with John? Even though they'd laughed about *Star Wars* and cars and seemed to be having fun. Fun, even with the horrible, awful way the day had started. Had Blue finally just gotten to be too much for John?

He fought off the memories of his family and how wondrous his childhood had been—making cookies with Mom, playing catch in the backyard with Dad, running around naked all weekend out at that hippy camp his parents loved so much, and the skinny-dipping and the freedom, freedom, freedom of being a part of the McCoy clan—before he went to live with his grandparents and lost his—

There was another cracking *ka-BOOM* of thunder, and he jumped and whimpered and cursed himself for being such a little girl.

Tonight in this old house, with the rain coming down heavier by the moment, all he could do was remember and try not to be lonely and—

"Blue!"

Shit! He was starting to hear things. For a second there, in the echo of that thunderbolt, he actually thought he'd heard his name being called out. Well, it certainly wasn't Gavel or Sly. They were gone. Apparently forever. And he couldn't imagine that Ruby, out for the evening, would be home so soon.

"Blue!"

He sat bolt upright on his mattress. Somebody *was* calling his name!

"Blue!"

Was… was that *John*?

Blue sprang off his mattress and dashed into the hall.

And there he was. John. It *was* John! Standing there at the top of the stairs, and thank God he'd lit a candle at the end of the hall because it cast just enough light to show off John's handsome face. Seeing a dark silhouette like that without being able to see who it was would have been something right out a horror movie.

John! It's John!

It was all Blue could do not to sprint down the hall and leap into John's arms. (And he could tell the big man could have caught him and held him tight and maybe even grasped his ass with those big hands of his and….)

And then he went right ahead and did it.

Ran, but not so fast as to maybe knock John down the flight of stairs. And he did jump, and damn if John didn't catch him as effortlessly as if he were a teddy bear and hold him just as easily. John's hands weren't on his ass, but they supported his upper thighs, and it was only with the greatest effort that Blue didn't wrap his legs tightly around John's waist. John would have felt his growing erection then, and Blue wasn't sure how the man was going to react to something like that—those damned mixed messages—and then, *then*, Blue felt John growing hard against the base of Blue's own cock and he breathed an inward sigh of relief, forgetting all about how he'd felt when he decided at the restaurant that John only wanted to sleep with him.

John trembled then and let Blue go but didn't drop him, allowing him to slowly slide down his body. He cleared his throat and backed off, and Blue grabbed his arm to keep him from going too far and toppling down the steps.

"I… I…." John cleared his throat again and then said, "I think you should come home with me tonight. If…. That is, if you trust me."

He trusted John. He did.

Blue nodded, and then John followed suit, and Blue warned him about a spot on the downward side of the steps that might break under John's weight. Once outside, they ran for John's car—it was pouring the proverbial cats and dogs—and not five minutes later (but an entire world away), they were at John's house.

It turned out to be as gorgeous on the inside as the outside, and Blue supposed that bank presidents must make really good money. There was lots of hardwood and glass and paintings and prints and bookcases and rugs (instead of wall-to-wall carpets) and a huge tank of saltwater fish (now how could anyone think *that* was boring?). The kitchen (where John made hot chocolate for them both "To warm our bones after that downpour!") was twice as big as Blue's room, with two ovens set into the wall and an island with copper pots and pans hanging over it and more counter space than Blue had ever seen. When John barely touched one of the cabinets, it lit up from within. John went into a little room off the side of that enormous kitchen, and when he came back, he brought a big T-shirt and a pair of pink sweatpants.

"Sorry about the color," John said. "They're my wife's, and I think mine would be ridiculously big on you. I thought you might want to change. We're both soaked."

"I like pink," Blue assured him, and John pointed the way to a little bathroom off the other side of the room (finally, something small about this house!). Even it was gorgeous, with a sink that looked like a big glass bowl, and damn if the toilet wasn't one of those silent kind that muffled sound (although Blue didn't know that until he used it).

When he came out, he saw John had changed into something similar (it kind of turned Blue on to know he was wearing John's shirt; it was so big on him that it had to be John's), and he was just finishing up the chocolate. He told Blue to sit down at a barstool along one of the granite counters. Blue tried not to look, but he couldn't help it, and he saw quite a bulge in the front of John's sweats, which made the front of Blue's begin to tent out as well. He sat down quickly before John noticed. In some situations it would have been just what they needed to get the ball rolling, but again there were those mixed fucking messages! One minute he thought John wanted him, and the next it felt as if the opposite were true.

He did get hard when he was holding me at home. He got hard at Temujin's too!

But did that mean anything? His wife had left him. Maybe he was just horny as hell and his body reacted to Blue's against his.

They sat in silence and drank their chocolate, and John apologized that it was instant, which made Blue laugh. Did anyone make real hot chocolate anymore?

"I should have offered you a hot shower," John said quite suddenly. "You're probably freezing. God, I didn't even give you a towel for your hair."

"It's okay," Blue said, and then John *did* ask if he would like a shower. Oh, that would be nice. A hot shower. It had been a week since Blue had washed off with anything other than the hose from his next-door neighbor. And if it turned out that John did want him, wouldn't he want to be clean? *Completely* clean? So he told John that would be nice, and John led him upstairs and then hesitated in the hall. Was he having second thoughts?

"Here," John said with a nod, and they went into a big bedroom with an enormous bed—the master bedroom, surely—and then to a bathroom with a shower and step-in tub that included Jacuzzi jets. It was an almost imposing room, and Blue wondered what it would be like to live life with a bathroom like this. Even the towels—surely John didn't want him to use one of those towels!—looked luxurious, as if one or two swipes would be all it took to have the water sucked off his body. What would they feel like?

With a nod, John left the room—

Guess we won't be showering together.

—and closed the door.

Blue got the shower going, and it was amazing. Hard not to stay in it half the night, because when was he ever going to shower like this again? He got hard but didn't do anything about it. There was still the possibility that maybe John wanted him, and Blue was surprised by just how much he wanted John. He'd read somewhere once that it was pretty common to want sex when thoughts of mortality were in the air, and every time Blue's mind strayed to Chewie, thoughts of mortality were indeed present. Was that it? Did he want John so much because of Chewie? Instead of being relieved that maybe, just maybe, someone was simply being nice?

When Blue was dressed again—the towels had been like heaven and had indeed dried him as if by magic—he found that the bed had been turned down on only one side, and he called out to John and found him across the hall in a smaller bedroom with a much smaller bed.

"You're sleeping in here?" Blue asked with a pang of disappointment.

John gave a single nod and then laid an eBook reader of some kind on the bedside table. "I have been since…." His voice faded away, and Blue realized what he'd probably been about to say.

Since my wife left.

So no reason to ask if John wouldn't want the bigger bed. Blue glanced out the door to the hall, beyond which lay a bedroom with a gigantic (empty) bed, and realized he was sleeping alone. He sighed and bit back a surprising desire to cry.

Instead he thought of all that John had done for him, and he smiled and went to him and bent and kissed him lightly on the mouth. At John's tiny gasp, he backed off. With a "Good night, John," he quickly left the room and went to be alone.

And realized he really wasn't.

Because for the first time in as long as Blue could remember, it seemed that someone was helping him with no ulterior motive at all.

So he crawled into the huge, gigantic bed (at least it felt like that) and stared up at the ceiling. Even shadowed as it was, he couldn't help but compare it to his own. This one was pristine white, his own blotched and stained and smelling slightly (or not so slightly, depending on the month) of mold. Thank God he wasn't allergic. And he wondered if John wanted him or not—why John hadn't pulled him into his own bed. Why hadn't John taken the advantage that was his? After all, he had given Blue a better place to stay and fed him and even let him take a wondrously hot shower. Didn't John have a right to his body?

He thought John wanted him.

John had gotten hard at least twice.

Was it possible that…? Could it be as simple as—

God.

—that John was a gentleman?

A short pause was all it took for Blue to realize it was more than possible.

And maybe it was time to show John one more time, for sure, that Blue wanted him.

At least for a night.

CHAPTER NINE

JOHN LAY in bed, completely unable to sleep, and stared up at the dark ceiling.

He tried not to think about Blue, but what else could he think about? Nothing, of course. Nothing.

His cock had finally softened, but only a bit. He'd thought about masturbating, but there seemed something so crude and wrong about jerking off picturing someone in his head who was only a room away. Almost as if he were taking advantage of him. Objectifying him.

And even picturing Blue confused him. He wasn't sure what he wanted from the young man.

But God, want him he did.

He near *ached* thinking about what it might be like to have Blue in his arms. To… to… kiss him again. But to actually *do* the kissing this time and not just be kissed.

What would it be like to really kiss a man? Not the gentle pecks he'd received already—those had sent his heart racing like nothing he'd ever felt before—but really kiss a man. What would that be like?

Especially one so exquisitely beautiful?

But then there was the whole Vivian thing.

Wouldn't it be cheating?

Or when Viv walked out that door, unwilling to tell him even where she was going, had that freed him of any oaths they had made? For better or worse (and could it be much worse?), for richer and for poorer (and poor they certainly weren't—even though she hadn't needed a cent of his money), in sickness and health (he'd seen her through several miscarriages before doctors had advised they stop trying for another child—for her sake), until death do us part (and he wasn't dead—far from it).

If he did bend to his desires, if he pulled Blue into his bed, was it cheating? Was it cheating when your wife left you? Told you she was bored? Said she wanted to go to the fleshpots of Bangkok? When divorce papers hadn't been signed?

He knew friends wouldn't think so. How many men had he known who had sex with other women when they were only separated? All of them?

John thought of Blue again and trembled. He trembled in wonder and confusing need and a little bit of fear.

A lot of fear.

He thought about getting up and going to Blue's bed (because Viv had given it up after all; it wasn't hers anymore!) and climbing in with him and finding out what actualizing a kiss with a man would be like.

But then....

Then there was a light at the door.

It was Blue, and he was carrying a big candle, which made him look even more like an angel than he ever had before. He paused there for an endless moment and then came slowly into the room, placed the candle on the bedside table beside John's Kindle.

Shaking as if possessed, John sat up and swung his legs out of the bed and sat there, staring at beauty.

Neither said a word for what seemed like a thousand years.

John gazed into that sweet, lovely face and longed to kiss that mouth and was too afraid to make the first move. Finally, thank God, Blue stepped closer, and that was what John needed. He leaned forward—the distance between them seemed to take forever to cross—and then he did it.

He kissed a man.

A rush passed through him like nothing he had ever experienced. He grew almost dizzy with wonder. With awe. It was... *power*. Just like waves crashing on a beach or the rumbling of the thunder outside. And he put his arms around that slim waist, even though he was still too hesitant to pull Blue closer.

Blue took care of that.

Blue stepped into him and pressed his mouth harder against John's and then used his tongue lightly to urge John to open to him.

Heart pounding, John did as silently bid, and Blue slipped his tongue into John's mouth and gently guided him, coaxing him to do the same.

When John moaned, Blue took a step back, and John echoed the sound in frustration this time. It had taken all his nerve to kiss Blue and now Blue was taking it away?

But that was when he saw what Blue was doing.

He was not ending things.

With one quick, fluid movement, Blue swept his borrowed T-shirt over his head and stood there, naked in the candlelight.

He was gorgeous.

Had John thought of Blue as a boy?

Was there a corner of his mind that perhaps thought him effeminate?

That was banished in an instant.

Blue stood before John, revealed as the man that he was.

Slim but beautifully built, lightly muscled, and reminding John of a colt. His chest was well defined, his nipples magenta in the candlelight and surrounded by just a few hairs, enough to make sure John knew this was a man's chest. Lower down a hint of abs, and then a hairy tummy that almost—but not quite—hid his navel, all of which led to lush blond pubic hair frosted with white. His cock, startlingly large for such a small man, hung heavy, his balls loose and hairless, the right a little beneath its twin. Blue's penis was uncircumcised, the head a lovely pink, and it gave a slight jump as if compelling— begging—John to touch it.

To, for the first time ever, touch another man's cock.

And compelled, he did so.

John reached out and, hesitantly at first, cupped Blue's balls— surprised at their weight—and lifted them, letting Blue's cock rest against his wrist.

His own cock surged erect, and any doubt left him, although he still trembled with want and need and not knowing what to do next.

Then Blue stepped into him, reached for his T-shirt, and lifted it over John's head so that when he pressed himself to John, they were bare chest to bare chest. Amazing then how they seemed to fit together, and John moaned again, and then they were kissing. Kissing with urgency and desire, and Blue pushed him back onto the bed and climbed on him, straddled John and pressed the cleft of his ass onto John's aching hard cock. Blue kissed him again and rocked on John's need, and just as John thought he would cum from that alone, Blue lifted up and began to struggle with John's boxers.

John helped him, pushing and shifting until the underwear slipped off and fell to the floor, catching for a moment on one foot before falling away. Blue stopped kissing his mouth then—just as John had come to accept it as the near perfection it was—and trailed his lips down John's jaw and Adam's apple, lower down his neck, down his chest, then stopped to suck on his nipples—God, why did something he'd never cared for now seem like exquisite fire?—and then down and down and down, tickling, inducing shivers. And God! Oh God, oh God, oh God, Blue took John's now-throbbing cock into his hot wet mouth, and once more John almost climaxed on the spot. But Blue did something, something painful, grasped John's balls and the base of his cock, and hurt though it did—for just a second—it stopped his orgasm and let him slide into pleasure he had never known was possible. Magic was happening as Blue bobbed slowly up and down John's length, his tongue doing impossible things, that painful pressure applied each time John thought he would explode.

But then—*no!*—Blue stopped and climbed back up John's body and… what? John knew in that instant, as he saw Blue's cock getting closer and closer, what Blue wanted from him.

To his surprise he did want to try doing what Blue had been doing to him. Imagine! But then Blue shifted, and his erection turned away as Blue reached over to the bedside table, picking up something beside the candle.

Condom.

Blue was opening a condom packet.

God, that meant….

Blue rolled the condom down John's cock—he almost came again—and then opened a tiny tube and squirted wetness onto his throbbing length. Then climbing and shifting again…. *Oh—my—God!*

Heat, tightness, unbelievable bliss overwhelmed John as he slid into Blue's body.

Nothing had ever felt like this.

John had had no idea he *could* feel anything like this.

Blue grunted, winced for a second, and then sighed as he took John in completely. John's cock pulsed with his heartbeat, and a tremor passed through him. He waited in longing and overwhelming need, and finally Blue began to rock back and forth, sliding upward and then taking John deep again. Blue leaned forward and rested his hands on John's chest, and they stared into each other's eyes, Blue's lids heavy with desire. John grasped Blue's waist, then moved his hands up and down Blue's back, let them stop in his armpits, thumbs feeling wetness and heat, and then stroked up and down his back again. Finally he grasped Blue's perfect buttocks and guided the speed and depth he needed—needed ever so badly—and all too soon the world blotted out and he was cumming like he never had before. It was like he was shooting everything that he was into Blue—his very being along with his semen and perhaps a piece of his heart and soul. He was dimly aware then that his stomach and chest were being bathed in great spurts of wetness, Blue was cumming all over him, and his heart pounded in welcome. It was as if he were being baptized or some such fucking wonderful thing, and he pulled Blue down and kissed him, kissed him with everything he had and everything he was.

And when they finally came out the other side, John knew he would never be the same.

Baptized, he was.

Fallen and risen into the man he was always supposed to be.

JOHN WOKE to the sound of cardinals and the golden glow of sunshine.

He was looking into Blue's face. And it was beautiful.

There was a man sleeping next to him. It was morning. The man had spent the night.

He had had sex with a man.

God.

Blue was even more beautiful in daylight than he had been in candlelight.

I fucked him. I fucked a man.

Although it was more like Blue had fucked him, wasn't it? Not, but like. Because Blue had been almost fully in control.

I don't even know if Blue is his real name.

That nose. That nose was so… so damned cute!

John smiled and chuckled and then shook his head.

I fucked someone half my age.

I wonder if Viv would think I'm boring now.

Guilt.

It hit heavy and strong for a moment, and then… the guilt was *gone*.

A sweet little smile tugged at the corners of Blue's mouth (which made John's heart skip a beat), and the guilt was gone in an instant.

She left me.

For better or worse.

This is better.

My God, this is better.

This is what I was missing.

And I don't even know if Blue is his real name and this is better than anything I have ever experienced in my life.

Blue shifted and rolled onto his back. The sheet pulled down a bit, and John could easily see Blue's morning erection tenting the fabric.

John throbbed and smiled and thought, *We both have erections. We are both men.*

It might have been a rude thing to do, but John reached out and took the sheet and pulled it down so that he could see.

God, it's big.

In the morning light, it was beautiful as well. For some reason it was Blue's balls John was drawn to—they were fascinating. The way one hung just a bit lower than the other. They were both the same size as far as he could tell. Beautiful. And beautiful was not a word he thought he would have used to describe a man's balls. But it was true. The skin of his scrotum looked so soft. So silky. He wanted to touch it. No. He wanted to see what it felt like on his tongue. What it tasted like.

He looked up at Blue's sleeping face as if he were going to be caught doing something he shouldn't and then moved closer, pulled the sheet a little lower, and saw that Blue's thighs were surprisingly hairy—especially compared to the rest of him. He brought his face even closer and smelled... musk. Smelled man. So different from the way the women he'd been with smelled. Not that he had that much experience, at least in numbers. Vivian and two others before her. She for twenty-five years or so.

Blue's scent was so different. He understood why it was called musk. It was sexy. Sexier. He didn't know how to describe it except that it made him want to get even closer.

So he did.

John moved within inches of Blue's balls, and then throwing caution to the wind—unable to resist—he pressed his face ever so gently between and against those balls. Oh, the warmth and silkiness of them was incredible, and he breathed deeply, filled his senses with....

With Blue.

The flesh was so warm.

He opened his mouth, let his tongue rest against one ball, tasted salt and spice and... musk. John licked, and Blue shifted and moaned and then sighed. The skin was so soft and smooth and delightful against John's tongue.

Blue's cock jumped, and a pearlescent crystal drop formed at the tip—*precum*, John thought—and with *Do it, it's time* encouraging him, John reached out with a finger and carefully touched it. When he drew it away, it formed a thin shiny thread. Fascinating. And before he could stop himself, he touched it to his tongue and tasted... salt... and sweet... and....

He didn't know how to describe it.

But John wanted more.

And so he shifted again and almost reverently took Blue's hard shaft into his hand and carefully pulled it away from that flat furry tummy. Thinking, *This is it*, he took it into his mouth.

And now I can't go back.

The first time he took Blue's cock too deep and gagged—hoping Blue didn't hear the sound; he didn't want Blue to think it had made him want to retch—and he backed off and then took it again, more cautiously the second time. It slid in smoothly, and John shivered in delight—felt goose bumps—and rested his tongue against the underside, tried to echo the things that Blue had done, and thought, *I'm a cocksucker*, and he grinned—mouth full of cock—and liked it. *Liked* that he was a cocksucker—

God! I'm a cocksucker!

—and began to suck it in earnest.

One minute he was asleep, and the next he was cheerfully— *cheerfully!*—sucking this near stranger's cock.

Excited beyond belief, he began to hump his own erection into the mattress. He carefully took Blue's balls in one hand and gently rolled them around, tasting more and more of Blue as his fluid began to flow stronger and stronger. Then Blue's fingers were in his short hair, and Blue was moaning and then crying out, "Oh fuck, John, if you don't… if you don't stop, I'm going to…."

John, amazed at how much he wanted it, moaned and nodded, and then—whoa!—Blue was flooding his mouth in hard, heavy jets, and the flavor was very strong, almost gamey but exciting. *I'm letting a man cum in my mouth, and I am loving it*, and *Fuck! I'm cumming!* And he ejaculated against the sheets, the pleasure of both happening at once all but overwhelming.

It was almost as if he had sucked himself off!

The semen was still in his mouth, and before he thought any more about it, he swallowed it, swallowed Blue, and then Blue squirmed down and kissed him full on the mouth, and they shared the last vestiges of that semen, Blue moaning all the more.

They kissed and kissed and kissed and got hard again (not that either had really gotten soft) and got into a sixty-nine position and began to suck on each other again. Blue, who knew what he was doing, got John, all forty-five years of him, ready to cum again surprisingly quickly—

(it was all so mind-spinningly sexy: Blue's hairy thighs—a *man's* thighs—and his shifting balls and the taste and the smell of Blue's incredibly fucking hard cock and the way it felt in his mouth)

—and they almost simultaneously came into each other's mouths.

Blue flipped again and they held each other—clutched at each other—and laughed quietly and breathed.

They looked at the bedside clock at the same time, and since it was much too early to go see Chewie, they just stayed in each other's arms and slept for a while and then got up and went across the hall to the master bedroom to shower together.

In the shower Blue did something shocking. John almost ordered "No! You can't do that," but Blue had already begun, had buried his face between the cheeks of John's ass to kiss and lick his hole, and exquisite didn't begin to describe how it felt. Blue made him wonder what it was like to be fucked—that was something he'd never fantasized about, when he'd allowed himself to fantasize about such things to begin with—and he wondered if he even *could* take Blue's thick cock inside him like that. And then he remembered the paradise of being inside Blue and realized that fair was fair after all.

So he told Blue to fuck him, and Blue asked, "Are you sure?" and John told him he was *very* sure—

"Now, right now!"

—but Blue insisted they get in bed first because he needed a condom, and fuck, John hated that because he wondered what it would feel like to have Blue cum inside him. Here, though, Blue was the teacher, and Blue told him to never ever let a man fuck him without a condom—ever!—and then began to do that thing with his mouth again, what Blue called "rimming."

"Man, I love your ass," Blue said.

"You do?" John asked and blushed into the pillow.

"Hell, yes," Blue said. "I like how the skin is darker right in your crack and almost totally hairless so I can see everything. And your hole is gorgeous, like a starfish or something, and the little folds… they're all smoothing out." Then Blue licked and sucked again, and he got some more of the lube and teased John's hole and slipped—*Oh God!*—a finger inside.

It felt so weird at first, and then sexy, and Blue played him like an instrument and got two fingers inside him and wiggled them around like mad. *Whoa!* It felt wild—and soon he had to know, *had to know*, what it was like to have a cock inside him.

So following another "Are you sure?" John nodded and said, "Please, Blue. Please." Then Blue was on top of him, using his knees to urge John's legs apart, and then carefully and oh, so slowly pushing inside him….

Hurts!

"Push out," Blue whispered in his ear, and the stubble on Blue's chin tickled. John nodded and pushed out even though that sounded like it should be wrong and—*Oh!*—Blue was there, *inside* him.

It burned at first while he was being fucked, but Blue was a careful and attentive lover. Then something magic happened—there were sparks and little jolts—*oh God!*—and Blue really was *fucking* him (*I am being fucked. A man is fucking me. A man has his cock in me!*), and John pushed back and got up on hands and knees and met each thrust, and soon they were crying out and moaning and then shouting and finally cumming together—*again!*

Afterward, with Blue's delicious weight atop him, John wondered how many times this had been. With last night included, was this the fourth time?

They lay there awhile and then saw the time and got up and showered again, and John made toast real quick so they would have something besides each other inside them. Then—calling first to make sure someone was there—they went straightaway to Four-Footed Friends.

As he drove it hit him.

I'm gay.

No doubt. None at all. No question.

How did I not know?

John had known he was attracted to men, but he'd read somewhere that almost everyone was bisexual—it was the Kinsey Report; that's where he'd read it—to some extent or other, and he'd just assumed that was it. He was bisexual. And bisexual meant he was attracted to men as well as women, so he could choose, and he chose women because he did *not* want to stand out.

But now?

He knew as he drove that he wasn't bisexual. Not really.

He was gay.

Because sex had never ever, *ever* been the way it had been with Blue. There were no words to describe it. Only that what he'd had before hadn't really been sex. He knew clearly why he'd been so indifferent to it before. It was because he'd been sexual with women instead of men. For him being with both sexes wasn't variety. Not different flavors of ice cream (purple yam or green tea). No. For him it was men.

The sex was stunningly different.

I'm gay! he marveled and found himself smiling.

Despite the joy of what he'd discovered, he had some lingering guilt.

No wonder Vivian had left.

Indifferent.

Who wanted to be treated with indifference?

She deserved the joy he'd had these past twelve hours or so. Instead she'd had an indifferent lover in her bed. So unfair.

But now she could have more.

He smiled again.

They both could.

That's the way it should be.

And that's the way it could be now.

CHAPTER TEN

HOUND DOG met them at Four-Footed Friends.

Dr. Lee was there too. Although he introduced himself as Dr. Garrow, which Blue found confusing until H.D. whispered that *everyone* called him Dr. Lee. He didn't understand, but all he cared about was that Chewie was awake.

Chewie's tail went a mile a minute when he saw Blue, and that felt good. Really good. He whined and mushed his face against Blue's hand and licked his fingers.

"Oh, my Chewie," Blue cried. "My big strong boy. Look at that cast!"

Blue turned to H.D. and the vet.

"Can I take him home?"

The two men looked at each other, then at Blue.

"It might be good to leave him another day," Dr. Lee (Garrow?) said. "Just so we can keep an eye on him. And he can stay relaxed."

No! Blue looked to Hound Dog for help.

Except he didn't. "You know he'll be jumping all around and everything," H.D. said. "And that leg is in a poor way."

H.D. was agreeing? Rebel of the world? The guy who followed no rules? Of course, that's what Blue liked about him. He'd seen so much of it at Men's Festival. But thinking of Festival made him recall something he didn't want to remember.

Blue turned to John. John bit his lower lip. "Maybe they're right," he replied.

The only reason Blue didn't burst into tears was because the big strong man had said it.

"Can I see him again later today?" Blue asked.

Now it was Hound Dog's turn to bite his lip, but after a pause he said, "Oh, what the fuck. I'll want to check up on him and see how he's

89

doing anyway. He'll want to use the bathroom. He's refusing to go in his cage, so I was going to have to carry him outside anyway. So fine! Why not? How about I call you about an hour before I leave the house, and we can meet here?"

"Sounds good," Blue said—lying because he wanted Chewie with him right *now*. He told John that in the LS 600.

"I don't think it's a good idea," John said.

What? What had he just said? Blue tried not to glare at him. They were at a stoplight, and John looked over at Blue, his expression unreadable again.

"You don't think it's a good idea for Chewie to be with someone who loves him?" Blue asked.

"Of course I do," John replied. "I just want him to be safe."

Safe? *Safe?* "And you don't think he's safe with me?" Oh hell, of course he didn't. "Because it's *my* fault he got hit by the car?" Was that what he meant?

John threw him a startled look. "No!" He shook his head and started the car into motion again. "I…." He stopped talking.

"What?" Blue huffed at him.

"Your house…."

My house? "My house?" *What's wrong with my house?* "What's wrong with my house?"

"Blue…. You don't even have electricity. If you don't need it, don't you think Chewie does?"

Blue blinked at him. He couldn't help but feel hurt. "You mean because my house isn't as nice as your banker's house?"

"Blue! I have *electricity*. You have a weak spot in the foyer that Chewie could fall through. You have a step that could break. Don't you think—"

"I don't think we can all be bankers!"

John pulled the car over to the shoulder. Threw it in park. "Blue?"

"*What?*" Blue barked.

"Is that your real name?"

Blue's mouth fell open. "What?"

90

John gave him a weak smile. "I—I was just wondering. Is Blue your birth name?"

Blue nodded.

"Really?"

Blue nodded again. "My parents were New Agers. They were the coolest." And they were. So wonderful. "They thought names like David and J—" Shit! He'd almost said John! "Fred were boring. They thought unique names were more important."

"So Blue?"

"You don't like it?" he asked, trying not to feel hurt once again.

"It's just that... well, they say that there is power in our words. I read that in this book about leaping...."

"Leaping?" Blue asked.

John shrugged. "Isn't blue about being sad?"

Now Blue shrugged. "Sometimes. But it's also the color of the sky," he said, remembering his mother's words when he'd asked her the same question long, long ago. He never forgot her answer. "And the sea. It's a masculine color. And it symbolizes trust and wisdom, faith and truth, intelligence and sincerity."

John nodded.

"Heck, they named my—"

John kissed him.

It was a very nice kiss. And it was right there on the street where, even though they were in John's car, anyone could see. Blue's heart raced, and he could almost forget the fact that John had dissed the place where he lived.

John pulled back ever so slightly, and Blue looked at him in surprise.

"I'm sorry, Blue. I didn't mean to imply anything bad about your home."

Blue sighed. Felt a pang. "No. You're right." Of course he was. *I'm living in an abandoned house!* "Chewie does need a better place to heal. But I have what I have and—"

"You could stay with me," John said.

Blue was even more surprised.

"J-just… I mean, at least a few days, until Chewie was doing—is doing—better?"

Blue felt a hitch in his heart. John was looking at him with those beautiful eyes of his, and they were so full of kindness. Such a nice man.

But Blue couldn't do that to John. Stick John with *him*. Because in a few days the same thing would happen that always happened. He would get tired of Blue. Blue would do something stupid or upset him, or he would just start driving John crazy. He didn't want—

"Blue, I'm a little scared."

Then Blue was more than surprised; he was astonished. John? Scared? The two words didn't seem to go together.

"You?"

John nodded. "I've never done anything like this before."

"Never done what before?"

"You. Me. I've never…."

Shit. What was John saying? They'd just met yesterday.

"The gay thing," John said. "I've never…."

Oh.

But, then, he'd suspected, hadn't he? It made sense.

"I'm freaking a little…," John continued.

Blue sighed.

"But I am also more excited than I think I've ever been. I had no idea I could feel like this."

Feel like this?

"And I don't know if you and I… I mean… I know it's soon. I don't… I don't know what this feeling means. What I am feeling for…. God! I don't *know* what I mean! You're half my age, and you probably like guys more your age and—"

"I would be happy to stay with you a few days," Blue said suddenly, not even realizing he was going to. His heart was racing again. *What am I doing?* "At least until Chewie gets a little better."

Maybe there would be blueberry muffins.

John smiled.

"I WOULD be happy to stay with you a few days," Blue said suddenly, and John's pounding heart practically stopped. "At least until Chewie gets a little better."

John smiled.

There had been a moment there. When he'd told Blue he didn't think it was a good idea for Blue to take Chewie home. He'd upset the young man. But how the hell was Blue's dog going to recover in that falling-apart house? The pain that had been on Blue's face!

But he had to tell Blue the truth. He had to respect him enough for that. It hadn't been easy, though! He could solve any problem at the bank. He could wheel and deal and do magic. He could oversee scholarships, promotional material, media spots, website content, any events the bank sponsored and so much more. But he couldn't talk when there wasn't a desk between him and another person? Couldn't be *human*? Which is why he laid it on the line, just like he would with a client at the bank. Reminded him that Blue didn't even have electricity.

At least he found out that Blue was really his name.

"You don't like it?" Blue had said, and John was sure that he'd bungled things again, but then he'd explained himself. What's more, he kissed Blue. He didn't even know he was going to do it. He just leaned in and kissed him. It was quite possibly one of the most the most impulsive things he had ever done. He couldn't believe he'd done it. But as he captured Blue's lips with his own, really kissed him, he knew it might be the sweetest, most magical thing he'd ever done as well.

Am I boring now, Vivian?

When he pulled back, he saw that Blue just might be as surprised as he was.

But he also knew he needed to apologize. "I'm sorry, Blue," he said, deciding not to think through his words. He just threw caution to the wind. "You could stay with me." *My God! What did I just do?*

Oh, the look of surprise on Blue's face.

And why not! John had just shocked the shit out of his own self! *What am I doing?*

But the very thought of waking up with Blue in his bed again…. And again.

Not that Blue had to stay in his bed.

Just to make him coffee in the morning would be enough. Help him with Chewie. Hell, he'd carry the dog in and out of the house!

His heart pounded even at that!

Just because this beautiful boy gave himself to me so freely last night—his heart pounded so hard it hurt—*doesn't mean anything more than one night!* But as crazy as it was, John wanted more. He thought of waking up this morning to Blue in his bed and he knew he wanted to wake up every damned morning with him. Sure, it was crazy. He didn't know Blue. But he wanted to.

But that was when Blue had said the magic words. Words that made John's heart soar!

"I would be happy to stay with you a few days," Blue said. "At least until Chewie gets a little better."

For the first time in forever, John knew what leaping was all about. And that sometimes, nets did appear.

CHAPTER ELEVEN

JOHN ASKED Blue what he wanted to do to kill time—offered quite a few suggestions—and Blue blurted out, "Have sex?"

John looked at him in surprise and then blushed.

And nodded.

They drove back to John's place in silence, and Blue started to wonder if he'd said the wrong thing, but the minute they walked through the door, John turned to him and pulled him into his arms and kissed him like—well, he wasn't sure! He wasn't sure if he'd ever been kissed like this before.

It was almost like they were in love.

What a stupid thought.

Love.

How could it be love?

But then Blue decided to pretend, to melt with it, flow with it, and his heart began to rush, and his cock grew diamond hard and—*Yes!*—John's did too. He could feel it.

Then John picked him up and—*Yes!*—grabbed his ass with those big hands of his, and his asshole kegeled in anticipation.

I want to be fucked.

He almost said it aloud, but John still seemed so skittish. Blue had to find some other words to convey what he desired. He didn't want to scare the man! It was the last thing he wanted.

But sex? Sex he needed. He needed to plunge himself into it (have it be plunged into him). He needed to feel alive.

John actually carried him upstairs—after Blue wrapped his legs around John's waist and pressed the lower part of his ass (just below the base of his cock) against John's hard length. When they got to the bedroom, John still didn't put him down but kissed him. Kissed him hard and deep and took his breath away.

Then John sat him on the bed—and damn, it was the master bedroom, and didn't that mean something?—and pulled his T-shirt off and kissed him again. He got down on his knees—imagine a big sexy man on his knees in front of him—and took off Blue's sneakers and his socks and then....

Wow....

John was pressing Blue's damp feet against his face. It tickled, but not too much, and—*Gosh*—John was moaning. He started kissing the bottoms of Blue's feet and, holy cow, sucking on each of his toes, and yes, it tickled, but it was also sending shocks of pleasure through his whole body until Blue thought he'd cum in his pants. But John had him cum somewhere else instead. He unzipped Blue's jeans and pulled them and his underwear off and then took his cock deep, as if he'd been sucking dick since he was Blue's age. Damn, it didn't take long. He tried to warn John, but before he could say anything, he shot off in John's mouth, and John swallowed. It was fucking bliss!

BLUE SHOT into John's mouth, and he swallowed hungrily, as if he'd been sucking dick and swallowing cum since he was Blue's age. It was creamy and surprisingly sweet with only that tinge of gaminess there, as if to remind John he was swallowing a man's semen (as if he could forget). Oh, and Blue's scent! Strong, very strong, and... musky (that really was the word) and wonderful.

How had he *not* done this all these years?

How had he avoided it?

Why?

Because you were married.

Of course that was part of it.

But now?

Now he was still married, but surely that was only on paper. Vivian was gone, and he knew she wasn't coming back. Not to be his wife, that was. Come home and file for divorce and decide who would get what, probably. No, they might as well be divorced already, and John found he didn't feel the slightest bit of guilt anymore, kneeling there between Blue's legs—in the bed he'd slept in with Vivian for so many years—nursing Blue's softening cock and then nuzzling his nose up and down and around those sexy—so fucking sexy—balls.

No guilt except for the guilt that he had never given of himself to her as he was to Blue. Of course she had left him! He'd been so hurt, and he'd been angry with her. For leaving. For calling him boring. He'd made her the villain. But *he* had been the villain! He saw that now. Locked her up in a castle and kept her here for years. But finally she had escaped, and he couldn't be angry with her anymore. No. Happy. Because *he* was going to be happy. He was happy for her. And he hoped and hoped and hoped that she was happy, or finding happiness anyway. Finding at least a fraction of the happiness he was feeling with Blue.

He wanted to make Blue happy too, and that thought came with lots of questions about the implications of making Blue happy.

Work, for one. People would find out. They would have to. How could he keep this a secret? There was no way, not ultimately. And neighbors. They would see Blue coming in and out and wonder why he was there. And what would John say? At some point he'd have to tell them. And friends. They would have to know, although he didn't have that many friends.

Those thoughts near terrified him for a moment. But then he looked at Blue lying back on the bed, one arm tossed over his head on the pillow, and had a weird sense of déjà vu as he remembered picturing Blue this way while they were in John's car going to Temujin's Mongolian Grill for dinner.

He could scarcely take it in. A few days ago he'd never kissed a man (although one had kissed him on the cheek). And now here he was in bed with one. It had all happened so fast!

Quite suddenly, the idea of everyone knowing was a little less scary. He wasn't ready to step out on his front porch and shout it to the neighbors. But he couldn't deny this was who he was….

But for now, all that was important was Blue. A part of that meant making him happy in bed. He thought maybe he was doing a pretty good job of sucking his cock—*I'm a cocksucker!*—and who knew pressing Blue's feet against his face and inhaling his sexy scent could be so fucking hot? But there was something that Blue had done for him and he hadn't done for Blue.

The idea scared him a little bit—*Can I do that?*—because he was the guy who didn't like to share straws, and then he thought, *What the hell*, and taking a deep breath, he took the plunge. He nuzzled down beneath the base of Blue's cock... and a little lower... and a little lower yet until...

"Oh God, John. Are you sure? I.... Oh *please*, John!"

Blue grabbed himself behind the knees and drew his legs wide and back and high. His cheeks opened, and there it was. *I've been inside that*, John marveled, looking at something beautiful and pink and seemingly way too small for such a thing.

Then without allowing himself to think about what he was doing—and Blue was clean; they'd showered after all—he pressed his face into that cleft and kissed Blue right there. Right there against that pucker of flesh.

Interesting. Blue let out a long, loud sigh.

And daring more, John gave it a quick lick and found that— *Whoa!*—interesting too.

Another longer lick, and it was rather amazing....

Like... like....

A penny.

The taste of copper... and a little tangy... and it wasn't at all unpleasant. The wonderful kinkiness—to him at least—of what he was doing hit him full strength then, and he moaned and pressed his face hard against that secret place, and he licked and licked and sucked and then—*Am I really doing this?*—pressed his tongue inside as that tight ring of muscle loosened and loosened to let him in.

"John," Blue cried. "Fuck me! Please, fuck me."

John staggered to his feet and started to unbutton his shirt, and Blue looked at him with unbridled lust—it was almost crazed, the way Blue looked at him—and shook his head and said, "No! Don't. I want you to *fuck* me with your clothes *on*. Pull your cock out of your jeans and *fuck* me. Please!"

John shivered with lust. Really? A smile took over his mouth. It sounded crazy hot! And so he did as bid. He unbuttoned his 501s and pulled his cock out and—

"Your balls! Pull them out too! Christ!"

—reached in and somehow managed to fish his balls out too. Damn, did it feel sexy! Thank God there were still condoms on the bedside table, and he slipped one on, afraid that simple gesture would send him over the edge. It didn't.

He grinned and clambered onto the bed, lined his cock up with that tiny, tiny hole, pressed, and went in halfway just that easily. Blue wrapped his legs around John's waist again, locked his ankles behind him, and pulled hard, and then John was inside Blue balls-deep.

It was one of the hottest moments John could remember.

In full daylight, he could see the gorgeous young man before him without impediment, spread and ready for him, breathing hard and gazing at him with lust in his eyes and his big cock literally throbbing and leaking fluid. An instant later John was deep inside him, and it was hot and tight and wet and—*Fuck!*—the goddamned sexiest thing in all of time.

Fuck you.

Going to fuck you!

And he did.

With Blue's urging, he did. He fucked him. Tried to keep himself in check, not wanting to hurt Blue (it was the last thing he wanted!), but Blue just kept crying, "Harder, John. Please, beautiful man. Please. Fuck me *harder*!"

And so he did.

"HARDER, JOHN," Blue shouted. "Please, beautiful man. Please. Fuck me *harder*!"

And so John did.

It scared Blue that he was saying such words because, as much as he didn't want to think about it, he remembered the last time he'd said words like those and the living hell it had become. The horror.

But that other man?

That man hadn't cared shit about him.

He had only been two holes for that man and his friend to use.

Blue had realized that day last summer that he wasn't liking it—was it only last summer?—and wanted it to stop, but he couldn't stop it, and finally he just surrendered so it would be over.

But this time?

This time he was getting what he actually *wanted*.

This time he was getting fucked hard, but with something more.

He didn't know what he was to John, but he was pretty sure he knew one thing.

Blue was more to John than holes.

This… this thing that was happening with John could be over tomorrow—

Except he asked me to move in with him while Chewie heals, and does he realize how long that could take?

—or it might last longer.

Please?

He looked into John's face and saw that he was fucking *Blue*, not just a hole. Hard and rough and desperate, yes, but desperate for him. He wasn't imagining it! There was caring as well as lust and need in John's eyes.

It took a gloriously long time for John to finish this time. Blue guessed the fact that the man had cum at least four times in less than twenty-four hours, was over forty, and was wearing that fucking raincoat on his cock that took away 99 percent of the feeling had something to do with it. But whatever the reason, this time Blue wanted it to last forever.

It didn't.

But it lasted long enough, and Blue was thrilled that he was doing something he hadn't done too many times in his life. He was cumming without even touching himself, shooting in mighty jets between them. John's eyes went wide with lust, and then he shouted, and Blue could feel John's cock jerking and twitching. It was glorious.

Then John collapsed on top of Blue and tried to roll off—

"I'll crush you," John all but sobbed.

—but Blue wouldn't let him.

He wanted, needed, to feel John's weight on top of him.

Though John was much heavier than him, if he were to fall asleep, Blue believed he could manage to rouse him enough to get him to roll off.

Instead John did something, Blue wasn't sure just what, with his knees, tucking them to either side of Blue, and sadly slipped out. Blue's legs fell down around him, and John tucked his arms under Blue's neck and rested his face in the hollow between Blue's neck and shoulder.

Blue thought maybe John did slumber just a little bit before giving a little shiver, half untangling himself, and rolling to his side, still keeping Blue in his arms.

And then John said, "I love you," and began to softly snore. Blue's eyes went wide, and he wondered if it could be true.

And if he wanted it to be true.

And of course, the answer to that was yes.

Oh yes.

"I LOVE you," John said and, knowing it was foolish to say it but not caring one bit, drifted into a deep sleep and dreamed a dream where he and Blue had been together for a very long time, and everyone was very happy.

BLUE WOKE from his dream with a scream, and when he saw where he was, the relief was gigantic. He looked at John in alarm, sure he must have awakened him.

He hadn't.

John lay there with a happy smile on his face, like a sleeping baby. Thank God.

Blue slipped out of bed and went first to the bathroom, changed his mind, went to the other bedroom, changed his mind there as well, and then went downstairs so that he could finally cry.

He wept. Wept in great painful lurching sobs.

In the dream he was being held down on a stone slab that had once been one of the most wonderful places on Earth.

"Take it!" the man who was fucking him yelled. "Take it, you goddamned *bitch*."

He wanted to tell Big Sir—that was who it was, or at least what he was called at the Heartland Men's Festival—to *stop*. To *please* stop. That this wasn't what he'd expected. Not at all. But he couldn't. His head was hanging off the end of a slab—an altar to the Green Man (who couldn't approve of this!)—and the other man was fucking his mouth, so he couldn't tell Big Sir that he was hurting him. Hurting him *bad*.

"Gonna *breed* you," the big man had growled. "Fill your sweet little ass with my cum. Fill you until you drip."

He wasn't wearing a condom! Blue always insisted his sexual partners wear condoms and hadn't realized Big Sir wasn't until it was too late and he could no longer protest. Big Sir was hurting him... hurting him so bad. And the cock slamming in his mouth—he didn't even know who the guy was other than some friend of Big Sir—was choking him, and he was seeing spots in front of his eyes from the lack of oxygen. Blue thought he was going to suffocate—

"Yeah," cried the man fucking his face. "Gonna fill you from this end. Choke you with my jizz."

—and God! Could he die this way?

He didn't die. But unlike with most dreams, the ones that were simply fantasies of his sleeping mind, the images and memories didn't fade. Blue couldn't stop them from playing in his head. They were seared into his memory.

Blue cried until his eyes burned and his chest ached, and then he snuck back upstairs and showered. He thought that it was the intensity of their lovemaking that brought up the memories Blue had tried to put behind him.

And yet something still felt good.

As he quietly went back to bed, climbed under the sheets, and snuggled up to John, something—somehow—was slightly better than before.

Because John would have stopped.

If Blue had asked, he knew *John* would have stopped. John had done what he did at Blue's urgings, fucked him hard because he'd wanted it. Wanted it hard for the first time since that horrible day. But John would have stopped.

Somehow he *knew* John would have stopped.

All he would have had to do was ask.

CHAPTER TWELVE

THEY HAD lunch. John made them grilled cheese sandwiches and tomato soup, and they ate in their underwear, which made John feel very daring and not at all boring. What would Vivian think? Had he ever been downstairs in his underwear? He got up after sex and put underwear on, and it had always driven her crazy. But otherwise he felt so… vulnerable. Exposed.

But that wasn't true with Blue, was it? Every time they'd had sex, John had drifted off to sleep naked and woken naked and cuddled naked and hadn't even thought about putting anything on. In fact, he hadn't even wondered about it. Until now.

Blue was transforming him in so many ways, so fast.

Yes, there he was, stodgy John, who wore suits to pet rescue centers, downstairs in the broad daylight in his underwear.

What if someone saw him? What if someone rang the doorbell?

He grinned and realized he didn't care.

And Blue looked so glorious in those blue underwear that made his cock look huge because of the way it cupped everything and his ass look like proof there must be a God after all, because how could something so majestic be a random mistake of nature?

"Want to eat on your patio?" Blue asked, standing next to the glass sliding doors and taking a bite of sandwich.

Wait. Not only be downstairs in their underwear, but outside?

Blue's eyes flashed. "Afraid?"

A little.

But excited by the idea as well.

And when he thought about it, John realized they probably couldn't be seen. There were trees in his backyard, enough to keep his neighbor to the rear from seeing anything. The couple to the south only had one window facing into John's backyard, and it was upstairs and seemed to always be curtained. And the neighbor to the north was a very old lady who had lived there all her life, and he doubted very much she would even be upstairs this time of day. Her grandson said she slept downstairs most of the time as the steps were too difficult for her.

So John smiled, went to Blue, opened the door, made an *after you* gesture, and followed him out onto the patio. They sat at the little table under the eave because John wasn't quite ready to expose himself totally to the world, but he was close. And it did feel so exciting to be outside like this.

Would someone boring do this?

He was just about to tell Blue that he wished he looked half as sexy in his underwear—simple boxers—as Blue did in his tight ones when Blue said, "You look so hot." He leaned in. "I can just see the head of your cock through your fly."

John blushed.

"I want to suck your cock right here."

John blushed all the harder. "Maybe next time," he whispered.

And then they chatted. It was nice. They just talked. John found he wanted to ask Blue all kinds of things, but he just didn't know where to start. It seemed wrong somehow to ask him why he was homeless. How he survived. And why he was interested in a man twice his age. Which only made him wonder what he was doing sitting here in his underwear with a man half his age. *What am I doing?*

"You okay, John?"

He almost startled at the question. Had he not looked okay? Was his confusion written on his face?

"I just can't believe what's happened in the last day, Blue. Until… until you, I'd never been with a man."

Blue nodded. "I figured that."

He had?

"I've avoided it all my life!" And that was true.

"You sure took to it like a duck to water, didn't you?" Blue said, eyes sparkling, cheeks turning pink.

"I guess I did," John said with a long sigh.

"You regret it," Blue said, in such a way that John couldn't tell if it was a question or a statement.

Regret it? "No." John shook his head. "But I still can't believe it. So fast. To not have allowed myself…. To have denied myself for so long…. And now I've done all I've done… I'm like… just sort of drifting here. In a fog or something."

"You denied you were…." Blue paused. "That you were attracted to men?"

John sighed again and shook his head. "No. I've always known. But I figured I was bisexual, and in my mind that meant as long as I was attracted to women, I had a choice. And I wanted a choice. I've tried all my life to just… blend in, you know?"

Blue cocked his head, brushed bleached blond hair from his forehead, and leaned back. Somehow John didn't think Blue had ever "blended in" a day in his whole life.

"I was afraid," John went on. "I knew if I ever tried sex with a man even once it would be over. I would be addicted." And was that what this was? Blue was his hit from the crack pipe, and now he was hooked?

Wait…. Crack pipe? Suddenly he was laughing, and Blue gawked at him—of course he did. John shared his inner thought, and Blue burst into giggles and told John he could have a hit of his crack anytime he wanted.

"Want a hit right now?" Blue asked, eyes flashing, and he started to rise to his feet, hands at the waist of his blue underwear.

John held up a hand. "No," he said quietly. "Give an old man a rest."

And there it was, wasn't it? Old man. What was he doing? Not only had he had sex more times with a *man* in only one day than he could count, but with a man who was the same age as his son. Hell! What would Alistair say?

Of course, it had been forever since he'd even talked to Alistair, hadn't it?

But Blue was shaking his head. "Old man? I don't see any old man!"

"I'm twice your age," John exclaimed. He'd caught himself looking at his image in the mirror this morning and being struck once again that it wasn't a man in his early twenties (Blue's age!) who looked back, but a man in his midforties. With lines around his eyes and the beginnings of a paunch. And he'd wondered then what he was doing. "I could be your father."

Blue leaned in, eyes flashing again. "John... you most definitely *aren't* my father."

John swallowed hard. "I... uh...." Confused. Blue confused him so much.

"You've got to let go of this father/son worry you've got going. I see it in your eyes. Let it go, okay? Please? I'm not your son."

"Not my son," John whispered in reply.

"And I'm not looking for some daddy-thing either."

"What are you looking for?" he asked quietly.

"What are *you* looking for?" Blue asked just as quietly.

The question startled John, but as he thought about it, he supposed it shouldn't have. Why wouldn't Blue ask? It made sense. He'd just been realizing that he hardly knew anything about Blue, but what did Blue know about him? That he was a banker? What kind of car he had? The LS 600h L that Blue said was like a robot from *Star Wars*. Where he lived? That he liked the music of his namesake?

What was he looking for? Hell. He had no idea. All he could do was think... Blue. Did that even make any sense?

"I don't know," John whispered. "I have no idea."

"Are you looking for a son?" Blue asked.

John jolted back. "No!" *I have one.*

"Are you looking to replace something you don't have in your life?"

Like my son? No!

Alistair's image came to his mind once more. Alistair the way he had looked the last time John had seen him. Indifferently saying that he was moving to Santa Fe, New Mexico, to pursue his dreams, and if John didn't want to help him with the expenses, that was okay. He didn't need the money; he could afford it himself. Then a new image. Alistair graduating high school. And Alistair showing him and Vivian some of his art on parent-teacher night one year. His sophomore year?

107

Junior? Unusual pieces. They'd surprised him. They weren't just pots or bowls like the ones he'd made as a kid—and oh, the hours he would sit in the basement over his wheel, spinning pot after pot after pot when all John wanted him to do was get out of the house. Have fun. Join Little League. Play football.

But Alistair wouldn't. Wouldn't even throw a few balls with his "Old Man," a phrase John hated but would gladly have accepted if his son had just played a little ball with him.

He'd never known how to relate to Alistair. And that rested inside his chest like a stone. Sometimes it was like his son was a changeling, switched at birth by fairies.

And yet John missed him. He felt it hard and strong quite suddenly, and it almost took his breath away. God, he missed his son. To his surprise the thought threatened to bring tears. But no! He would not cry.

And looking at Blue, he knew something else. He might not know how this all happened or why it had happened or how it'd happened so fast. But Blue was not his son, and he was not trying to replace Alistair with Blue. This was something entirely different.

Blue nodded. "Maybe we should just take it one day at a time?"

"Maybe one hour at a time?" John asked, and he suddenly thought he didn't want to imagine more than the hour he was living in this very moment. It was all just too big.

"Sounds good to me," Blue said.

AFTER THEY ate, they cuddled on the couch—*I am cuddling with a beautiful young man!*—and watched *The Clone Wars* on Netflix because, dammit, Blue liked *Star Wars* too.

Then for God's sake, Blue was massaging his cock through his underwear, and how could John help but get hard? Blue pulled his hard-on out through the fly (right there in the living room) and sucked his cock (Blue looked so hot on his knees between John's legs), and he didn't last long at all despite the fact that he'd cum about a million times in the last (in less than) twenty-four hours.

What do you think of that, Vivian?

Then Blue crawled up his body and whispered in his ear, "That's so you can relax." And when John reached for Blue's crotch—he should return such a favor after all—Blue shook his head. "Later. I wanted that to be all for you."

So they got dressed instead and went for a walk, and John was surprised by the urge to hold Blue's hand but couldn't quite yet (it would almost be shouting from the porch, after all). Then Blue—as if reading his mind—asked him to take him to Liberty Memorial (what Blue called Kansas City's great erection in the sky). John had never thought of it that way, but the words were no sooner out of Blue's mouth than he wondered why it had never occurred to him before. The monument couldn't have been more phallic without being obscene. He chuckled and then wondered what else Blue would show him. Tell him. Teach him.

The first thing was that Liberty Memorial used to be a big gay hangout. There had been lots of what he called cruising (which wasn't what John thought of as cruising), driving up and down the main drive and up and down the surrounding hill looking for someone who wanted to go off into the bushes and have sex. Had Blue done that? And then, even if Vivian might think it was boring, his gentleman's instinct kicked in and John did his best to sweep the thought from his mind. He certainly didn't ask. It really wasn't any of his business.

Should I worry about his sexual past? Is it something I should be concerned about?

And then he decided to not worry about it.

What was past was past. The only Blue he needed to be concerned about was the one walking at his side. Still, gay people walked the great length of the plaza before the towering pillar of concrete—a tribute to all who had died in "the Great War"—with the rest of the crowd. Blue nodded at a few of the men now and again. Almost all of them young. Blue's age. Some of them skateboarding. Friends, John supposed, and fought off a tingle of jealousy that some of them might be more. And if they were? None of his business. But then he did think to ask what had happened to Blue's skateboard. Hey! Something to ask.

"I had to sell it," Blue said. "It was that or starve." And then he shrugged and rolled his eyes comically, and that kept John from feeling sad for his new friend.

I'm one of his friends now. He hoped. He smiled.

And realized they were holding hands.

Outside.

Where people could see them.

It was thrilling. Scary. Exciting. His heart started to pound.

When had that happened? And then he remembered Blue lightly slipping his hand into John's, and it had been so natural, he hadn't even noticed.

It felt right.

And if anyone thought it was weird? John's heart skipped. If someone thought they were father and son? If Blue's friends thought something bad?

Oh, John. Fuck it! He's here with you now. Live in the moment. Live!

And enjoy just how wonderfully right this felt.

WHEN THEY still hadn't heard from H.D., they went to dinner at Gates Bar-B-Q, and it was wonderful even though the waiter gave them that look—that are-they-father-and-son-or-what? look. John didn't give a shit. How delightful!

The waiter should be so lucky as to be with Blue.

While they were eating, it suddenly hit John that he had told Blue he loved him. It just came out of nowhere. Hit him between the eyes. Rocked him back in his seat.

Why the hell had he said that?

And did he?

He looked at Blue. Could he love someone, especially another man, after so short a time? He didn't know.

What he did know was all this was going to turn his world upside-down.

But no, not upside-down. This was certainly turning his life around, no doubt, even if it ended today. But upside-down? Somehow that implied something bad, and John didn't think this—what he was experiencing—could possibly be considered bad. Experiencing not just with Blue, but with himself.

He was leaping. He was doing something he'd never dared do. He was taking a chance. Now would the net appear?

He knew one thing: he was happier right now than he had ever, *ever* been in his entire life. That made him smile. It made him smile so big that his heart swelled until he thought it might burst.

Then, as if being polite, Hound Dog called just as John was signing the check for their dinner.

THEY DASHED off to Four-Footed Friends, and when they got there, it was time for the decision whether they could take Chewie home.

Chewie was very happy to see Blue; that was for sure. John smiled at the dog's antics.

H.D. took Blue's shoulders in his hands and bent slightly so he was looking him in the eyes. "Now you see how he's bouncing?" he asked.

Blue nodded solemnly—looking ever so much like a boy instead of the young man he was.

"That is just what Dr. Lee was afraid of. Chewie needs rest. *Lots* of it."

Blue nodded.

"Can you promise me he won't be jumping up and down on things?"

"I can try," Blue said, looking even more like a little boy. Maybe it was that button nose and the fact that he was sticking his lower lip out ever so slightly.

"How about going potty?"

Potty? Had H.D. really said "potty"? He didn't seem like the type.

It's Blue, John thought. As if he were a child that needed to be taken care of. But John knew one thing: Blue was no child, even if he needed some protecting. He brought that out in people.

Just like he brought me out. John's cheeks warmed at the thought. But it wasn't the boy in Blue that had done it. Young Blue might be, but it was the *man* in him that had done that.

Made me want to suck cock.

John blushed all the more.

Made me like it.

Of course, he'd wanted it for a long time, hadn't he? Blue hadn't made him suck cock. He'd *let* him.

John stepped forward. "I can take charge of the potty stuff, at least most of the time," he volunteered. "While I'm at home. And Blue is going to stay with me for a bit."

H.D. stood up and eyed John, raised an eyebrow. "Oh?"

"At least until Chewie is out of the cast. I'll carry him out to the lawn and back inside."

Blue looked at him in surprise. "You will?"

"Do you know that is going to be two months?" H.D. asked, the other brow rising to join the first.

John fought to keep his mouth from falling open. Two months? It was a little shock.

Blue live with him for two months?

He gulped, looked at Blue, and saw the expression on his face.

Expectation. But not the good kind. Like he was expecting to be hit. Like he was expecting John to say "No way!"

Hitting Blue was the last thing he wanted. Telling him he didn't want him around was a close second. In fact, his heart was suddenly doing weird and wonderful little pirouettes. Two months to get to know Blue. He figured in that amount of time he would know what this was. This crazy turn of events in his life. Midlife crisis? The wild rebound? Meeting his destiny? That last felt the best.

He smiled, and so did Blue, and the pirouettes turned into grand jetés and tours en l'air, and what would Vivian think if she knew he knew what those words meant? Boring?

John found he didn't care. His heart was too busy making an entrechat.

Leaps of joy and fear.

He was going to grab and hold on to every minute of joy he could get.

And he might just get two months of it.

"Two months sounds just fine," he said.

In fact it sounded like… well, heaven.

JOHN CARRIED Chewie out to the car effortlessly—and a labradoodle wasn't a small dog. Somehow it was one of the sexiest things Blue had ever seen.

"Why don't you get in the backseat with him," John said. "Even in this car there's not enough room up front if poor Chewie gets upset and gets to thrashing."

H.D. had warned it could happen, but somehow Blue didn't think so. His dog was all woggy with painkillers, and that was a good thing. For now at least.

They had gotten a quilt from the closet this morning so that Chewie could be more comfortable. He looked up at Blue with complete trust and then at the back of John's head and back at Blue. He blinked contentedly, lowered his head, and went right to sleep.

Good drugs.

But something told Blue that wasn't all it was.

And then he looked at the back of John's head—even that was sexy. Who would have thought the back of a man's head could be sexy?—and something skipped around inside him and made him feel wonderfully content.

How could all this be happening?

Blue decided not to worry about it.

They got back to John's (wonderful, big) house, and John scooped up Chewie (who gave only a slight little yelp), carried him to the door, and had Blue unlock it with his keys. "I'll have to give you a set," John said, and Blue's heart did some more of those delightful skips—

He's going to give me a key to his house!

—and then John told him the code for the alarm system.

The code for the alarm system!

Then John told Blue to dash upstairs to the bedroom and arrange the blanket on the floor for Chewie—

"Which bedroom?" Blue asked.

"The big one, of course," John replied easily. "*Our* room."

Our room!

—and John followed Blue up the stairs carrying Chewie as if he weighed no more than a stuffed toy.

Blue fluffed and twirled the blanket and tried as best he could to make the blanket a nest he thought Chewie might like. As John effortlessly settled Chewie into the midst of it, Blue wondered if his dog might like his own blanket more. If it would help him feel more at home.

Home.

More heart skips.

John stepped back and sat on the edge of the bed, and Blue got down on his tummy, propped his chin on his upturned hands, and watched Chewie watch them both before resting his head on his paws and seemingly going to sleep.

After a moment John said, "I should go down to the car and get his food."

Blue looked up at him and said he could do it—surely he could do that much—but John shook his head and got to his feet.

"Nah, I got it," he said as Blue tried to build up the courage to ask if they could go to his place and get his blanket for Chewie.

He didn't succeed.

And he didn't know what to do. Stay up here with his sleeping dog or go downstairs. His indecision meant he was still there when John came back into the room carrying the big bag. He'd insisted on the fifty-pound bag. "A dog his size can eat a lot of food in two months," he'd said.

Then to Blue's surprise, John got down on the floor with him, rested his chin on one propped-up hand, and after a long moment said, "How shall we do this?"

Blue looked at him. Do this? Do what?

"I mean, I brought Chewie up here because I figured he'd want to be near us. So we probably need to set up everything up here.

We could make the guest bathroom his. That way if he goes to the bathroom on the floor if we're not here, it will be on tile instead of the carpet. Do you know if he's paper trained?"

Blue didn't think so. After all, H.D. had said he hadn't liked going to the bathroom in the kennel at Four-Footed Friends. "I always take him outside, and he does his business there. He's never made a mistake inside."

"*Hmm*," John said. "The guest bathroom seems so far from us. Of course, we could just put him in there if we're both gone. Matter of fact, we could put him in the master bath then."

Blue didn't know what to say. This was all in John's court.

"Yeah. I think that would be best," John continued. "We'll have to find a better bed for him too." He looked thoughtful for a moment, and then one of his eyebrows rose. "I bet Alistair...." He paused, a funny look on his face. John took a very deep breath. "I—I bet Alistair's baby mattress is in the attic. Viv had some crazy idea about saving it for his kids, but I don't know if he has the slightest idea we have it, let alone if he wants it."

"Alistair?" Blue asked before he could stop himself.

"My son," John said quietly. He sat up.

Son? John had a son? He hadn't mentioned him, and... and now John had a sad look on his face.

"He lives in Santa Fe," John said very quietly.

Blue nodded, at a loss for what else to say.

"He's your age," he said even more quietly. Gave a deep sigh. Got to his feet.

"We don't have to use his baby bed," Blue said.

John looked at him, and oh, the look on his face!

I did something wrong! What did I do wrong?

John has a son?

"WE DON'T have to use his baby bed," Blue said.

John looked down at him and saw the strangest expression on Blue's face.

"It's okay," John said, at the same time wondering what the fuck he was doing.

I am sleeping with a man who is the same age as my son.

Stop it! Let go of it. Blue is not Alistair.

But….

Holy shit. Am I trying to replace *the son I've lost? Is all this affection I've built up some kind of fucking redirection of my emotions?*

His stomach clenched in aversion at the thought.

Is that what I'm fucking doing?

But looking at Blue's lovely face—filled with confusion that John knew he'd put there—he was certain Blue wasn't some attempt to fill in for an apathetic son.

No! He'd thought about it already, and he knew that wasn't what was going on. Yes, he missed Alistair. Yes, he wondered why they had never seemed to have a real relationship—as if there had always been a little chasm between them that they couldn't cross.

You couldn't cross came that inner voice of his, and it all but made him gasp.

No. Don't even go there. Not right now. Because all that had nothing to do with Blue. This was something else—he just wasn't sure exactly what. Not yet.

Was it like all those men he'd known through the years who had cheated on their wives with women so much younger than themselves? Something that had always made John feel rather contemptuous of them.

Was he doing the same damned thing?

But one look from those beautiful brown eyes banished that idea as well. He didn't think it was that either. He always figured those men had done what they had done because they were feeling old and having a young girlfriend fed their egos. Those young women made them feel young again. John wasn't sure he even *had* an ego. And he was content with his own age. Didn't feel….

Wait….

Blue was sitting up now, the look of worry on his face growing stronger.

Could it be something far simpler?

John's mouth almost fell open at the idea.

Content with his age as he was, sometimes the man who stared back at him in the mirror made him want to say, "Who is that guy?" As if the college picture of him that hung on the wall in the hallway should be staring back instead. Because in truth, that college guy was the best of who he'd been. If he'd ever been happy, that was when it had been. If he'd ever dreamed of seeing the world, or at least the country, it was with dreams of being a professional football player. It had been crushing to discover he just wasn't good enough. And yet still he'd been happier than he'd ever been at home. Home had meant a weak mother who bowed to his father's whims. Home had meant a father who thought he was the lord and master of his house. And a small little house it had been.

Ugly place. Squat and square, missing siding showing black paper beneath. But the real ugliness was his father, a man who had never been happy a day in his life. And shit rolled downhill. John had figured that out after he'd left to make his own life. The man hadn't been happy and didn't want anyone else to be happy either.

Home had been all those things and worse.

Happy had meant getting away from all that and beginning his own life, no matter what that was. Not football after all. But he found that once he was out from under his father's thumb, he had an affinity for both people and numbers. An unusual combination, he'd been told. Maybe something like being an investment banker was in his future. A switch in degree to finance, accounting, or mathematics.

And he hadn't quit football. He figured he'd never be carried off the field on the shoulders of his team. But so what.

John had been happy.

He'd even been tempted by another player. A long-haired blond who gazed at him across rooms with big brown flashing hope-filled eyes. They'd even had a drink at a party. The kid—*Marty! His name had been Marty*—had asked him if he wanted to go back to his dorm room and showed him a half-concealed half-bottle-size container of some cheap scotch.

They were heading for the door when a friend pulled him aside.

"You ain't going off with Marty, are you?" the friend had asked, his own alcohol rolling off his breath.

"What?" he'd replied and glanced over at Marty, standing at the door with those hope-filled eyes.

"Marty's a faggot," the so-called buddy had said, and John had frozen as if turned to ice. "You go off with him and he'll be trying to suck your dick. Anybody sees you going off with him and everyone will think you're a fairy. You ain't a fag, are you, John?"

"Of course not!" John had cried, yet somehow muffling his voice. Felt for sure the shame that could come with words like fairy and faggot and fag. And knowing—knowing—that wasn't what he wanted to be. Someone to be spoken of with such derision. Hell, looking at that "friend's" face, he'd seen outright horror. Even hatred.

John hadn't gone off with Marty. He'd turned his back and felt shame for it and yet relief at the same time. Along with a heavy, hard need in his groin, a pounding in his chest, and some difficulty catching his breath. Simply from the thought of sharing a few swallows of cheap scotch with that boy. If he'd have gone to Marty's dorm room, he would have been lost.

Lost? But I would have been happy. How different would my life be today if I had spent that night with Marty? Would I still be with him today?

With all these thoughts in the forefront, he looked into Blue's eyes, and an idea—very powerful—began to form.

Maybe it wasn't that this young man *made* him feel young....

It could quite simply be that he'd actually never let himself *be* young.

Whoa.

His heart skipped a beat.

By turning his back on Marty, had he cut himself off from being... himself?

Looking at Blue and trying not to stare, he wondered, *Are you my youth?*

John got off the floor, sat back down on the bed, and patted the space next to him. "Come here," he said.

Blue slowly got to his feet and came to him only a little hesitantly. *Oh God, Blue.*

Then before Blue could sit down, he put his hands on Blue's narrow hips and pulled him between his open legs and kissed him. He meant it to be light—like those first kisses Blue had given him—but instead it was much more. He opened his mouth, and after a moment Blue followed his lead. Then John moaned and Blue echoed the noise and they had sex again.

Only this time they made love.

CHAPTER THIRTEEN

AFTERWARD, SPOONED together, Blue found his thoughts returning to John's revelation. A son. John had a son. Wow.

But the pain that had come into John's eyes....

Ask him?

Blue shook his head inwardly. He thought that maybe now wasn't really the time. So instead he asked something entirely different. "Do you think we might go back to my place and pick up a blanket? I think Chewie might like it. It has my smell on it."

"Of course." Then after a pause, John sat up. "Hell. Shouldn't we get all your stuff? If you leave it there, somebody might take it."

Blue rolled over and looked up at him, wonderfully surprised. Did he mean it? "Really?" he asked.

John smiled and nodded. "Of course. We should do it right away."

Blue's mouth fell open.

John nodded enthusiastically. "Yes! I'll take Chewie out for a quick pee, and then let's do it."

And that's just what he did.

Giggling, Blue had to remind him to put some clothes on first.

"Why?" John said, laughing. "Aren't you the one who dared me to eat outside?"

"In your *underwear*," Blue said. "You're naked!"

Something happened on John's face then. Something magical and powerful. Something actually *changed*. Blue felt as if he had witnessed something important, something significant. He just wasn't sure what.

Not yet.

Laughing again, John slipped on a pair of discarded (sort of tacky) boxer briefs and, by God, carried Chewie outside all *but* naked. Something that Blue wouldn't think twice about doing—hadn't he spent a happy childhood naked most of the time?—but he knew was a very big deal for John. He was a banker, after all.

And fuck what John's wife said.

Not boring.

So very *not* boring.

Although he was going to have to do something about those plaid boxers. With a house like this and a car like he drove, why such Walmart-like underwear?

Chewie staggered about a bit in the grass, did his doggy business, and tried not to fall over backward. He looked up at them both in obvious doggy embarrassment, and bless John, he looked away (mostly) to give Chewie his privacy (but watched over him as well).

Blue felt something swell inside his chest then and knew it was something very much like love. Oh God, could it be? Would falling in love with this man who had already said "I love you" first be a bad thing? Because even though Blue thought that maybe John had said those words in his sleep, did it count?

Something was happening inside him.

Something wonderful and scary and powerful and maybe totally fucking foolish.

Did he go for it?

Or had life taught him that would be a stupid thing to do?

In that moment, Blue decided *What the fuck.*

Just see what happened next.

WHEN JOHN scooped Chewie up to take him outside, Blue said, "John! You better put your clothes on first!"

Whoa! He was about to go outside naked.

Him!

John "Boring" Williams.

And he laughed, and it felt so damned good, titillated him to the core. Walk right outside naked! Right out in the sunlight. Him. Who a week ago wouldn't go downstairs without a bathrobe.

He looked at Blue, sitting there cross-legged, naked on the bed, and he realized he meant it, and something... something inside him *changed*. Something wondrous. Something powerful.

Was this what people meant by... whoa... a religious experience? Enlightenment? Because it was compelling. It felt incredibly important. Mighty and forceful and paramount and—dare he say it?—miraculous. Not to be ignored. Ha! Impossible to ignore.

John knew in that second this was something he would remember for the rest of his life.

And he owed it all to a naked, beautiful young man named Blue.

He almost put Chewie down and leapt onto the bed to make love to Blue again—imagine!—but instead, laughing more, he carefully put Chewie down and pulled on a pair of underwear—

Mine? Must be, because I'd never fit into Blue's!

—and then he carried Blue's sweet dog (who gave him doggy kisses on the way) downstairs and outside and then stood there on the patio—in his underwear!—and bounced on his toes. He felt so wonderful, so incredible, so free! And oh, look, Chewie was the one who was embarrassed—

Well, you are watching him do his private thing after all!

—and so he looked away (mostly, he wanted to make sure Chewie didn't fall over) and locked eyes with Blue, and it was like they merged, went into each other's souls—

(at least that's what it felt like to John, who had never believed in souls until that second)

—and then he blurted it out—

Full speed and damn the torpedoes!

—before he changed his mind.

"I love you, Blue."

And thank the God he'd never quite believed in either—

(until that second?)

—Blue said, "Oh, John. I love you too!"

CHAPTER FOURTEEN

WHEN THEY got to Blue's place, John took one look at the stuff scattered about the room and thought, *Fuck it*, and told Blue the car was big enough. They would try to take it all.

The mattress wouldn't fit.

It wasn't a very nice mattress.

But God, the look on Blue's face. Nice or not, it was Blue's mattress, and who was he to say if it was good enough or not? It had been a resting place for Blue for who knew how long? They needed to take it (although he hoped Blue would never sleep on it again).

"We'll need some rope," he said.

Blue paused and then cried, "I know where to get some!"

He started to run out the door, but John laughed and told him to wait until they loaded the car.

So they did. They collected clothes and some paperback books, including *Stranger in a Strange Land* by Robert Heinlein (one of John's very favorite books—it had been too long since he'd read it) and *The Outsiders* by S.E. Hinton (nice to see people still read the book; he'd read it in high school) and *To Kill a Mockingbird* by Harper Lee (which he had never liked and had gotten hell for it) and *The Perks of Being a Wallflower* by Stephen Chbosky (which he hadn't heard of, but he was certainly intrigued by the title and thought he would have to ask Blue if he could read it). He was happy that Blue liked to read.

Blue had a harmonica and some of those rubber-band bracelets that he'd seen young people wearing (*young like Blue*. And somehow that made him laugh), as well as a leather one.

The handful of CDs and DVDs Blue owned bemused John. He wasn't sure how Blue would have enjoyed them without electricity (but they could certainly do so at John's house!). Maybe they would watch *Avatar* tonight.

And then there were the candles. Several boxes of candles of every shape, size, and description, including….

His eyes went wide.

Penis-shaped candles.

And it was clear even to John that these were far too real just to be simply *shaped* like penises. He tried, but his eyes wouldn't go back to normal. They stayed wide.

He blushed and put down the candle he'd picked up. The texture of the head was far too real, and he'd seen a penis up close lately after all, and he knew that it was far too real for a sculpture.

John looked at Blue, who was also blushing—furiously—and looking downcast, ashamed, scolded, and… afraid.

"I… I cast them," Blue said. "I don't know why. I always thought it was kind of sexy."

John didn't know what to say, but somehow he knew he needed to say something, and fairly quickly. But *damn*! This was *way* out of his league!

"It makes me know it happened. That someone wanted to be with me, even if only for a day or a night. But now… I… I should throw them all—"

"Who *wouldn't* want you?" John blurted, hoping and hoping and hoping it was the right thing to say. "How could anybody *not* want you? God, Blue. I resisted myself, I resisted men my whole life. Then you came along, and that was it. I was lost."

Lost? Had he said lost?

Blue looked at him, and John cried, "And I never ever want to be found again."

Blue smiled. It was radiant. It didn't stop a single tear from rolling down his cheek, though. "R-really?"

"Would you make one from mine? And"—now John was grinning—"can we make one of yours?"

Blue's wonderful Cheshire grin was back then, and he said, "Yes! If you want."

And John did want.

Wasn't that crazy?

Wasn't that wild?

Wasn't that delicious?

Wasn't that *not* boring!

John burst into laughter and realized he was getting hard again. He wanted to make love to Blue right here on this soiled mattress, but Chewie… they had to think of Chewie.

So they got everything out to the car and dragged the mattress out there and got it on the roof. Blue held it there precariously with one hand out the window as John drove very, very slowly to another house for one more stop before they went home.

BLUE TOOK John's hand in his and led him up the little winding walkway to the front door of Mom's house. There were lights on inside, so he knew she was home, and he knocked and then rang the bell.

"Jesus H. Christ!" came a bellow from the other side of the door.

Blue turned pink and looked up at John. What would he think of Mom?

The door flew open, and there she was. Mom, in all her glory. Her hair was tameishly wild, and so were her eyes, and she was wearing a black and blue-green flowing top and a huge clunky turquoise necklace with matching bobbing earrings.

Mom.

"Oh! It's you, Kidness! I was just about to give you hell, knocking and ringing before I had a chance to even get up off my couch and…. And…. Why, who is *this*?" she said, pointing at John with her chin.

"This is John, Mom."

John gave him a startled look, and Blue opened his mouth to explain, but she pushed the screen door open and stepped out, offering a hand. "Miriam Sheridan," she said. "He calls me Mom. And that's okay with me, even though I'm old enough to be his grandma."

125

"John Williams," he replied and then surprised himself by cutting right to the truth and saying, "He calls me John, even though I'm old enough to be his father."

Her eyes went wide, and she let out a bark of laughter. Elbowing Blue, she invited them in.

"We really don't have a long time," John said. "Chewie is at the house, and we've already been gone for nearly an hour."

"Then why are you here?" she asked.

"Rope," Blue said.

Now she looked back and forth between them. "*Rope?*" she asked in a way that said she was drawing only one conclusion.

John blushed despite trying to put on a brave face, and Blue burst into giggles, and then they stumbled over each other trying to explain about the mattress.

But she held up a hand, showing today's rings were turquoise as well. "Nit, nit, nit! I *don't* want to hear. You're both adults. If you want rope for your mattress, who am I to criticize or ask for details?"

She did command them to make a reappearance, and soon, "And you bring that dog of yours. I need to meet him!" But John countered with a proposal that she come to "their" place instead—

Blue thought he'd swoon.

—for dinner, and that way Chewie wouldn't have to be moved unnecessarily.

Blue sighed happily, and Mom elbowed him again, a little more discreetly, and whispered, "What a *hottie*. I'd hold on to this one for a while."

If Blue had anything to say about it, he would.

Blue'd had too much taken from him in his life—takings that left him devastated. Instead he decided to take some advice he'd heard going to Camp Sanctuary each year, where only one bad—very bad—thing had ever taken place.

He decided to hold on to John all right. But with an open hand. Not grasping. But certainly not pushing away. He decided in that very moment that he was going to enjoy every minute with Mr. John Not-boring Williams and thank God for each and every one.

And when it was time for John to go away?

Maybe—just maybe—it wouldn't be so painful.

CHAPTER FIFTEEN

BUT JOHN didn't go away.
And neither did Blue.

CHAPTER SIXTEEN

JOHN DID go to work and found people looking at him... funny. Especially Janet, his assistant. He'd look out the glass wall of his office and see her there at her desk, peering at him curiously over her glasses.

It was while she was taking a letter that he asked her what was up.

Her cheeks pinked a bit, and then she burst out with a, "That's what *we've* been wondering."

John leaned forward on his desk. "We? What's going on, Janet?" People were wondering about him?

She looked down and then up, down, and then up again. "You're so... happy."

John sat upright. Happy?

"I mean, you've been so... well, solemn since Mrs. Williams vanished into the night."

John gulped. "Ah... Janet.... Vivian, Mrs. Williams, didn't exactly 'vanish into the night.'"

She gave a little shrug. "She left. Which is crazy. I can't imagine why any woman would be so stupid."

John gulped again. What?

"I mean, we all think that you're, like, the best boss we've ever had. You're a good man, Mr. Williams, and you're fair. And...." Her cheeks got a little pinker. "You're very handsome. Anyone would be lucky to have you."

Now it was John's turn to blush. He could feel the heat on his cheeks and hoped it wasn't too noticeable. "Why... thank you, Janet."

Her eyes went wide behind her fashionable glasses. "Not that I... I mean... I'm happily married, Mr. Williams. It's just. Well. The girls talk." She smiled. "And one or two of the boys too. And they all agree that she—Mrs. Williams—must be crazy."

Well, she thought I was boring, Janet. I probably was. I know I was. She left to see the world. And have three-ways.

Then he saw Blue's upturned ass in his mind, waiting for him, and he really did flush so hard he knew his cheeks were blazing. Something happened in his pants, and he tried to think about Blue's face instead—which wasn't difficult, Blue had the most beautiful face in the universe. *If you could see me now, Vivian.*

He wished her the best. He wished her fine cabana boys with butts as nice as Blue's and safe travels and climbs to the top of one of the Mexican pyramids they still let you climb and hoped she was fleshing in Bangkok to her heart's content—if that's what she wanted. He found he wished her not the slightest ill will. Vivian had been unhappy.

And he'd come to see that he had been as well.

That he'd never been truly happy.

And now he was.

Happier than he'd ever been in his life.

How could he wish her anything else?

Wait. Had Janet just said one or two *guys* found him attractive?

He smiled shyly and wondered which ones. Not that he was interested in them. But how had he missed that? How had he missed that men were attracted to him?

Blinders, he supposed. He had spent his life looking straight forward—ever since that night in college—and never to the left or right except when it came to business.

Viv had really had a host of reasons to have been so unhappy.

John found he really did wish he could see Vivian. See her and wish her well.

He looked across his desk at Janet—whose chair was at the same level as his because he'd never believed in that bullshit of having a big chair so that he was above the people who came to see him, figuratively or physically—and she gazed back and then asked, "You seeing someone, Mr. Williams?"

And John grinned. That fast. He couldn't help it.

"I—well, yes I am, Janet."

Her smile was huge. "Oh, that is good news! We were afraid— or I was at least—that you'd mope around here forever. Where'd you meet the lucky lady?"

John opened his mouth, shut it, and found himself flummoxed. He could lie. It would be so easy. Hell, he could tell half the truth. *I met her at an animal shelter. I was thinking of getting a dog. I found a human instead.*

But he thought of Blue smiling at him across the dinner table or cuddled up in the crook of his arm watching television—they'd watched *Avatar* again last night, this time with the extra footage, and Blue had loved it—or asleep next to him in bed and found saying such a thing would be a betrayal. The idea hurt his heart.

And hadn't she told him that a couple of men thought he was attractive? Hadn't she said it without blinking an eye, as if it were the most normal thing in the world?

Before he could think about it too much, he said, "Guy, Janet."

She looked at him curiously.

His heart skipped a beat, and whether it was the image of Blue's smiling face or a bit of fear (maybe both?), he said, "A guy. I met a *man*. I was thinking of getting a dog, and I went to this animal shelter and found a human being instead. And I'm the lucky one."

Her mouth opened halfway, and it was clear she was surprised. But then she gave a nod and a little gulp and smiled as if the sun had come out on a rainy day. "*Wow*! That's wonderful, Mr. Williams!"

"Surprised?" he asked. *Because I sure was.* "I was as surprised as hell."

"A bit. Let no one say you've ever acted even a little light in your loafers. But I think it's great. Chad will be crushed—" She covered her mouth and ducked her head, an "*Ooops*!" if John had ever seen one.

Chad? Chad Harris? Really? He thought of the man, curly hair and big glasses, and realized the idea that Chad was gay had never occurred to him. Not that anybody's anything had ever concerned him.

"Don't tell him I told you, Mr. Williams!"

"That he's gay?" he asked.

She rolled her eyes. "*No*! Who can miss that Chad is gay?"

Apparently me.

"No. That he has a crush on you."

A crush. An actual crush?

John gulped.

Took a deep breath.

"Then maybe we should keep me getting involved—

(*Falling in love*)

—with a man between you and me. Just for now."

She nodded and looked at him very seriously. "Sure, Mr. Williams."

At least until I'm fully ready.

And thinking again of Blue cuddled next to him on the couch, John thought maybe that wouldn't be too long from now.

AND BLUE? Why, for Blue life was grand. Wonderful. Wonde*rous*.

He didn't know when he'd ever been so fucking happy.

Living with John was like… like playing house. And he tried not to hope too hard that it wasn't only playing.

Could a man twice his age—so smart and sophisticated and worldly—stay interested in him?

But as each day passed and John didn't seem to lose interest, Blue found it harder and harder to keep his resolve to hold John with an open hand.

They did so much together!

They went to the Nelson-Atkins Museum of Art, and what a delight it was when they shared what they knew about the art instead of each seeing it just one way. Blue had learned a lot taking notes for students after all. He knew more about the queerness of world art while John knew the history. One day they had sat cross-legged on the floor for what seemed like forever looking up at the Nelson's wooden figure of *Guanyin of the Southern Sea*, which was famous for being the finest sculpture of its kind outside China. John knew that it had probably been stolen, and Blue knew that it wasn't really female.

"See?" Blue had pointed. "No breasts? This was back when the bodhisattva was transitioning from male to female for those cultures that needed a goddess figure."

And John knew all about Emperor Hadrian and the power he had brought to Rome but hadn't known that the Roman ruler was gay and that the beautiful bust of the male youth that faced him across one gallery of the museum was his lover, Antinous. Hadrian had deified him after he died. "Antinous was much younger than Hadrian."

"How much younger?" John, curious, asked the much-younger Blue.

"Well," Blue said, and then his mind did that thing it did, recalling information that he'd learned before as if from some file opened and read. It was something he'd never understood. "Antinous was nineteen when he died, and Hadrian was sixty-two. They were thirty-four years apart."

Thirty-four years! John thought, and suddenly the twenty-some years between them mattered just a little bit less.

"How about Samuel Johnson and Elizabeth Johnson? They were married in 1735 when he was twenty-five and she was forty-six. Twenty-one-year age difference. Or Rebecca Rolfe, who we know as Pocahontas, and John Rolfe, married in 1614. She was eighteen, and he was twenty-nine, eleven-year age difference. King Willem III and Emma of Waldeck. Married in 1879. She was twenty-one and he was sixty-two. Forty-one-year age difference."

Uh-oh. It was happening. The file had been opened! The horses were out of the barn. Soon they would start galloping. And when was it going to stop?

"King William IV and Adelaide of Saxe-Meiningen," he continued, the words flowing faster and faster. "Married in 1818. She was twenty-six and he was fifty-three. Twenty-seven-year age difference. Grover Cleveland and Frances Folsom. Married in 1886. She was twenty-one and he was forty-nine. Twenty-eight-year age difference."

Stop talking! Stop talking before he knows you for how weird you are.

"And that is heterosexual couples. Men? Well, there was a male couple of Ancient Greece: Nero—not the crazy Roman one—and Sporus. They were married in 67 AD. Sporus was somewhere around seventeen years old and Nero was around thirty, sixteen-year age difference. More recently, of course, there was Oscar Wilde and Lord Alfred Douglas. Met in 1891. Oscar was thirty-seven and Alfred was twenty-one. Sixteen-year age difference. And Noel Coward and Graham Payne? They met in 1942. Noel was forty-three andGrahamwastwentyfournineteenyearagedifferenceand—"

And just when he was losing it completely, John reached out and took Blue's cheek in the palm of his hand and said, "God," and sighed happily. "You know all this stuff! You are *so* smart."

And Blue was back on Earth—himself again.

Smart?

John had just called *him* smart?

His heart pounded harder by far than anytime a man had told him he was sexy.

John stepped forward and leaned down so their foreheads were touching. "I am so proud of you."

Blue all but melted.

"Isn't that nice?" came the voice of a woman. Blue broke their hold and saw a woman who had to be in at least her seventies with a much older man. "Isn't it nice when a father and son can express their affection in public?" She smiled at them.

"Oh, but we're n—"

Blue squeezed John's hand.

And then the old lady's eyes went wide, and she winked and bobbed her head in the older man's direction. Without another word the couple went on ahead of them into the Medieval Hall.

"So you can stop worrying about the difference in our age, okay?"

"Okay," John said. "But we're equals."

It was all Blue could do not to cry. Equals. He nodded, not knowing if he trusted himself to speak.

The days flew by.

Mornings started with John taking Chewie out—despite Blue's argument that they were equals after all. He wasn't weak. He could do it—and ended the same way. John insisted.

"You can take him out while I'm at work," John said.

Chewie seemed to love the spoiling.

And when John wasn't at work, they did the things they could do and not be away from home for long. For the most part, home was where they stayed. They watched movies and played games—cards and otherwise—and Blue whipped John's ass at chess.

They gardened, something John had been interested in but never taken up. That had been Vivian's domain, something she wanted to do by herself. But she was gone now, and the gardens out back needed care, and Blue was thrilled. They went to local nurseries and downtown to the City Market and picked out plants and flowers *together* and planted them together.

Museums were a big part of what took them away from the house. They went to the American Jazz and the Negro Leagues Baseball Museums. John had a love for jazz that he delighted in sharing with Blue, and Blue knew baseball. Vivian had hated baseball, mostly because of the length of the season.

This only led to John and Blue heading to several games.

And they went to the ballet. John had dreamed of going (secretly) for years (something else Vivian did with her female friends. *"Imagine, a man wanting to go to the ballet!"*) Pretty much all he'd had the opportunity to see before that was *The Nutcracker* at the Kansas City Music Hall, dance routines in musicals at the Starlight Theater, and many late-night secret viewings on YouTube.

And then there was the fun of dressing Blue up. They'd had to go and buy a suit of course.

"Do I really need one?" Blue had asked. "I'm sure I've got *something* I can wear."

"I'm sure you do," John said. "But you'd look beautiful in a tux."

Blue's eyes had gone wide at that. "A *tuxedo*?" he'd whispered. As if it were a magic word. "I can't really afford a—"

"I've got it," John told him.

Blue shook his head. "No, John. You've been paying for everything and I'm starting to feel like some kind of kept boy. Tuxedos aren't cheap, and they're something you wear once in a blue moon and—"

John sucked in a breath. God. Making Blue feel bad was the last thing he'd wanted. "Blue. Let me do this. I really want to. You should see all the crap I've bought for Vivian. Have you peeked in that walk-in closet? There must be a hundred pair of shoes in there. If I can pay for a pair of Alexander Wangs for her, I can buy you a simple tuxedo. Hell. The tux will probably be cheaper."

Blue bit his lip. And finally nodded.

It had made John very happy.

And it was surprisingly sexy to get Blue fitted. It was all John could do not to pull Blue into a booth and take the thing off him. Blue would be more than happy for him to. But as far as John had come, he wasn't quite ready for that.

So John bought Blue the tuxedo and then they went to the ballet.

John loved it.

And so had Blue.

"My God," he'd whispered in John's ear. "It's like they're floating. It's like they're… *oooh*, look! Like they've just stopped in midair!"

It was a big step when John accepted Janet's dinner invitation. He asked Blue, who was shy but all for it, and they went. Thankfully it was just Janet and her husband and one other couple who were surprisingly also far apart in age—although they were a straight couple. A man who had to be in his sixties with a wife no older than thirty. It made everything very comfortable. The only odd thing that happened was that the wife, a woman named Amélie—

"Like the movie?" Blue asked.

"Oui," she answered in a delightful French accent.

—kept looking at Blue and swearing she had seen him before. But try as they might, they couldn't figure out where.

And for those times they were out late?

Well, Mom watched Chewie.

After the three of them had their dinner date, that was.

JOHN GRILLED, but Blue did everything else while he was at work. Miriam arrived on time, and she brought two bottles of wine. "A red and white," she said. "I wasn't sure what you were grilling."

They opened both.

And Blue was thrilled.

Because the evening was a hit.

"You're bisexual, then, John?" Miriam asked.

"No. I don't think so. I'm gay."

"You know, just because you're madly in love," she said and sipped from her wine, "doesn't mean you have to forgo being bisexual. There is such a thing, you know. As bisexuality, that is."

John shrugged and gave her a lopsided smile. "I guess?"

"I'm bisexual," she declared.

His brows shot up but then settled gently. "Okay."

"So there's nothing wrong…."

"Maybe I am in some degree," John replied. "I was sexual with my wife for twenty years. But there was no… passion. It wasn't bad. Just not…." He looked at Blue. "Miriam, the first time Blue and I kissed—hell, that first time we met when he barely kissed me on the cheek—it was like… like nothing I'd ever felt before. Ever experienced before!"

She eyed him.

"I was reading this story in this book once. It was this story about Socrates, I think. Or Plato? He was talking about these people who had lived chained in a cave all of their lives, facing a wall, and all they'd ever been able to do was watch shadows projected on that wall. The shadows were all they ever knew. And then one day they were freed from the cave and marveled that the shadows they'd seen on the wall did not make up reality at all. But once they'd seen the truth, they couldn't go back. I read that and thought about what's happening to me now that I've been with Blue. I didn't know reality. I could only go by what I'd read or what I feared. And now? Now I see that I'm not straight and I'm not bisexual. I'm gay. Now that I see it, I can't unsee it. And I know a woman won't come along that can make me feel these things. I know I never gave my wife the passion that she deserved. I want to do that for Blue. I want to do that so damned bad. I'm worried a bit. Scared to take the full plunge. Coming out is the term, right? I'm not ready to march in a parade. But I want to give Blue all the passion in my heart."

Miriam fanned herself. "Oh my!" She looked over at Blue. "What did I say about holding on to this one?"

Blue grinned.

"I think the biggest thing that still gets me is our difference in age. Blue's teaching me. All about Hadrian and Antinous, Pocahontas and John Rolfe, Grover Cleveland and Frances Folsom, and Oscar Wilde and Lord Alfred Douglas, but...."

"I'm not at all bothered by the age thing," she said with a wave. "I hung out with the beatniks in California way back when." She turned to Blue. "Did I ever tell you I knew Allen Ginsberg?"

Blue shook his head. "Really?"

John obviously hadn't heard of him and asked who he was.

"Amazing poet," she said. "He wrote a book of poetry called *Howl and Other Poems* in 1955." She shook her head. "*Whoo-wee*, did *that* ever cause a stir. When he published it, it got him arrested for obscenity. Went to trial too. Very homosexual—emphasis on sexual."

"Really?" John asked, obviously surprised.

"I have an autographed copy in the house," she said, pride clear in her voice. "First printing. Got it at City Lights Books the day it came out." She nodded and smiled wistfully. "I knew a lot of those people. Neal Cassady, Jack Kerouac, William S. Burroughs, James Broughton. I was a dancer. We were all artists. *Artistes*, as some people said." She cackled, and as usual with her, the sound was delightful. "We danced and performed and made movies and thought we were changing the world." Then she sighed and looked out into the distance.

"You've met some famous people," John said, and Blue could see he was impressed, and that made him happy. Mom was not your average lady.

"Yes," she said quietly. "But it was James Broughton I wanted to tell you about, the Big Joy himself. I was in several of his films.

Some of them were terrible and some a total delight. I have a copy of *The Bed*, which was nothing but nudity—but tasteful and delightfully innocent. He couldn't find anyone to develop it and finally had to go to a porn company. I was *not* in that one!" Again she laughed, and again she seemed to go off into another world as she spoke. "It made him famous on the West Coast!

"And holy shit, I loved James's poetry!" She sat back, closed her eyes, smiled blissfully, and then began to recite.

> *Big Joy   have mercy upon us*
> *Deliver us from dread*
> *from fret funk and glum*
> *scowl sneer and fidget*
>
> *Big Joy   have pity upon us*
> *Deliver us from droop*
> *from flinch fuss and squirm*
> *sham shame and dither*
>
> *Big Joy   shed grace upon us*
> *Deliver us from daunt*
> *from whine whimper and pout*
> *chafe vex and blooper*
>
> *O Big Joy   rescue us*
> *from the petty the inane*
> *the vacuous the mediocre*
> *and the triumphantly stupid*

WITH THAT she laughed, bobbed her head back and forth happily, opened her eyes and rolled them, and said, "*Gods*! That is *so* James!"

She sighed once more and drank from her wineglass and seemed to come back to reality. Were there tears in her eyes? Mom? Tears?

Then she was looking at them both, pointing wildly with her glass but not coming close to spilling a drop of her wine. "But the point. This wine has made me miss the point! What I wanted to say was that *James* didn't meet Joel Singer, the love of his life, until he was *sixty-two*. Delightful young man! Who was *forty* years James's junior. They were together forever after that too. I think Joel kept James young, although Joel might have said it was the other way around. They were such a joyful couple. I envied them."

Blue giggled happily—he couldn't help it—and looked at John, and to his surprise, he saw tears in John's eyes.

"John?" he asked.

John shook himself, grabbed a cloth napkin, and wiped at his face, and they both caught Mom looking at them. Her expression? Why, bliss. *Big joy*, Blue thought.

Later, after she left, that's what John replied. "Joy."

"Big joy," Blue said.

Of course, they were both stoned to the gills.

Miriam had insisted. "I got something here that will make your socks switch feet without you moving to help!"

John, bless his heart, joined them, and from what he said, he had never even indulged in college. Luckily he didn't have to drive. And luckily he didn't have to work the next day. Luckily Chewie was on the patio and could get to the lawn to pee on his own by then. Luckily he'd been sleeping downstairs of late, and they wouldn't have to carry him upstairs. And luckily that sock-switching pot produced some of the best sex Blue had ever had.

And from the moans and groans and exclamations, it seemed to be true for John as well.

IT WAS.

It was about the best sex John had ever had, and he'd had some pretty incredible sex lately. Now that he was having sex with—what was for him—the right gender.

Who knew sex could be so fantastic?

140

Who knew touching could be so grand?

That *being* touched could be so intense?

That orgasms could be so powerful?

He also decided—and thankfully Blue agreed—that smoking pot should be a sometime thing instead of a normal thing (despite the fact that Miriam told them she could help them grow an excellent plant behind the lilac bushes along John's back fence).

Because John wanted their sex to be real. No additives. No alterations.

Because it was perfect as it was.

A symbol of their love.

Love.

He was in love!

But he thought that maybe what had made the evening so perfect, and maybe why the lovemaking had been so grand, was Miriam's story about James Broughton and Joel Singer. How Joel was the love of James's life and how late in that life it had been when he met Joel. How James kept Joel young as much as Joel had kept James young.

It was one thing to think about Hadrian and Antinous, or Oscar Wilde and Lord Alfred Douglas. But they were so long ago. They lived in worlds where an age difference was common. Today was a different world.

James and Joel bridged that chasm for some reason, had set his heart free. He'd felt it take wing. Felt a weight lift off his shoulders!

> *Big Joy   have pity upon us*
> *Deliver us from droop*
> *from flinch fuss and squirm*
> *sham shame and dither*

Tonight John felt as if he might have finally let go of shame and was fully ready for Big Joy….

AND SO April went into May and into June.

It was magic.

It *was* Big Joy.

And soon not a day passed that John didn't tell Blue that he loved him, and thank God—that ephemeral being—Blue loved him back.

Because there must be a God, right?

A God who invented love.

And created Blue.

And put him in his life.

Those months were all Big Joy.

At least until the end of June. Two days before Chewie had his cast taken off.

That was when the trouble happened.

CHAPTER SEVENTEEN

IT ALL started at The Male Box. It was the first time John had ever been in a gay bar, and his heart was pounding and he was sweating despite the near gallon of underarm deodorant it felt like he was wearing.

At first he wouldn't have known it from any bar he'd ever been in before. They walked in, and the bar itself was directly in front of them. A few older men sat about nursing beers. It was early...

"For gays anyway," Blue said with a toss of his hand. "Gays are like vampires. They don't go out until well after dark. I thought I would start you in the kiddie pool. Let you get your toes wet."

To the right were a couple of pool tables and to the left a dropped-down area with a dance floor and stage as well as steps leading to an upper floor. Immediately to their left were several round tables, only one of which was occupied. Three women sat there, one with blue hair and—God! Elaine from Four-Footed Friends. One of the baristas from The Shepherd's Bean, a coffee shop that John liked, was the third, and Elaine and the barista were holding hands. Well, damn....

John laughed.

"What?" Blue asked.

"Is *everybody* gay?" he said, pointing at the trio at the table.

Elaine noticed them and motioned them over, so with a deep breath, John plunged into a new experience.

"Sit," Elaine said. "Join us."

The lady with the blue hair eyed them both from top to bottom, and Elaine's companion, the barista, told her to stop being so rude. "They come to The Shepherd's Bean," she said. "They're cool."

Elaine made the introductions. Blue-hair was "Tiff," and the barista (John was embarrassed he didn't know her name, as many times as she had served him coffee) was Mara.

143

"I should know your name," John said, voicing his apology aloud.

Mara just laughed and waved it off. "The only reason I know yours is that I saw it on your credit card enough times. That and you're always sweet enough to put the tip in the jar instead of on your card."

Which left the unsaid message that all cash tips weren't necessarily reported to the tax man.

"How's Chewie?" Elaine asked, bringing a smile to both John's and Blue's faces, extra helpings for Blue. "He's supposed to get that cast off any day."

Blue nodded energetically. "He's awesome. He even sleeps with us."

Now Tiff was really eyeing them.

"Get your eyes back in your head, Tiff," Mara said, rolling her eyes behind *huge* glasses.

Tiff shrugged and then nudged John, looked at Blue, looked back at John, waggled her eyebrows, and said, "Good for you, pops."

John sighed and then put on his fake business smile. But it was only fake until he glanced at Blue, and then it turned very real.

Good for him, indeed!

"He doesn't jump off the bed in the night, does he?" Elaine asked.

"Jump *on* is more like it," Tiff answered and then pretended to look aghast. She wasn't very good at it. "Oh! You mean the dog."

Everyone laughed, even John. He might as well get used to it. Actually, hadn't he been getting slowly acclimated to his new life for the last two months or so? He knew what people thought. Or wondered. First they would look at the two of them and assume he and Blue were father and son—John *knew* that. It had really bothered him at first, made him supremely aware of the disparity in their ages, made him feel like a dirty old man or something. But then he remembered Hadrian and Antinous and Oscar Wilde and Lord Alfred Douglas and James Broughton and Joel Singer and Noel Coward and Graham Payne....

And now John Williams and Blue McCoy.

They were of one clan.

And he didn't care what other people thought of him.

Being with Blue wasn't about trying to recapture his youth.

Being with Blue was... being with *Blue*. Blue was the first man he'd ever had sex with. His first time got to become a second and third and tenth and fiftieth time—and it had become love. And it wasn't until Blue that John really knew what love was. The depth of it. The power of it. When he and Blue were around other people, it really began to hit him. Being gay wasn't just about loving cock (and oh, he *loved* that, which was a delightful surprise). It was about loving *man* and all that represented. It was about discovering himself and the world, the family of men loving men.

And if he and Blue did anything in public that was decidedly *un*-father-and-son-like—gazing into each other's eyes the way they still did, touching across a table, holding hands in the park, getting caught kissing behind a statue at one of the museums they still loved going to—and someone looked at them with surprise or gave them a look of disgust, John had learned to think, *Fuck them if they don't approve.*

He'd spent his whole life trying to get the approval of people he thought mattered. He was done with that. He didn't care what anyone thought. Neighbors, strangers, waiters, coworkers. For the first time in his life, he was truly happy. And he was going to guard that happiness. And guard Blue as well.

Strangely, it still hadn't become an issue with the bank. He was sure everyone must know by now. Not because of Janet either. He and Blue had bumped into Chad from the bank at the Kauffman Center Theatre when they went to see the Kansas City Ballet, and the way they'd been sitting at the bar—shoulder to shoulder, heads practically touching—there was no way Chad could assume anything other than the fact that they were a couple.

Couple. Imagine! I'm part of a gay couple.

A part of him expected the CEO to give him a call or show up at his office, or for him to get called before the board of directors.

"Mr. Williams, word is that people have been seeing you all over the city with a boy who obviously isn't your son, and we just don't think that you project the image that should represent Heartland United Bank."

But nothing. Not a word. Not even when he'd proposed that they become a sponsor for this year's Kansas City Gay Pride. After all, gay people needed banks just as much as anyone. And with same-sex marriage being legal nationwide now? Wasn't it a smart move? He was still waiting to hear back on that one.

What would happen if he was fired?

He wasn't sure.

But looking at Blue, he figured that in the end it didn't matter. Because it was true. He was in love. More so than he'd dreamed was possible. And he thought that Blue loved him too. Blue said it was true. John was pretty damned sure it was true. He didn't think he was just some passing fancy for Blue. And he was sure that Blue wasn't just a rebound after Vivian had left him. He'd never felt anything more real in his life.

That's what really mattered. The rest? Why, he would just have to leap and trust in the best outcome.

"John?" Blue asked, pulling him back to the table and their companions.

He smiled. "Yes, Blue?"

"I love you."

"I was just thinking about how much I love you," he said, glowing.

Just then the front door opened, and what at first seemed like a host of people came in. On second glance, it wasn't a host, but it was… eight people.

And of course, Blue knew them. Or at least some of them.

"Little Bear," he cried and leapt off his stool and rushed to the slightly chunky one. He threw his arms around the young man's neck and kissed his cheek.

Nothing to be jealous about. It was a gay thing. Not John's thing yet, but then at one time, neither was eating ass.

The "bear" (that's what big gay men were called—especially if they were hairy) hugged and kissed back and made loud cries of happiness, and then a few more hugs followed. After which Blue herded them over to the table.

"Everybody, this is my boyfriend, John."

Boyfriend! John's heart rushed. *I'm a* man's *boyfriend.* He found himself grinning like a fool. *I'm Blue's boyfriend!* And would he ever get over the rush? Somehow he didn't think so. He hoped not.

John nodded, and then Blue at least tried to continue the introductions. "This is Little Bear," Blue said, waving to the man he'd initially hugged. "And he has a new boyfriend! This is Hodor."

"Kevin, actually," said the big, rugged-looking man with a beard cut in a style that almost reminded John of muttonchops. "Hodor is just a nickname I use when we go to camp."

"Hodor like in *Game of Thrones*?" John asked.

Kevin/Hodor nodded. "'Cause I don't usually talk all that much."

They shook hands. Kevin had a big hand.

"And this is Scott and the Jockster," Blue said, indicating a slim man and his companion, a blond with a fauxhawk.

"Jockster?" he asked, and tried not to laugh.

"Another nickname," said the Jockster. "Call me Cedar."

"Cedar *Carrington*," Blue said conspiratorially, leaning into John. "He's the son of *Cyan* Carrington."

John blinked in surprise. "Of Rumors?" he asked, referring to the world-famous rock band whose every album he owned.

"I ask people not to do that," Cedar said, narrowing his eyes at Blue.

Blue bounced. "I'm sorry. I can't help it." He turned to John. "And he sings sick too!"

Sick? Oh, yes. *Sick* as in cool. Now he did laugh. Offered his hand and had it taken. "An honor to meet you."

"Ditto," said the son of a famous rock star who was also "sick."

"I'm just the son of kooks," Scott said, and then they were shaking hands as well.

"Me too," John said.

"And this is Asher Eisenberg," Blue said, indicating a man who looked familiar. "He's one of the stars of the show *Drunks* we watched the other night on HBO."

John's eyes went wide. *Whoa*, the people Blue knew!

Another handshake.

"And I'm blanking on the other names," Blue said, blushing a deep red.

It turned out the others were Sloan, Max, and Peni.

They chatted a few moments, and John found himself fluctuating between "Oh, wow, I am a part of this gay world and I'm not the only one!" and being a tad overwhelmed. Blue was right. Coming in the early evening before the crowd was the right move.

Then, just before he got completely overcome, the small crowd said they had a date with the "back patio" and would make sure to say hello later, and off they went to the rear of the bar and out a back door.

Blue climbed back on his stool, and the five of them remaining discussed… well, for the most part "normal" things. For some reason it was a very powerful moment, and John found himself realizing he liked being a part of this gay world. He felt at home. He felt welcome. He felt a part of something greater than himself. He didn't remember ever feeling like this before.

It was wonderful.

It was about then that Blue indicated he was going to the restroom, and John nodded and felt safe being left alone (because after all, he wasn't really alone, was he?).

It was one more nice feeling to be added to an ever-growing list.

LITTLE BEAR—WYATT—HAD been looking at him funny. Of this Blue was sure.

Had he even known that Little Bear's real name was Wyatt? Oh, wait! He had. He'd met him at Peter Wagner's huge annual big gay Fourth of July party! Was that last year? In fact, he'd met most of them there, including the pretty dark guy—Peni. Was he Polynesian? Some Pacific Island for sure. But…

Wyatt had been looking at him funny.

Blue tried to let it go. Tried to ignore it, but… it could have been anything. Maybe Blue had something on his face? But surely John would have let him know. He wasn't the kind of man to let a person sit at a dinner table with a piece of spinach stuck between their teeth.

Blue ducked into the bathroom and smiled, checked his reflection. Nope. No spinach.

Wyatt had been…. It was almost like the bear was trying to beam him some mental message.

But, then, of course, there was the fact that he'd had sex with Big Sir—Wyatt's husband. Maybe Wyatt just didn't like him?

And even though the two of them had had an open relationship, and even though that man was now an *ex*-husband, and even though the sex Blue had with Big Sir had hardly been a pleasant experience (for Blue at least) and had turned into a nightmare, it was hard to separate feelings from logic. Open relationship or no, sometimes you just didn't want your husband to go off in the woods and fuck another man.

So maybe that's all it was. Maybe the look was nothing more than "You're the one that was the center of something *very* bad my husband did, and maybe if you *hadn't* gone off with him, nothing bad would ever have happened, and I would still be with him."

Natural.

He hoped, though, that Wyatt knew what Blue had figured out pretty damned fast.

Wyatt was far better off without Big Sir.

"Like Kleenex," Mom had said. "They blow their loads and use you to wipe it up and throw you away!"

So exiting the bathroom, he glanced back to the front of the bar to see if John was looking his way (he wasn't, thank God), took a deep breath, squared his shoulders, and headed through the glass door that led to the back patio.

And there they were. A small happy army. Laughing, joking, drinking. Friends. Good friends.

And Wyatt was leaning up against the big, very handsome Hodor—ah, *Kevin*—instead of Big Sir.

You can do this!

Turning on a smile as if by a switch, Blue headed into the breach. "Hey, guys, good to see you!"

They turned as one and greeted him once more with, "Hey, Blue," and "Good seeing *you*," and "How are you?" and "Goddamn, is that hunk your *boy*friend?"

(The last was from Cedar, of course.)

And he answered with "I'm doing *great*!" and, "Why yes, Cedar. Goddamn, he is. Two months now!"

Asher jumped up and declared he was getting the next round and, "Can I get you something?"

Blue accepted, a gin and tonic—extra lime. Since John liked the stuff so much, he was trying to acquire a taste for the juniper liquor. And interestingly... Asher ordered a Coke for himself....

Blue tried to catch Wyatt's eyes, but the bear seemed to be avoiding just that. Then, as Blue was about to give up (for some reason he couldn't just lean in and ask if there was something wrong) and back away from the group, Wyatt suddenly disengaged from Kevin with a whisper in the big man's ear and told Blue he was going his way.

Blue's heart started to pound in premonition.

It wasn't a *good* feeling.

Wyatt went with Blue into the bar and then asked him if he would join him in the bathroom.

Now Blue's heart was pounding twice as hard.

He's about to tell me something big. And once I hear it, I will never be the same.

With a hard swallow, Blue nodded and followed Wyatt into the small restroom. Wyatt walked ahead and then turned around.

He offered a weak smile—one Blue saw right through.

"I... I...." Were those tears forming in Wyatt's eyes?

Wyatt took a step forward, then leaned on the sink. Even in the dim light Blue could see his hand was white-knuckled.

God....

"I've got something I have to tell you, I think. Has Howard contacted you, by any chance?"

Howard?

Who the fuck was Howard?

But of course, he knew.

Blue shook his head anyway.

"Howard moved to Birmingham—"

"*Who?*" Blue blurted. Asking—pretending he didn't know who Howard was—to delay the bad news he knew was coming. Giving him one last moment to avoid whatever it was.

"Oh! Sorry." He looked away. Sighed. Looked back. "Howard is Big Sir. My ex."

The cold feeling of foreboding doubled as it washed over Blue. God…. *God, God, God*….

Big Sir…. Blue cleared his throat. "Oh," he said.

Wyatt let go of the sink and took another step toward him. Blue actually stepped back.

"*Gods*, Blue. I gotta tell you. I haven't seen you in months. Not since…."

Since the nightmare ending of Heartland Queer Men's Festival last July, Blue thought.

"Blue…."

Spit it out, Blue tried to say, but found he didn't have the spit to do so.

"Howard… Big Sir…. I think you're okay, but… he's HIV positive."

And there it was.

"H…. H…," he managed and tried to swallow but couldn't. "H… I… V?"

Wyatt took another step, and this time Blue found he couldn't back away. He was feeling dizzy. The world had gone wonky. The planet Earth was tilting off its axis, and he had to reach out and lean against the wall to keep from falling. It only sort of helped.

Wyatt took Blue's shoulders in his hands. "I'm okay and…. Well, there was more recent sex between him and I. I tested out negative. I bet you're *fine*. But you need to get checked out."

Gray spots. Swirling gray spots. He staggered.

"Should I get your boyfriend?"

John.

Blue started to fall.

HIV positive.... Please, God. Not that. Not when the world finally seemed to be going right.

Chewie. Someone would have to take care of Chewie...! Who would take care of...?

Shit! Had he infected John? They'd been using condoms, and....

He started to fall, but....

Wyatt grabbed him. And little man that he was, he still outweighed Blue easily.

"Let's sit you down," he said, and he helped Blue to the only place he *could* sit down. The toilet.

Wyatt squatted down before him. "I'm going to go get your man, okay? His name is James?"

"J-John," Blue managed through the spots before his eyes. *But no! Don't tell him! He won't want anything to do....*

Only Blue hadn't said this last out loud, and Wyatt had already scrambled to his feet and was dashing out of the bathroom.

Blue trembled and dropped his face into upturned palms. Shuddered.

HIV positive....

God!

Tears filled his eyes, and he wiped at them and shook his head. Saw graffiti on the stall wall.

Love your Crocs... said NO One EVER.

Carl Loves Ned, with "Loves" crossed out and "Loved" added.

Haikus are easy
But sometimes they don't make sense
Refrigerator.

WWJD? followed by, He wouldn't vandalize bathroom walls.

And of course, many, many pictures of cocks and balls and assholes and blow jobs and....

God, God, God… I'm going to have to live with….

"Blue!"

It was John, and he was here, and he was kneeling on the nasty floor in front of him and looking into his face like….

Like he loves me.

Blue burst into tears.

THEY WERE home and sitting on the couch, because Blue knew he couldn't make it up the stairs, and he didn't want to be carried up them. Not this time.

John had knelt on that pissy bathroom floor and held him for a long time. Held him and told him he loved him and everything would be all right, and then Blue had told him that he might be HIV positive, and damn if the man froze for only a second—even less than that— and then told him that everything *would* be all right.

John was sitting next to him now on the couch, and fuck, his knees were wet!

"Water?" John asked.

No. Piss. That's piss on your knees. And suddenly Blue thought he would vomit, although it wasn't like pee had ever scared him before.

But this was *John.* This was *non*kinky John (for the most part), and John should never have piss-wet knees!

That's for someone like me. Someone who would go off in the woods with two men to play kinky games…. John didn't deserve that. *He doesn't deserve me! What if I've infected him?*

"Blue? Do you want some water? Something stronger?"

Oh. John was asking if he *wanted* water…. "Something stronger," he managed and then wondered if he would even be able to keep water down.

Big Sir is HIV positive.

The man who raped him—all but raped him—was HIV positive.

John came back with a screwdriver, and that almost (but only almost) made Blue laugh. The first drink he'd had with John. It did make

153

him smile, if only a little. He took a good swallow, and it was strong, really strong. Just what he needed.

Because it was Sunday evening, and the Kansas City Health Clinic wasn't open, and it would be tomorrow at least before he could be tested, and then it would be a toss-up if it would be a day they were doing rapid testing, or if he'd have to wait two or more weeks before he got his results.

Once again Blue thought he might throw up.

But not here, not now, and not in front of John. No way, nohow.

So he took another big swallow of orange juice and vodka instead, and John didn't tell him to be careful, just nodded in encouragement, so Blue gulped it all down and held out the empty glass for more. And without a word—only a nod—John got up and got him another.

And they cuddled on the couch that had become so significant to Blue. Couches were where families gathered, and it had been a very long time since he'd thought of himself as being part of a family. Sure the gang that hung out at the Wyandotte house were a family—but one where two of them would just up and leave without telling him (as if that had never been done before). Blue had been back to the house several times, only to find they were indeed gone.

But with John and the recovering Chewie, he had been made to feel that maybe, just maybe, he'd finally found a family to call his own. Now he could only wonder if he'd keep that family.

But then he looked at John and was astonished at what he saw there.

Love.

That was love in his eyes.

They watched a little television, although Blue barely paid it any attention. He usually found *Unbreakable Kimmy Schmidt* a hell of a lot funnier.

He knew he shouldn't focus on the worst possibility. He knew it was possible he was okay. Wyatt was okay, after all. He had a chance. He knew he needed to be positive—and *that* word had sure become ironic, hadn't it? Because positive was what he didn't want. Negative was what he wanted to be. Fuck! It was enough to drive him crazy.

Blue climbed the steps on his own, even though he was pretty damned tipsy by then. Of course, John was at his side, arm around his shoulder.

And then… John got amorous? Really?

"I don't feel like…."

"*Shh…*," John said. "Don't worry. Just touching. That's it. Close your eyes. Give me a few minutes, and if you still want me to stop, I will. It's called effleurage."

F-floor-wha…?

"Touch, my love."

My love. He called me "my love."

"It's touch. Nothing else. And if you don't want me to touch you, I won't."

And that momentary instant of not wanting to be touched went away—because this was John, not Big Sir, and he was touching him with love, not hate or hurt. So Blue closed his eyes and just… felt. Felt John's fingers lightly, lightly touching and stroking his skin. Tracing muscles. Back, arms, buttocks, legs. And that first impulse… to flee… it was gone. Because he did want to be touched. Oh God, he did.

But by John alone.

Forever and ever.

Just John.

IT SURPRISED John how quickly Blue fell asleep.

And how something powerful happened to John. With Blue, powerful seemed to be the name of the game. Because in the instant he'd heard that Blue might be HIV positive, he'd almost panicked. He'd *almost* leapt up and run away as fast as his feet could carry him.

But it was only an instant. A half instant. Less than that!

And then something else happened. Just like that, the fear was gone—*completely*. A total calm took over. A knowing. Knowing that it was his job to take care of Blue, no matter what.

Because if Blue did have AIDS—no wait, *not* AIDS. He'd done enough reading, enough research in the past weeks, to know differently.

If he was to be a gay man living and loving and being sexual in this world, he knew he had to be responsible and learn. And among everything else he was learning, he researched AIDS. Having the HIV virus was *not* having AIDS. Just like people didn't die of AIDS. They died of complications due to AIDS. It might seem like a small distinction, but it wasn't.

He also knew this: people lived a long time with HIV now. It wasn't the death sentence it was in the eighties and early nineties. Having HIV certainly wasn't "as easy as living with diabetes" either. Too many gay men pronounced it thus and became irresponsible—figured they should just run out there and catch the virus so they wouldn't have to worry about it or practice safer sex. Which was bullshit. Ask anyone with diabetes if it was "easy."

But the fact was, people did live with HIV. It wasn't an incurable type of cancer. There were people who lived with HIV for decades. And while he didn't want Blue to have the virus, he knew one thing. He—John—wasn't going anywhere. Maybe he wouldn't be able to swallow anymore—and the jury was out on the safety of that one still—who really cared? He'd lived over forty years without doing so. He could live a lifetime more.

What he couldn't live without was Blue.
So what he really knew was this: He was not going *anywhere*.
Not without Blue.
Because he had found his life.
And it was worth any price.
And he would touch Blue for as long as he lived.

CHAPTER EIGHTEEN

THEY MADE it to Monday.

John called in to work and let them know he would not be there—no, not at all, and maybe not Tuesday—

"Do you have the flu, John?" Janet had asked. "You need to watch that! Stay in bed. Drink plenty of fluids. Soup! You need chicken soup. Want me to bring you some—"

"I'm fine...."

"—soup? You know what they say. Starve a cold, feed a fever. Or is it feed a cold, starve a fever? God. I'm not even sure what that means...."

"I'll be okay, Janet. I promise."

—and after he spoke to Janet, he made a few other calls too. He found what he needed to know, and he made sure some other things happened as well.

Because being in charge was something he was very good at.

He made sure the clinic was doing rapid testing today, for one thing. At least for Blue. It was interesting to throw the name of the bank around for himself for once, something he rarely did. Because couldn't the Kansas City Health Clinic use a friend like Heartland United Bank? Maybe what John had implied wasn't entirely ethical, but why be a bank president if not to use the title once in a while?

"Well, I'll be damned, John" came Vivian's voice in his head. *"I'm impressed...."*

So then John got Blue up and tried to get him to eat some breakfast, but Blue said he wouldn't be able to keep it down.

"At least some toast? One piece? With some jelly for the blood sugar?"

Blue had sighed and then looked at him with such open, naked trust that it both filled John's heart and almost broke it at the same time.

"Okay," Blue said, conceding. "The gooseberry?"

157

John had nodded. "The gooseberry it is. Although you know that's awfully special to me, and there isn't much left, and...."

And then John saw that Blue wasn't really up for jokes, his expression showed that—as if he wasn't sure if John *was* joking—and John stepped in and kissed him. Really kissed him. And then made several pieces of toast and slathered them with purple-blue gooseberry jelly that he'd gotten from the Amish table at City Market, every last bit of it, clinking the spoon at the bottom of the jar, and then informed Blue they would just have to go back and get more. That finally earned him a small smile, and Blue ate not one piece but two.

That was good.

Then he got Blue dressed and into the car, and they started the day's journey.

BLUE TRIED not to be scared. Told himself over and over and over again that he had a good chance. After all, hadn't Little Bear said that he was fine? That he had checked out negative? And that he'd had sex with Big Sir since... since Blue had?

But what gay man got tested and wasn't a little bit nervous every time—even if he knew he had to be HIV negative?

Or at least thought he knew.

Because who *knew*, really? Knew for totally absolutely sure?

Why, Blue had known a guy who "knew for totally absolutely sure" that his lover would never ever cheat on him. But then it turned out he had. Once. And he'd gotten it. Gotten HIV. And passed that little present on to Blue's friend.

Thank God John was there with him.

And he wanted it to stay that way.

He wasn't sure how all this had happened, how he had a man like John in his life, but he wanted him to stay. So he decided right then and there—sitting in the car before they even went inside the clinic—that he wanted to clear the air. To come clean. To say it all. And to let John know why he might have HIV in the first place.

"I've had a lot of sex," he said, looking down at his hands, which he was wringing between his knees. *What if this makes him run?*

"Okay," John said quietly.

And then they talked.

And then, thank God (again), John didn't seem to be going anywhere. Except into the clinic.

At the counter was a lovely African American lady who asked him to sign in and had him fill out some small bits of information—first name, birthday, last four of his social security number—on a clipboard. He was in a sort of cloud through it all, with John at his side helping him. The nurse looked it over and then nodded. "Yes, Blue. I've got your name on my list. Why don't you sit down? I'll let Geoff know you're here. He's been waiting for you."

Waiting for me? he wondered. He looked at John—handsome beautiful strong John—who nodded.

John guided him to a couch, and they sat. John put his arm around him right there in front of everyone, and it felt so good. He rested his head against John's chest and closed his eyes.

He didn't have to wait long.

"Blue?" came a soft but strong voice.

He looked up and saw an older man with stylish glasses who offered his hand and told him, "My name is Geoff. How are you doing this morning?"

"*Not* too good," Blue said and then tried to smile.

Geoff nodded, bit his lower lip, and said, "I imagine not. But it's going to be okay, Blue."

"Promise?" Blue asked.

"One way or another," the man said. "Now why don't we get all this anxiousness over?"

Blue looked at John and then at Geoff and asked, "I don't suppose he can come with me?"

"I'm sorry," Geoff said with a single shake of his head. "Totally against any and all rules." He looked at John. "I'm sorry, Mr. Williams."

Mr. Williams? Geoff knew John?

"I understand," John said, and then stood and helped Blue to his feet and hugged him and then even kissed him lightly—yes, right there in front of everyone. And somehow that helped. The day brightened just a bit with hope….

"I'll be okay," he whispered aloud, and both John and Geoff asked him what he'd said, but he just shook his head and said, "Nothing."

So then, with one last look, he followed Geoff through the security door—it had one of those little boxes with numbers to be typed at the threshold, but someone buzzed them in—and then down a hallway and left and into a small but pleasant room. Or as pleasant as such a room could be.

They sat, and Geoff asked if he needed a drink of something.

"Screwdriver?" Blue asked.

"I *wish*," said Geoff. "I'd join you."

Blue found himself liking this man—slim, around sixty, black hair gone gray at the temples and slicked back from a style a million years old—who patted Blue's knee. It wasn't at all uncomfortable.

"This isn't going to take long," Geoff told him. "Less than a half hour."

"Half hour," Blue echoed, and Geoff nodded, smiling, so kind and sympathetic.

"No needles… not really. Just a tiny little prick on the end of one finger, and I am happy to say I am very good at it. You'll barely feel a thing."

"Okay," Blue said, and then Geoff did some shuffling and moving around of things and opening little packages and getting it all laid out on the small table to their side.

"Ready?" Geoff asked then, and Blue nodded. Geoff did something with a little bitty plastic orange box that looked a lot like a pencil sharpener, and there was the tiniest little blink of pain, barely anything—Geoff had been right. Then he did something else, but Blue decided not to watch. His stomach was doing these little flippy-floppy things, and he certainly didn't want to faint. That would be a scene, wouldn't it? What would happen then?

160

"Alrighty, then!" Geoff said with much enthusiasm, as if they were about to do something wonderful—get a big ice cream sundae or go for a ride in the country in a car where they could put the top down, maybe to Temujin's for one of those amazing dinners—and then began to ask him a series of questions.

Blue tried his best to answer them all.

"Now just so you know—I am sure you do, but—what we are testing for are HIV antibodies, not the virus itself. If a person is infected with HIV, it takes the body two to twelve weeks to start producing antibodies for the virus. Sometimes as long as six months—but that is rare."

Blue swallowed hard and started to do math in his head—as well as he could—and missed the first question.

"Blue?"

He started and said, "Huh?"

"I was just asking if you'd received oral sex recently."

"It's been over six months," Blue cried.

"Since you had oral sex?"

"No! Since I was raped." Blue trembled. "Sort of raped. Whatever the hell it was."

Geoff looked at him with big concern-filled eyes and asked him what he meant.

So he explained.

"I see," Geoff said. "God, I'm sorry that happened to you. I really am. I hear about stuff like this all the time. People think it's just women, but it isn't. Men are raped all the time. And you're such a little guy, it would be easy to overpower you. This man should have checked in with you to make sure you were going along with the scenario the two of you created."

Blue didn't even know what to say to that.

"But I can say this. If that incident is the one you're worried about, we will know with 99 percent certainty whether you've been infected—in my opinion, 99.9 percent."

Blue didn't know if he should be relieved or not.

161

So he went on and answered the rest of the questions—if he'd given or received oral sex and if he'd swallowed (yes, yes, yes), and if he'd given or received anal sex and if he used condoms (yes, yes, and yes) and if he'd had vaginal sex (Blue had barked with laugher at that one, and Geoff said he'd had to ask), and how many sex partners he'd had in the last three months (counting John and Gavel and Sly, it was three—no, shit, there had been a couple of others. "What is wrong with me? Am I some kind of slut?" And Geoff had assured him he wasn't). There were more questions, including if he'd been paid for sex or paid for sex himself (not so much with money…) and if he'd had sex with a known IV drug user (probably), and somewhere along there Geoff's timer went off, making Blue jump a foot despite how tiny the noise had been.

And then Geoff gave Blue his results.

CHAPTER NINETEEN

JOHN LOOKED at the clock on the wall. Ten minutes. It had only been ten minutes. It seemed like an hour since they'd sat in the car. But ten minutes was all. Maybe fifteen.

"My parents were the coolest," Blue had told him. "*The coolest.*" He smiled wistfully. "Mom was beautiful and petite and had very long hair, and we called her Michelle because she didn't believe in authoritarianism and wanted us to mind her by choice, not because it was expected."

Blue called his mother by her name. Interesting. John didn't call his mother by her first name. Not that he talked to her much anyway. Why should he? He'd never been the son she wanted. The feeling was mutual. She'd never been the mother he'd wanted either.

A thought shot up out of the dark. *And I've never been the father Alistair wanted.* The thought hurt.

"My dad was big," Blue continued. "People used to tease them. Said they looked like a father and daughter although they were the same age. He was so muscular. He had blond hair and the biggest brown eyes." Blue sighed. Got that faraway look in his eyes. Blue had obviously cared for his father. John's father had cared for him less than his mother had. The only thing he'd ever done that had gotten him any approval from the man was playing football. And when that finally became clear, he'd quit.

It had been an ugly, explosive argument. Luckily football wasn't John's strength in school. Math was. And that's how he'd gotten his scholarships. Scholarships he'd needed. Needed to find something he really wanted to do. Needed to escape.

"We did cool things. Yoga classes. We meditated together." Imagine.

"We went camping together. Clothing *optional* campgrounds. They said that we shouldn't be ashamed of our bodies."

John forced himself not to react. Nude? He couldn't imagine being naked in front of his parents. He wouldn't want to. Wouldn't have wanted to. He had to fight a shudder.

"They never got married. They said they didn't need a piece of paper to show they were in love."

But then it hit him. "I... I...." He was confused. What did all this have to do with what Blue had been talking about? He'd been admitting an extensive sex life. But it wasn't like John hadn't already figured that out. And hadn't cared. Because what was past was past. So what did Blue's parents have to do with his sex life? "What...?"

"They died in a car accident when we were ten...," Blue said.

John froze. *Oh no. No. Died? Oh no....* But then something else hit him. *We?* "Wait... we?" Because suddenly he knew "we" didn't mean Blue and his parents. But what *did* it mean?

Blue gave him a curious look. A confused look. "Yeah," Blue said, "we."

"Who is 'we'?"

"Me and my brother," Blue replied.

John's mouth fell open, and his eyes went wide. "*Brother*? You have a brother?"

"Well, yeah," Blue said matter-of-factly. "I told you that."

You certainly did not. "No, you didn't." Stunned.

"Sure I did."

"No, you didn't," John said firmly. "I would remember something like that." Of course he would. A brother?

Blue looked even more confused, obviously lost in thought.

Then it hit him. Of course. Why hadn't he seen it? "Wait a minute." All those times Blue had said "we," John had assumed.... "All those times you said 'we.' You didn't mean just you and your parents? You meant a brother."

"Yeah," Blue said. Something happened to Blue's face. A sadness. A *supreme* sadness.

No. Had something happened to Blue's brother as well? His sweet Blue had lost his parents in a car accident. And then something with his brother? "What happened to him?" Unable to help himself, he reached out and cupped Blue's beautiful cheek in his hand.

"He ran away," Blue said, and his eyes began to fill with tears. "He left me."

Oh, Blue. My sweet, sweet Blue. And before he even knew what he was doing, John pulled Blue into his arms. Rocked him as best he could, the two of them sitting in the front seat of his car. "Oh, baby," he said. Today was yet another day that it proved to be a good thing he had such a big car. It allowed for more holding room than the average front seat.

"When our parents died, my grandparents took us in." He trembled in John's arms. "They weren't like Mom and Dad. They were fucking crazy. They were super religious. Crazy religious. Not the good kind. Not the 'Jesus Loves Me' kind. When they were making us go to church I met some good Christians. Mom and Dad didn't like Christians, especially my mom. But it wasn't because of *Christians*. It was because of my grandparents. Her parents. So when she left home, she made sure to bring us up in a way that was totally different from her parents." He shuddered then and buried his face against John's shoulder.

That brought something out in John. That feeling of protectiveness. Selfishly, it made his heart swell. Someone who really needed him. Had anyone ever needed him?

And then he knew something else. There was nothing that Blue could tell him that would make him love Blue any less. He didn't care if he found out Blue was one of those prostitutes that dressed up like a woman and worked on Main or Troost Streets. He didn't care if Blue had had sex with a hundred men, a thousand, a million.

All he knew was that he loved Blue. Loved him in a way that he'd never loved anyone before. And that he wanted to be there for him no matter what.

"My grandparents were crazy. They told us that God allowed our parents to die so we could be saved. They made us read the Bible before school and every night before we went to bed. We went to church all the time. They weren't as bad as Carrie's mom. No prayer closet, but it was pretty awful. And they *did* punish us. They would make us stand and hold buckets of water out to our sides, and if we lowered them they would hit us with a switch. They said it would make us better Christian soldiers. Then one day Indigo—"

"Indigo?" John asked. *Indigo?*

Blue looked at him and smiled, but his eyes were swimming with pain. He nodded. "Indigo was—is—my brother. Did you think Blue was the weirdest a name could get?"

John's heart felt heavy at those words. "I like Blue," he whispered. Then louder, "I *love* Blue."

Blue blinked at him. As if he were worried a smack would follow the compliment. God. Just what had Blue's grandparents done to him? To them? Blue and his *brother*. "I like Indigo too," he added. "Much better than plain old boring John."

"*Not* boring," Blue said. "Manly. Strong. And you can find it on those little license plates with the names on them that you get for your bicycle. Do you think I ever found Blue on one of those? Or a magnet? Or a keychain? Or a coffee mug? Anything?"

John chuckled. "I suppose not." He shook his head.

Blue nodded and a tear escaped, dropped down into his lap. "We were both fourteen when he left—"

"You were *both* fourteen?" John interrupted. "You were born within a year of each other?"

Blue blinked at him. "Of course. He's my twin."

"I CAN'T take it anymore, Bro," Indigo said. "I'm outta here."

Blue could only stand there. *Out of here?* Then he tried to play it off. He rolled his eyes. "Yeah, right. That's what you *always* say."

"Nope, Blue. I am *done*. Super done." Indigo nodded firmly and shifted his weight from one foot to the other, adjusted his backpack. "Can't take it. Can't take *them*. They're fucking *crazy*."

Fucking. Indigo said "fucking." He'd been saying it more and more lately. He'd even used the F-word once right in front of Grandpa. He'd gotten knocked down for it too. Grandpa had bloodied his mouth. The glare Grandpa had gotten in return actually made the old man back up, a look of... had it been fear? Blue was pretty sure it was.

An ache started in Blue's heart. Because he suddenly knew his brother meant what he said. He knew Indigo wasn't just blowing off steam. This time he meant it. Indigo really *was* leaving. And it wasn't just the backpack slung over his shoulder that told him so. It was in his stance. In his *eyes*.

This can't be happening. "But where are you going to go?"

"New York City. I'm going to be a model."

A model? "You're *fourteen*," Blue said, picturing the runway his brother was always dreaming about. "You can't be a model."

"What about all those kids you see in the ads and catalogs? They have to get those kids from somewhere!"

"But Indigo! You have to have connections. What are you going to do? Just walk into the offices of Land's End or L.L. Bean and shout 'Here I am'?"

"They'd be lucky to have me."

"Of course they would!" Blue cried. "But do you think it will happen?" Not that he wanted to be like his grandparents and tell Indigo that his dreams were stupid—or worse—the Devil's dreams for him. But he had to be realistic. They were only fourteen!

Indigo tossed his head back (like he had when he had hair long enough to throw back, before their grandparents made him cut it) and smirked in reply. "There are other kinds of models. You don't think men will want to take pictures of me?"

Blue's eyes went wide. *Porn?* Was Indigo talking about *porn?* "P-porn?" he managed aloud.

Shrug. "Why not? I'm pretty. *We're* very pretty. Don't the girls tell us that all the time? And some of the boys too? You don't think men would want me? Either of us?"

Now Blue had to sit down on his bed. What was his brother suggesting? That he would do more than let the men take pictures? That he would have *sex* with them?

"B-but Indigo," Blue cried. "That's big city! We've seen online what those big city gays want." Leather. Tying each other up! *Orgies.* Peeing on each other. Doing things with their.... Blue shuddered. With their fists! "You're ready to have sex?"

"I already have," Indigo said. Said it in a tone of banality, as if he'd just announced which of the old ladies had won their grandmother's weekly mahjong game that afternoon.

Blue would have fallen off his feet if he weren't sitting down. What? Indigo had... *been* with someone? And for some reason, it felt like an ice pick to the chest, even though they'd decided they didn't want to be "that way" with each other. That they would want their own boyfriends. But it was simply the fact that Indigo had already done it. Hadn't told Blue. Hadn't told Blue he'd even found someone he wanted to do "it" with.

"Wh-who?" he asked, fearing the answer. Would it be Johnny, the cutie who was so good in track?

Barry, who had been asking them both to come spend that night at his place, "We could have a lot of fun!"

God! Not Jack, the senior who had told them both they had asses sweeter than any girl's in the whole school. Because he was like, yeah, a senior!

"Mr. Weberman." Again, stated so matter-of-factly that it took Blue a moment to really grasp what he was saying.

"Mr. Weberman?" Their shop teacher? The guy who was second only to the football coach in manliness? *That* Mr. Weberman?

Indigo nodded. "He's got a super bod," he said, finally getting some feeling in his voice. "And a huge cock."

Blue reeled.

"You did it with Mr. Weberman?"

Indigo nodded.

Indigo had fooled around with Mr. Weberman! Blue felt another stab to his heart. And then imagined the shop teacher naked. He couldn't help it. It wasn't like they hadn't seen naked men before. At camp when they were kids—although that really had been marvelously innocent. Natural. And then lately, much more sexually, they had looked at men on the Internet. Men doing things with men. And stories that told them what men liked to do to each other. Some of it they found sexy. Some of it pretty gross.

What had Indigo done with Mr. Weberman? Had he done something to him? Or had Mr. Weberman done something to Indigo? No! Not…. He hadn't… stuck his dick in….

Indigo laughed, and when Blue looked back at him, heart breaking, his brother sighed and sat down next to Blue. Took Blue's hand in his own. "We've talked about this. I want a boyfriend. Don't you?"

Yeah. He did. He'd imagined a lot of them too. Big hunky men. Like Marcos Ferraez or Peter DeLuise from *Stargate* or Jeffrey Dean Morgan, the beefcake dad from *Supernatural*. So yeah. He knew. But…. "But Mr. *Weberman*?"

"How else do you think I got a *B* on that piece-of-shit bird feeder I made? Besides, it was kind of hot with a *man*. All those muscles. That…."

And Blue cringed at the things he said next. Things that helped answer his question about what he and their teacher had done. "Indigo! It's against the law!"

"Only if someone finds out."

Then a new realization hit him—one he'd already known but had refused to let surface. About what Indigo would be doing when he went to New York City. "You're not talking about getting a boyfriend!" Blue cried. "You're talking about selling yourself!"

Indigo gave yet another shrug. "I bet I can make a lot of money too. There are men out there who like boys."

"No!" Blue cried and then let out another sob. "You can't, Indigo. Please!" *Please don't.* He pictured the pornographic images from the Internet in his head, but with Indigo in the middle of it all. Not loving. Not love.

Then Indigo leaned in and kissed Blue's forehead. "Come with me."

Blue drew back despite himself. "Wh-what?"

"Just think!" Indigo's eyes were sparkling. Flashing. "What they'd pay for two of us. Two identical twins. My God, Blue. We'll be fucking rich!"

Fucking rich. Said it again. The F-word. But more. Because it *was* fucking. Literally *fucking*....

He shook his head.

"*Come on,*" Indigo said, and finally there really was passion in his voice. *Pleading* now instead of the matter-of-fact tone he'd been using for things that should never be talked about ordinarily. So candidly, without concern. "Rich. The two of us will be unstoppable."

Blue shook his head adamantly. "No! Indigo, sex should be special."

Indigo scoffed at him. "It's like anything else for sale," his brother said.

Blue whimpered. To think of Indigo having a boyfriend was one thing. But to sell himself? To be so darned callous about it?

"You could die," Blue said.

Indigo just looked at him.

"You could get AIDS. Some serial killer could get you. A gay basher could kill you."

Indigo shook his head. "Nope. I'll be careful." And then he did something else that shocked Blue. He pulled out a knife, and with a *snikt* sound, the blade popped out—a switchblade.

"Indigo! Where did you get that?"

"Where do you think?" And when Blue didn't—couldn't—answer, Indigo said, "From Mr. Weberman."

"He gave it to you?"

Indigo nodded.

Blue closed his eyes, suddenly so dizzy he thought he might collapse, sitting on a bed or not. He opened them when he felt Indigo getting up off the bed.

Indigo was looking at him, brows together, eyes dark, mouth a straight, hard line. Then he asked it. "You coming with me or not?"

Because he really was leaving.

"What if I yell for Grandpa?" he asked, desperate, the tears starting for real.

"Then I will hate you for life!" And the slash of his mouth was now a snarl.

Blue gasped, hurt now beyond anything ever.

They looked at each other for what seemed the longest time.

And then Indigo went to the window and opened it, lifted the screen upward in its track. He looked back at Blue, the question unasked. Because they both knew what Blue was going to say.

He was not going to go with him.

He couldn't.

He was far too afraid.

Indigo had always been the brave one.

What would he do without his brother?

"Please don't go," Blue sobbed.

Indigo sighed again, then shook his head resolutely. "I have to. I can't stay here."

"Something bad will happen."

Indigo shook his head. "No. I'll be fine."

"You're so little!" *We're so little.* "You won't stand a chance." *Something bad will happen!*

Indigo shushed him, fire in his eyes again. But dangerous fire. Blue drew back and then suddenly thought, *He is dangerous.*

And God help anyone who tried to hurt him.

"One last chance," Indigo asked.

Long pause.

Blue shook his head.

It near killed him.

Then Indigo shocked him again. Rushed forward and kissed him—really kissed him—hard. Then bit at his neck. And said, "Love you forever, brother."

And an instant later, he was out the window and down the trellis and gone into the night.

CHAPTER TWENTY

"I NEVER saw him again," Blue told John. "Never even saw a letter. Not until I ran away myself."

John was still holding him, again truly glad Vivian had talked him into the big car he'd never really needed, since they used her Tesla when they did anything social—if they did.

Now he was finally seeing that they hadn't done much of that.

That he'd claimed—to himself—that he wanted a normal life with a wife and a house and a white picket fence (which he didn't have; it was a privacy fence, but only in the back) and social dinners with other couples. But he hadn't wanted that at all, had he?

If he'd given Vivian that, maybe she would still be with him.

What he'd been suspecting was true. She wasn't the villain.

He was.

Of course, if he had given his wife the life she wanted, if he'd been the husband she wanted, he would never have met Blue. Except for that day he almost ran over him with his car.

And so life went the way it went. Right now that meant holding this young man he had inexplicably fallen completely and totally and madly in love with. A lifetime avoiding men… and now hopefully a lifetime loving one. No matter what that involved.

No matter what.

"When did you run away, baby?" *Not that I would have blamed you for running away the next day from what you've said so far.* He'd had no idea that things had been so bad for Blue. But it explained a lot.

"My junior year," Blue said, pulling back a bit. "Grandpa sent me to the attic to get some storm windows, and I found a different box entirely. It was letters. From Indigo. Like something right out of *The Color Purple*. He had written me on and off for two years. Told me everything that happened. He was alive. At least he was for two years. But then he stopped writing. The last letter…."

> *I don't know why you won't write back, but I can tell you're not going to. I'm giving up, Blue. If you ever decide to look for me, well, I don't know. Me and Jimmy are going to London. I don't know how you can find me. But things work out. And if you ever decide to get away from those two fucks, remember what I told you. You don't have to stand on street corners. And men will do all kinds of favors for a night with you. Food and all kinds of stuff.*
> *Love you,*
> *Indigo*

"That was it."

Oh God, thought John.

"Finally I had had it. Indigo had been writing me for two years, and they kept it secret! I… I lost my mind, John! I went to them, and I was screaming, and—"

And?

"—I pulled a knife on them!"

GRANDMA SCREAMED, and Grandpa went as pale as milk.

Oh, the way they were looking at him.

They were scared! They were *fucking* scared, as Indigo would say.

Blue looked down at the knife in his hand—it was fucking huge—and that made him laugh because… *him*? Holding a knife on someone! Why, it was like something from *Alice in Wonderland* or some British sitcom like *Absolutely Fabulous*.

He threw the knife then, far to his right—practically over his shoulder—and nowhere near either of the old fucks, and then Grandpa pissed himself.

He actually peed his pants.

Blue could hear it.

They all three did.

The front of Grandpa's khaki pants went dark, and then a long wet path went down his leg and puddled on the floor.

Blue shook his head and wondered why he'd ever been afraid of this pathetic old man. He turned and left the room, and he crammed some shirts and underwear and two pairs of jeans in his backpack and left.

He never looked back.

"AND SOMETIMES I've had sex with guys because… when I don't have any food or money or anything!"

Tears were pouring down Blue's face, and the apprehension in his glassy eyes as he peered at John made John's heart hurt.

Oh, my sweet Blue…. God, I wish I could have been there for you. The world can be a cold place. And…. That look….

"Do I…. Do I disgust you?"

What? Disgust? "No, Blue! I don't care," John said.

"Wh-what?"

"I mean, I *care*. I do. I care about you. I care that you had to do things you didn't want to do." John cupped Blue's cheek in his hand and said, "It kills me that you had to do those things. But it doesn't matter."

"But it *does* matter," Blue said.

John frowned. Had he messed up again?

"It matters that all kinds of shit like that happens in the world," Blue went on.

John nodded. "Yes, it does. Of course it does."

"Then why did you say…?"

John wiped one of Blue's many tears away. "What I mean is that I love you. I don't know how it happened. I don't know what it was about you that let it happen. I resisted men for thirty years. I didn't even jerk off with friends." John turned away and looked out the car window. He was fighting tears and didn't want Blue to see. But then it occurred to him that he didn't have to hide anything from Blue.

Shouldn't hide anything. Not from the man he loved. John looked back and smiled.

"You know that movie?" he asked.

"Movie?" Blue said.

"The one with the famous line? 'You had me at hello'?"

Somehow, through some miracle, Blue smiled back. "*Jerry Maguire*."

John ran his fingers through Blue's hair. "Except you had me at 'Sorry, dude!'"

Blue's eyes went wide, and he laughed. "What?"

John leaned in close. "That was what you said to me when *I* almost hit you with my car."

Blue's eyebrows shot up. "I did?"

John nodded and rested his forehead against Blue's. "And something about being late for a very important date and then…."

"I kissed you."

John nodded. "And I've never been the same."

"Really?" Blue asked.

"*Really*," John replied and nodded again—once. Twice. "And I thought about you for months, when I would *let* myself."

"Really?" Blue repeated.

"Really." He closed his eyes and opened them and said, "And then I decided to get a dog. Because my wife took our dog when she left, and I sure missed *him*."

Blue laughed at that. Only a little laugh. But he laughed. It lifted John's heart.

"So I went to an animal shelter and—"

"And?" Blue asked.

"—I saw an angel and forgot all about getting a dog."

"I'm not an angel."

"You're *my* angel," John replied and kissed him lightly, ever so lightly, on the mouth.

Blue's expression darkened, and he shook his head as if in denial. "I went in the woods with a man," he blurted. "I wanted him to force me to have sex."

John kissed him again. It didn't matter.

"I'd never been *forced*."

And John kissed him again. *Go ahead. Tell me if you need to. But it doesn't matter.*

"But I wanted to be. I wanted to be *forced*. Just once."

Blue closed his eyes, but he didn't stop. "It was supposed to be a game. Role-playing. *Pretend*." He opened them again, looked away. "Like having sex somewhere you could get caught, you know?

"Or a cop fantasy. Blow me so I don't give you a ticket."

John nodded. He was new to this gay thing, but not so new he couldn't understand the desire for new experiences, for exploring everything it might mean. Not that he could imagine ever wanting those particular experiences himself. Or, well, maybe he could. But now was not the time for speculation. Now was the time to be here for Blue. He kissed Blue again. "He didn't stop. He wouldn't stop. It was supposed to be a game, and when I realized I didn't like it, that I wanted it to stop, he wouldn't." *They wouldn't.*

That caused a pang in John's chest. He couldn't deny it. But not a pang of horror or disgust. Except for the horror and disgust that someone could do that to another human being. Especially one like Blue. John looked him in the eyes, trying to show Blue his love. Because he wasn't sure just what to say. "I'm sorry" sounded so hollow.

"It was *horrible*," Blue said, and tears flowed again. "And that's why I'm here today. Because he's HIV positive. And he might have infected me. And it's my fault."

And then for the longest time neither of them said anything.

"And now I don't think I can ever go back to camp," Blue said. He looked so sad, like someone who had lost a beloved friend. "Camp Sanctuary was one of the only places on earth that I felt safe. But now…?"

John wasn't sure what to say, but he knew what *not* to say. He didn't say "What's past is past." He didn't say "Shh. There, there." He didn't say "I can imagine."

In the end all he said was, "I love you. And if I have anything to say about it, nothing like that will ever happen to you again."

This time Blue kissed *him*.

Then John said one more thing, and he believed it with all his heart. "It wasn't your fault. And God help that man if I ever meet him."

Blue curled into John's arms then. Not speaking, no longer crying, simply accepting the love and comfort John wanted so much to give him.

After that they went into the clinic.

CHAPTER TWENTY-ONE

THE DOOR that Blue had disappeared through opened and brought John out of his musings. At last it was Blue.

And even though John knew it couldn't have been even a half hour since Blue had gone through that door, it seemed like forever.

His heart was pounding.

Blue…. *God, please have him be okay….*

Blue was smiling!

He gave John his results, though the outcome was already written all over his face. Blue needed to say the words, so John let him. He was negative.

To John's surprise, he found himself thanking God, and he meant it with all his heart.

Thank you, God. Thank you for sending me an angel and for letting him be negative. And forgive me for not believing in you. Thank you.

After that, all John could do was kiss Blue. His angel.

John didn't wonder again how it had all happened. How he fell so fast.

But he did decide to thank God every day from then on.

THEY STOPPED at home only long enough to pick up Chewie. It was his day to get the cast removed.

To Blue's surprise his dog perked up and seemed excited when they pulled up in front of Four-Footed Friends. He'd been worried that Chewie would be afraid. After all, his only experiences with the place had involved pain. But no. He began to bounce about and bark as if he were about to see long-lost friends.

It hit Blue then, of course.

Chewie knew.

Dogs were very intelligent, and he *knew*. Knew these people had helped him. Knew they hadn't been the source of his pain.

John was smiling at them both from the front seat. He reached out with that big hand of his, ruffled the hair on Chewie's head, and said, "Good boy," and, "I love dogs. He knows something good is going to happen."

Blue grinned.

And was pleasantly surprised at the joy the love in John's eyes brought him. More love than Blue ever thought he would have, ever dreamed he could have.

"I love you too, Blue."

Blue felt almost light-headed. "Good," he said. "I live for your love."

John's eyes widened slightly, and then he smiled and the world was good.

So they took Chewie inside, and surprise, surprise, the whole gang was there. Not only Hound Dog and Elaine—who owned and ran the place—but Mara, Elaine's girlfriend, as well. And of course, Dr. Lee, who said that anyone could have done what needed to be done today, but he wasn't going to miss it for the world.

They clapped when Blue and John came in, and Chewie barked happily and did his magical hobble on his cast, which after all this time looked almost graceful, and then sat and gave them all a big happy doggy smile.

"You ready to get that thing off, big boy?" Dr. Lee asked, bending and resting his hands on his knees.

Chewie barked as if to let them know that he had never been more ready for anything in his life.

Everyone laughed at that, and then Dr. Lee took Chewie to the back. There were far too many of them to join him, and Elaine assured Blue that his dog would be just fine. She offered them coffee, but Blue was already so high-strung with all that had happened today he might simply explode if he had any caffeine.

They sat in the little break room—and little was the right word considering there were four of them. H.D. was helping Dr. Lee, which made Blue feel good. Hound Dog was almost magic.

"Well, how have you been?" Elaine asked and then took a drink of coffee, apparently not worried in the least about caffeine consumption.

"I'm negative!" Blue blurted, as usual not thinking before speaking.

Mara's eyebrows shot up. "You seem awfully cheerful for someone who's negative!"

"Huh?" Blue asked, confused.

John put an arm around him, gave him a squeeze, and explained. "We just got back from the health clinic. Blue is HIV negative."

"Oh!" said Mara.

"Great news!" said Elaine.

And classy as they both were, neither asked if Blue should have been concerned either way.

Friends, Blue thought. *They're my friends.*

He had friends.

Real friends.

The happy couple—Mara was leaning her head on Elaine's shoulder—certainly didn't want or need anything from him. They were simply his friends. No ulterior motives. The only place he'd felt like that in a long time was camp. Heartland Queer Men's Festival. Those men had loved him with no expectations either.

Until Big Sir.

Would he ever be able to go back to camp again?

But no. He couldn't think of that today.

This is a good day!

They didn't have to wait long. In a surprisingly short time, Chewie came all but bounding into the room and ran straight to Blue. Chewie barked, looked at his shaved doggie leg, and then gave Blue a curious look and another short bark.

"Yup," Blue said. "That's your leg, all right!"

Happy dog smile. Soon replaced by that soulful look he got when he wanted something.

"You need to go potty?" Blue asked.

No response.

"You thirsty?"

Nothing.

"Walk?"

Almost something. A furry doggy brow seemed to lift a bit within all the hair that surrounded it.

It was John who said it aloud. "Treat?"

Chewie came alive with joy and many loud barks amid even more laughter. John pulled a dried duck foot (Chewie's favorite) from somewhere and slipped it into Blue's hand, fooling Chewie, who had shoved his face into John's lap, completely (for all of twenty seconds). He smelled it then, though, and practically jumped into Blue's lap.

"I wouldn't let him jump or put all his weight on that leg any more than you have for the past two months," Dr. Lee said, seeming to almost magically appear in the doorway. "At least for a week or so."

Blue nodded solemnly but then couldn't help but laugh as Chewie began to desperately circle his chair, like a shark that had sensed blood in the water. So he opened his hand, showed Chewie the duck foot, and then handed it to him. Chewie snapped it up, missing Blue's fingertips by the usual mere millimeters.

Then he was in a corner, snuffling and snorting in joy over his mummified delicacy.

Somehow it was easier to talk after that, and talk they all did, giving Chewie time to devour his cast-removal award (which didn't take long), and then Blue got a surprise when Elaine revealed they would be at his and John's place at six with brats and coleslaw.

She said, "Your all's place," and not "John's place," and Blue finally believed it was true. Somehow he'd gone from squatting in an abandoned house with no electricity and sleeping on a piss-stained mattress to living in a big beautiful home with a big beautiful man and... it was his place too. He thought so. He was pretty sure so. He didn't know how it had happened, but it had.

Then Chewie's face was in his lap and his tail was moving so fast it could barely be seen, and Blue knew this dog had somehow helped change his entire life.

"Just promise me you'll never leave me."

"I'll try my damnedest," Chewie yipped back (Blue was sure that was what he said), and after that the day only got better.

THEY TOOK Chewie to the dog park—still the small dog side although Chewie looked with open longing at the other side—and he socialized and peed everywhere (only one of his favorite things in life).

It was on their way to Costco that Blue saw something that made him shout. "Oh my God, John! Look!"

He pointed out the window.

"A dollar forty-nine! Chicken nuggets at Burger King are only $1.49. For ten of them! If only I had known!"

At Costco, they picked up an apparently preordered cake, an enormous thing that would take an army to eat, and Blue began to wonder how many people were showing up at "their place."

(Happy giddy feelings at those two words! *Their place.*)

And then that niggling little fear hit. Was it "their" place? Now that Chewie could get up and about, would Blue still be welcome to stay with John?

Please.

Oh please.

Turned out it wasn't too many people for dinner, just Elaine and Mara and H.D. and the handsome Bean—the owner of The Shepherd's Bean, which was just around the corner from Four-Footed Friends. They brought their dogs, a Yorkie/miniature dachshund mix named Sarah Jane and a sheltie named Rammstein. Chewie was overjoyed.

It could have been quite overwhelming for poor Chewie, but he was all but exhausted by this point, and after only the slightest bit of circling and butt sniffing with his two canine guests, he settled in a corner and mostly watched—rising only when a bratwurst somehow broke into three pieces and fell from the grill to land on the deck.

And here Elaine had claimed to be a master. Imagine dropping meat from the grill so carelessly!

There was a final late guest. When the doorbell rang, John asked Blue to answer it, and he was thrilled to see Miriam at the door. Once again she'd brought two bottles of wine. He turned and saw John waiting in the doorway to the kitchen, eyes glowing, and Blue's heart leapt with joy.

"Let's get this party started," she said.

Conversation over dinner was mostly casual. Hound Dog mentioned that Dean's (aka Bean's) mother had finally seemed to not only be used to his presence in her son's life, but to actively seek him out. "She actually has me over for tea and ladyfingers," H.D. said.

Dean rolled his eyes.

"I think she's hoping she can use me to influence what Dean does. His parents were very independent—"

"*Are* very independent," Dean interjected.

"—and basically let him sort of raise himself."

"And *then* thought they had the right to question my decisions in life," Dean continued. "They didn't think a coffee shop was a suitable career for their son, for instance."

"Of course she changed her mind about that," H.D. said.

"What happened?" Blue asked.

"She found out that The Shepherd's Bean won an award and is considered one of the best cafés not only in Kansas City, but the Midwest."

"Wow!" exclaimed Blue.

"Which is why it's the only coffee I'll drink anymore," Elaine said.

"That, and it's where her girlfriend works," said Mara, pointing at herself.

"It was actually Dean's coffee that brought us together," Elaine said with a big smile.

Couples, thought Blue. *I'm surrounded by couples.* It felt good, these gay couples, proving to him that it could happen. That it did happen. He looked at John, who was looking at him, and his heart skipped at least one beat.

Am I in a couple?

John reached out and took his hand. Brought it to his lips. Kissed it. Blue's heart swelled.

I think I am.

Of course, Miriam was single. But Blue couldn't quite imagine the magical lady with anyone. She was like a force of nature. Too powerful for any man (or woman for that matter).

And while dinner conversation was casual, it wasn't boring. Miriam made sure of that. Made sure of it with a few tales of her beatnik days. She didn't forget her beloved James Broughton either. "One of his highest moments came when he made *The Pleasure Garden*. That film won him a special award at the Cannes Film Festival in 1954, which was presented to him by none other than Jean Cocteau—a hero of James's. Oh, I must have heard that story a hundred times!" She began to laugh and Blue could feel the room filled with even more joy. Big Joy.

While they were eating a fraction of the gigantic chocolate sheet cake—the icing was amazing, neither too thick nor too sweet—one more surprise was revealed.

John presented Blue with the most oddly wrapped gift he'd ever seen. It was flat on one side and weirdly lumped on the other. What could possibly be under that paper...? And then it hit him.

It couldn't be.

Could it?

But all he had to do was lift it to know.

Blue tore open the gift and found out that it was indeed what he'd suddenly suspected.

"A skateboard!"

He looked up at John, stunned.

"H.D. helped me pick it out," John said.

Hound Dog nodded happily. "He knew you liked purple. I convinced him on the silver streaks."

"It's like my birthday or something," Blue cried.

"That's *just* what it is," John said, leaning in close. "Your birthday. Time to leave your old life behind and take on the new. Will you make it official?"

"Official?"

"I spoke with a lawyer Friday—"

A lawyer?

"—and I've started divorce proceedings. I think it's only proper since I want you to officially make this your home and, I hope, make me your man."

Blue's mouth fell open. And then a joy so great it could not hope to be contained swept up through him and out into the universe! "You *mean* it," Blue cried. Literally, for tears were welling up in his eyes. For one reason or another, he cried a lot with John. Happy and sad tears—and cleansing ones.

John leaned farther forward and cupped Blue's cheek in his big hand in that way he did (which always made Blue feel safe). "Of course I mean it. If you'll have me...."

And the look on John's face was so impossible, Blue had to clap a hand over his mouth to keep from bursting into laughter. Because how awful would that have been when John was looking at him in.... Was it fear? Could John possibly think Blue would say anything but yes? It was hilarious to think that Blue would make any other choice.

Then something else totally impossible occurred to him.

He had a choice.

He really did.

He could stay here with this man. Or he could leave. He could go live in that house with the sagging floor. He could do anything he wanted.

But all Blue wanted was to stay here with John.

THEIR COMPANY lingered long enough after dinner to have Miriam's bottles of wine between them all, plus at least one more, and then they made their good-byes and departed.

Perfect.

Blue let Chewie out to use the bathroom, and it was so nice to see him doing it without waddling. He seemed awfully proud of the fact himself.

Then they locked up and went upstairs and made love.

And Blue drifted off to sleep with promises of waffles in the morning.

Waffles.

He sighed contentedly.

Imagine.

Someone was making him waffles....

CHAPTER TWENTY-TWO

JOHN DIDN'T have to go upstairs to wake Blue. He'd wondered there for a bit, though. Blue had been so soundly asleep, snoring his soft little snores, that John hadn't wanted to wake him.

His angel.

Resting on the big white pillow, hair like a halo around his face one arm tossed over his head, Blue reminded John of when he had imagined him that way the first time they'd been in John's car.

Blue's hair was shorter now, and the bleached blond was almost gone, replaced by a beautiful golden color (the fluff in his armpits and his pubic hair had returned to their natural color as well).

John hadn't asked Blue to stop bleaching it, but he was glad that he had. Not that he minded. Not at all. But he liked Blue the way God had made him. When he'd casually mentioned that, Blue had made a big ceremony of throwing his hair products away. Even his gels.

John liked that too. The better to run his fingers through the silky strands.

But this morning John was glad Blue hadn't hung on him as he rose from bed, hadn't pulled him back, pressed his erection against John's hip or side or buttocks and asked for loving.

Or at least he was mostly glad.

No.

He wanted to do something really special.

He'd carried Chewie downstairs. He didn't need to anymore, but why overexert the dog? Then he started breakfast in his underwear— soft, very short boxer briefs that Blue loved. He said he loved the way they clung to John's ass and "goodies." Which made John blush. He blushed now at the thought.

But he also liked the idea of Blue coming downstairs and seeing him that way.

Me.

He sighed happily. Not only was he downstairs practically naked and loving it, but the patio doors were open, the morning breeze was coming in, and Chewie was in and out at his doggie leisure, and it all felt like *home*. Not just a house. But *home*.

John got fruit out—blueberries and strawberries—as well as pecans and real whipped cream, and put it all in bowls. He made the batter from scratch, something his grandmother had taught him. No premade boxed mixes for them. The waffle iron was out and working beautifully, and that was nice because it had once belonged to his grandmother as well. There were easier ways to make waffles, but doing it all the old-fashioned way made everything more like home.

Why, he even squeezed fresh orange juice, and it all took a long time, but thankfully Blue slept through it all.

Yesterday had been quite the emotional roller coaster after all.

John stopped and looked out into the sunny backyard and thanked a God he'd had so little use for most of his life. Felt curiously nice that he could want to thank "God." That the idea of someone watching over him was no longer a dark one. Maybe because somehow he'd linked the idea of "God" with his father? Isn't that what God was supposed to be? A father? And what a horrible example his own father had been.

But somehow he'd been freed from all that, and this morning he quite happily thanked God that Blue was healthy and safe and *his*.

Love.

He was so in love.

The very thought of Blue lying on the mattress upstairs, barely draped in white sheets, made John's heart swell, along with a little swelling down below. John arranged himself in his underwear and got back to work, pouring the batter, closing the heavy iron lid, flipping it, and setting the timer.

Nothing worse than burned waffles!

Except for maybe popcorn.

Then he ground coffee beans—a gift from Dean from The Shepherd's Bean—and started a pot of coffee. Soon the entire downstairs was delightfully heavy with the smell of both waffles and coffee.

And it was that smell that brought Blue down.

John turned and saw Blue standing in the wide doorway between the dining room and kitchen, and the sight took his breath away.

An angel.

So graceful and beautiful and sexy. Those lovely eyes and that button nose, the golden hair, long neck, and pale perfect skin. And the way he stood there, weight mostly on one foot, one arm casually at his side and the other raised high and taking his weight against the doorjamb, the fluffy patch of underarm hair nearly the only hair on his perfect body.

John almost cried.

Such beauty.

His.

Oh, and he was wearing those sexy blue briefs!

John felt his cock shifting and had to shake himself to get his mind off sex. Breakfast first!

"Coffee?" he asked.

"Love some," Blue said.

Then before John could serve him, Blue drifted into the room almost magically and got two mugs down from the cupboard, rising up on tiptoe and showing off his lovely blue-clad bottom and those beautifully muscled legs covered in fine, soft dark blond hair. *Even his toes are sexy. Is that crazy?* Then Blue poured them both coffee, brought the mugs to John, handed one over, kissed him, and said those wonderful words.

"I love you, John Williams."

"I love you, Blue McCoy," John answered.

Blue *oohed* and *ahhed* over everything set out on the granite counter and asked when they could eat.

"Any minute," John replied. "Your timing was perfect."

Chewie gave a bark at the patio doors, and Blue went to him, got down on one knee, and told him what a good dog he was. A delightful dog. A simply terrific dog in every way. Chewie gave another little bark that clearly said he knew Blue was correct but was happy to hear that Blue knew it too.

The timer went off, and true to his word, John got the last waffle from the iron and served them two apiece.

"Come pick out how you want them," John said, gesturing at the bowls. "And we've got real fresh butter and maple syrup from City Market. I heated some up because I didn't know if you like your syrup hot or cold."

"I'm just thankful to have anything at all," Blue said, coming to him, rising up on those delightful toes again, and kissing John. Their bodies pressed against each other, crotches touching, and it was all John could do not to moan and make love to Blue on the spot.

"Can we eat on the patio?" Blue asked.

"We can do whatever you want wher*ever* you want," John answered, and Blue looked at him, eyes flashing, and told him that would come later.

So they sat at the lovely black iron patio table in the morning sun and ate and even fed occasional bites to each other, sucking syrup and butter from each other's fingers. John was hard and wanting Blue desperately when Chewie suddenly let out a series of barks and ran into the house.

"Now what's that about?" John asked.

Blue shrugged, and when the barking continued, louder, John told Blue he'd see what was going on. Blue said he'd bring the dishes in. "Chewie is probably only barking at a fallen leaf or people walking by," he said.

But it wasn't a leaf.

It wasn't passersby either.

It was Vivian.

JOHN WAS stunned.

She was standing in the middle of the living room, eyes wide.

And when she turned from the barking dog and looked up at John, her eyes went even wider.

Vivian could have stepped out of a fashion magazine. Her hair, long and dark, fell around her shoulders, perfect, shining in the bright morning light. She wore a lovely blue-and-silver sundress (revealing her famous long legs), matching high heels (not too high or too low and accentuating her legs), and a pastel blue jacket and gloves (and of course, a clutch).

Vivian stood there, frozen, staring at John.

And suddenly he realized he was standing there in only his underwear.

"Viv," he somehow managed. "What are you doing here?" He was amazed that he hadn't stuttered. At least he didn't think he had.

Chewie began to growl.

"Chewie," he cried. "Back."

Chewie gave John a startled look—all, "Really, Dad? Are you kidding me?"—and took two steps back.

"Go on, now. Go out back. You did your job. Good boy."

The "good boy" apparently placated Chewie, and he took one long last look at Vivian, seemed to furrow his brow at her, and with an "Are you sure?" expression, trotted proudly out of the room.

"You got a dog?" Vivian asked.

"I did," John said and tried to figure out what to do with his hands. Place them in front of him? Vivian had seen him naked a thousand, thousand times. Wouldn't covering himself be stupid?

Of course, those times were different. That had been when they were husband and wife. And paper or not, as far as John was concerned, they weren't married any longer.

Yet his lack of clothes and her dazzling outfit did make him feel vulnerable. He couldn't help it.

John decided to face the lion.

He stood up straight, squared his shoulders, and locked eyes with her, daring her to look down.

"What are you doing here, Vivian?" Strongly. But without malice.

She squared her shoulders as well, pulled off her gloves (a soft blue to match the jacket), and (impossibly) said, "I *live* here, John."

She almost flummoxed him.

Almost.

He didn't let her.

"No, Vivian. You left. And you took Moxie with you. Did he enjoy Cancún?"

Her shoulders dropped a little. She gave a slight laugh. "I didn't take him to Mexico," she said. "He stayed with my parents."

John nodded. "I see."

"Something smells wonderful," she said. "Not just coffee…."

"Waffles," he said, and quite suddenly and stupidly remembered Blue.

He stiffened. What was she going to think?

Blue is in his underwear too.

"Really? You haven't made waffles in years."

"I started again."

Really? Am I standing here in my underwear talking about waffles with the woman who left me? And my lover likely to walk in the room any second?

"Vivian, what *are* you doing here?" he asked again. Trying to say *What the fuck are you doing here?* without saying it.

"I got your divorce papers," she said. She opened her large clutch, started to pull something out, and stopped. "I figured it was time we talked."

God. How can she look so composed? So beautiful still?

But then he saw it. Living with her for so long allowed him to do so. The ever-so-slight break in her mask. At the corners of her mouth. The twitch of one brow.

"You surprised me with that, John."

"Why?" he asked, even though he knew the answer. *She figured she would file first.*

To his surprise, she answered truthfully. "I guess I thought I would file first." She gave one tiny tremble and then raised her head high. "Oh, for God's sake, John. Could you please put something on?"

And with that Blue strolled into the room.

"Holy crap," he said, eyes almost comically wide. "Who the heck are you?" John might have laughed had the situation not been so serious.

Vivian's mouth dropped open, her composure gone. She opened and closed it several times, fishlike, and then said, "I'm the wife. Who are you?"

Blue cocked his head.

"I'm Blue." He looked at John.

"The boyfriend," John finished.

CHAPTER TWENTY-THREE

THE WIFE? Blue shook his head. *The wife?*

That woman was Vivian?

John's wife?

The one who left him?

And crap. She was gorgeous! Her nose was a little big, but Jesus. Gorgeous.

Blue had been so shocked to see her standing there in the living room, looking like some kind of movie star, holding those gloves and that big clutch. When he'd realized he was in nothing but his tighties, he'd turned nineteen shades of red (at least). That's when he'd excused himself and gone upstairs.

Where he was now. Trapped. Because he didn't want to go back downstairs when the steps ended right there in the room where they were talking… or whatever they were doing.

God, oh God, oh God, oh God!

Blue began to pace.

He wrung his hands.

John's wife!

His gorgeous wife.

She was back.

To stay?

Was she back to stay?

"What if she wants him back?" he said aloud. "What if she won't grant him the divorce? She doesn't have to, does she?"

He searched his mental files, but there was nothing there on law or the like—certainly not divorce law.

"What if he wants her back? What if this is it? What if I have to leave? What if he tells me to leave?" The idea of going back to that abandoned house, the one he'd actually liked at one time, turned his stomach to lead. Not that he was ashamed. But this house was filled with love. The other was nothing more than a structure to protect him from the elements.

What about Chewie?

And as if psychically called, the dog's fluffy, curly head nudged his thigh. Blue reached down to pet him, only vaguely aware he was doing so.

I'll have to find a better place. But I can't afford anything. I'll have to get a job. Then find an apartment. Will John give me time? Is he getting ready to come upstairs right now and ask me to leave? Where would I go? Mom's? Does she have room? It's a small house! Elaine's? Would she take me in? For just a little bit? I could stay in a back room at Four-Footed Friends. God! What do I do? Shit. Oh God. Oh God, oh God. What can I do? No! This can't be happening. It can't. Please, God. Please no. I can't live like that again. I can't do it! I can't start again. Too good. It was too good to be true. Gone. He's going to make me leave. Start again. Be alone again. No! Nonononono. I don't want to be alone again. Don't want. Don'twanttobealoneagainpleasenonotaloneagain!

Chewie gave a loud bark.

And Blue snapped back to reality.

He trembled.

Chewie looked at him with big concerned eyes through curly brown bangs. He made a little *woof* noise.

Blue shook himself. Thought about how he'd just fallen into one of his word storms for the first time in weeks. Thought whirlpools. Because of John. John had helped him with that. Both because he joined in on the conversation so Blue had no panicky need to fill the silence, and because John never sat there slack-jawed, staring, as if there were something wrong with Blue.

Even better. Because it was also okay to be quiet with John.

Blessed relief.

But John wasn't here, was he?

He was downstairs.

With his wife.

"*Woof?*" Chewie asked.

Blue let out a very long sigh. Said, "I'm okay, Chewie."

Chewie cocked his head. Looked at him like "You sure, Blue? You're not shitting me, are you? Huh?"

Was he okay? *I'm not sure.*

Was he about to lose everything?

Then Chewie made another noise, shoved his head up under Blue's hand, and gave him another long look.

And for some reason it seemed to Blue that maybe, just maybe, Chewie was saying, "Trust him. Trust John."

Trust John.

Blue nodded.

He would trust John.

What else could he do?

JOHN STEPPED into a pair of sweats he found in the laundry room, as well as a T-shirt. No shoes, but that was okay. He was armored again. Covered. He had learned to love the freedom of his skin, but not now. Not today. Not with her.

When he stepped back into the living room, he found Vivian pouring herself some scotch. He clenched his teeth. She knocked it back. His scotch. Not hers anymore. She had left.

Sensing, perhaps, that he was back, she turned and asked him if he wanted one.

He did.

Vivian poured another for herself and one for him as well. Turned and stepped toward him. He reached out and took it. Made sure their fingers didn't touch.

For a second he thought she was going to try and clink glasses with him. He stepped back. Sipped. Sipped larger. But didn't knock it back. He was in control.

She was in *his* place.

"What are you doing here, Viv?" he asked. Again.

"Mind if I sit?" she asked calmly, seeming sure of herself. Or nearly so. He could tell he'd rocked her. She was regrouping. He'd seen her do it a thousand times.

He nodded toward the couch. "Sit."

She did.

Then she took a deep breath.

"The papers startled me," she said, and was that a slight tremble in her voice?

"Why?" he asked.

"As I said. I figured I would be the one to do it."

"That I'd be sitting here waiting for you?"

"You didn't."

"Didn't?" he echoed.

"Wait." Then she trembled. "You certainly didn't." She glanced at the staircase. "But good *God*, John? What is he? *Twelve?*"

"He's twenty-three."

Her brows rose slightly. "He doesn't look it."

"No, he doesn't."

Oh God, I'm doing this. I am talking about Blue. My lover. With my wife.

Ex-wife! Even if it wasn't legal yet.

"Gay, John? You're gay?"

"I guess I am." No. Not a guess. "Yes, Vivian. I'm gay."

Said it. Said it out loud. To her.

"Then why did you marry *me*, John? Was I some kind of beard?" She took a drink of her—*his*—scotch.

"I didn't think of myself as gay. Bisexual, I guess. And I loved you."

Now where did that come from? He'd surprised himself, and he saw by her expression that she was surprised too.

"You did?"

"I did, Vivian. Or I wouldn't have married you."

"So you knew you liked men?"

He clenched his jaw. Didn't know why. Relaxed it. "I knew I found men attractive. But I was never with one."

"Not once?" she asked.

He shook his head. Once. Twice.

"Not even that high school shit that boys do?" She raised a perfect eyebrow. "You know. Jerking off with buddies—"

"*No.*"

"But now?"

"Now I am with a man."

"A *boy!*"

"A *man.*" He grinned. Hoped his eyes said something. Something a little mean.

Now she nodded. Looked like she was about to say something. Maybe that this all explained why he'd been such a boring lover. He decided to say it himself. "I guess that explains why I was such a boring lover, Vivian."

And suddenly the mean was gone. He didn't have the energy for it. Or even the need. And why hurt her? Hadn't there been enough hurt already?

Because hadn't he figured out that she wasn't the villain in all this?

"*Not* boring, John," she said quietly and looked at him with those dark brown eyes of hers—nearly black they were so dark. "Just not...." She looked away. Sighed. "Inspired." She turned her eyes back to him. "God, John. I never suspected for a second...." Her eyes widened. "Were you the one who was bored?"

He shook his head. "I didn't think I was."

She glanced again at the steps, then looked back. "Does he inspire you?" Very quietly.

John let out a long sigh, finished his scotch, and then sat on the couch next to her. "He does, Vivian."

She shook her head. "Why did I not see it? Not once?"

Because I didn't even allow myself to look. Not while you were around. "Because when I married you, I vowed to be true. I didn't look." Then, admitting, "Not often."

Vivian nodded.

"I'm sorry, Viv," he said, not realizing he was going to say it.

"Sorry?" She blinked.

"For not being the man you needed me to be."

She didn't say anything.

"I am sorry I drove you away. I should have been a real man and let you go so you could have what you wanted. I just… I just didn't realize. Not until…."

"Until what?"

Admit it. Be honest. His heart started to pound.

"One kiss," he sighed.

"A kiss?"

"One little kiss. And I *knew*. Knew I wasn't bisexual. Knew I wasn't just attracted to men. One kiss and I knew I was gay."

And wow. Wow! A mountain lifted up off his shoulders.

Gay.

He. Was. Gay.

How could he keep realizing the truth as if it were something new? But now that he'd said it to her? Now it was realer than anything ever.

"I didn't cheat on you, Vivian. Not one single time. Not before you left. And after? When you left, you *left*, Vivian! I knew it was over, that there was no way you were coming back. Papers or not, we weren't married anymore. Because you *left*. Left me stone-cold."

She looked away and then back. Swallowed hard. "I didn't cheat on you either," she said quietly. "Not before I left. But while I was in Cancún…."

He nodded. It was okay. Because she had left. It wasn't cheating. Legal or not, they weren't together.

"Was it good?" he asked. Actually hoped it was.

It took her forever to answer.

Then she nodded. "Yes," she said quietly.

And he smiled.

"Good."

Neither of them said anything for a long time. Then finally he needed to tell her. "I'm not boring, Vivian. I was simply content. Is there anything wrong with that?"

She shrugged.

He gave her a wicked smile. "I'm definitely not boring now. Trust me."

Vivian blushed. Wow. "I do," she said. "How *could* you be with that stunning creature in your bed?"

"He is, isn't he?" Now he couldn't help but grin.

"Uh-huh," she said.

"So it wasn't you. It was me. Okay? I didn't know, Viv. I wouldn't allow myself to know any earlier."

"Until one kiss," she all but whispered.

He took a long breath. Let it out. "Until one kiss."

Neither said anything for what seemed an eternity.

"Thank you," he said. Knowing he needed to. How important it was.

"For what?" she asked, clearly surprised.

"For leaving me, Viv. If you hadn't, I might never have discovered who I really am."

"Oh." She bit her lower lip. Then rubbed her teeth. Probably didn't even know she was doing it. She was making sure she hadn't gotten any lipstick on her teeth.

Then she stood up, held up her empty glass. "One more?"

"Sure," he said.

So she went and took the—*his*—scotch and poured them both a generous two fingers, and this time they did clink glasses. Drank.

Was it happening this simply? Was it over this easy?

"I'll sign the papers," she said then.

"I would like to keep the house," he said.

"Okay," she said, still miraculously keeping it simple.

"I'll buy you out, of course."

"*Pffft*," she said with a wave.

"It's only fair."

"All right," she said. "Whenever."

She finished her scotch. He finished his. Then she stood again and headed to the door, pulling on her gloves as she did. She paused and turned around. "No, wait."

Wait? For what? It's been said. This is the perfect good-bye. No accusations. No anger....

200

And something fascinating happened. Her expression…. He couldn't quite figure out what it was he was seeing.

Then he saw it.

No mask. I am seeing her totally without her mask.

She reached out and touched his arm. Shook her head.

"I can't do this," she said.

What? Do what? No. Go. Go, Vivian.

"I can't let you take the blame. It's not your fault."

He narrowed his eyes.

She cleared her throat. "I've been feeling so guilty, and dammit, I almost let you take the fall. I can't. I won't let you. God, I need *another* scotch!"

Another?

She held up a hand, brows high. Made a noise somewhere between a cough and a laugh. "Don't worry. I'm not asking! I *do* have to drive." She cleared her throat again. "The last few years, John… I was shit to you." Vivian shook her head, and God, were those tears in her eyes? Vivian? She didn't play that card.

"The things I would say to you. How I *criticized* you." She looked up at him. "This part inside hated me for doing it. And then it just became easier to turn it on you."

"You hated me?" That stung.

Vivian shook her head. "No! Not that." She looked down at her hands. "But in the end it's the same. I turned that hating myself and my life…."

"You hated your life," John echoed.

Their eyes met again. "I should have been honest. With you. With myself. Before it went that far. You're right. We could have ended this years ago. You could have discovered yourself earlier. Had all this time to be with… with a…."

"A man?" he asked.

She nodded.

But then I wouldn't have Blue. "Everything happens for a reason," he said. "Everything happens when it should."

She pursed her lips. "Do you think we'll be able to be friends?"

"I'm willing," he said, further surprising himself when he realized he meant it. He liked her. And now that they weren't a couple, he realized he loved her.

"I loved you, John."

He smiled. "I did too. I do love you. I probably always will."

"You don't hate me?" she said, clearly surprised.

"Not at all." How wonderful. He didn't! "Do you hate me?"

She smiled. "Not at all." She leaned in and gave him the lightest kiss. Then she left.

And John went upstairs.

BLUE HEARD the creak of the second-to-top stair. Knew it was John. He was lying on the guest bed, arms around Chewie, who was spooned up with his back to Blue's belly.

"Blue? Where are you?"

John was standing in the doorway. "Why are you in here?"

Blue didn't say anything.

"Why aren't you in our bed?"

Our bed?

"Our bed?" he whispered.

John nodded. "Yes. *Our* bed."

Blue's heart skipped at least one beat. Relief immeasurable flooded through him.

John came into the room and sat on the edge of the bed, and Chewie sat up and gave him a doggy kiss.

"Where is your…" *wife…?*

"She's gone. For good. We're over." He reached out. Took Blue's hand. "And now *we're* forever," he said. "If you want me."

Blue scrambled up onto his knees and threw his arms around his man. His forever.

"Yes," he said.

Forever.

CHAPTER TWENTY-FOUR

THE PHONE call came less than twenty-four hours later. John glanced casually down at the screen on his cell phone and couldn't help but freeze.

Alistair.

Oh God....

His son.

Vivian. She'd called him.

Didn't wait long, did she? To tell their son he was gay? That he'd hooked up with a man half his age?

But then before he could get angry, he had a second thought. *Well, of course she did....* Alistair deserved to know. And after all, Viv and their son talked. *He never talks to me.*

And he didn't even know what she had told him, did he?

So why expect the worst?

"Who is it?" asked Blue through a mouthful of meatloaf. Good meatloaf too. He'd had dinner ready when John got home. He'd been doing it for weeks now.

"My son," John answered and pressed the keypad. "Alistair!" Brave voice. Happy voice. "What a surprise." Please have it be a *nice* surprise.

"Hey, old man," Alistair replied. Because that's what he'd called John for years, even though John didn't like it. At least Alistair sounded good. No tension. He sounded downright cheery.

Is he going to make fun of me?

"To what do I owe the honor?" John asked.

Alistair laughed. "I think you know."

Laughed. *He is going to make fun of me.*

"Oh?" John managed without his voice cracking.

"Mom called last night."

I bet she did.

"I guess I'm not surprised," he said softly.

Alistair whistled. "Twenty-three?" He laughed again. "You old dog! Traded Mom in for a much younger model? Is it a little red Corvette next?"

John's stomach started to twist, and then… it didn't. Wait. He isn't even mentioning that Blue is a guy? Surely she told him that—

"And a *guy*, Dad? A guy?" Alistair's tone was positively gleeful.

He looked over at Blue. Gorgeous Blue. Who was looking at him with some concern. John didn't like that. "Well, yeah, Son. He is."

"Mom says he's a hottie too," Alistair added, the glee amping up higher. If he didn't know better, John would have thought this was two men fist-bumping in a bar.

Blue blinking at him with those stunning eyes.

John sat up straight. "He sure is," John said proudly.

"God, this is so fucking great!"

Wait.

What?

What did he say?

"Great?" he asked.

"Yeah, Dad." Then there was a pause. And when he started talking again, it was Alistair's voice that cracked. "Dad… there's something I've been wanting to tell you."

Tell me?

"Been trying to tell you for a very long time. B-but I was afraid."

Afraid? Alistair? "But you're not afraid of anything!" John exclaimed.

"That's only what I wanted you to think. You're not exactly a *warm* guy, Dad."

John gulped. Not a warm guy?

Jesus.

"I'm not?"

Another pause.

"Well, you weren't."

"I'm sorry, Alistair. I never meant to…."

"It's okay, Dad." He could almost hear the shrug in Alistair's voice. "Who knows what's going on? Kids can be hard on their parents. I know

I was being pretty hard on you. Then I got out here in the fucking real world—if you can call Santa Fe the *real world*, that is—and I found out that it can be tough. *Real* fucking tough. Suddenly I realized that when you're a kid, your parents aren't much older than kids themselves. That you and Mom weren't more than kids. It's an eye-opening experience."

Wow. John blinked. *Wow.* And he had no clue what to say. "I… ah…."

"Anyway, Dad." Pause. "Whew!" Another pause. "Dad? I'm bi."

He's bye? What? "Huh?" he grunted.

"Bi, Dad. Bisexual."

What? Alistair is what? He's…. My son is bisexual?

"And… I'm in a triad."

A what? "*A what?*" He tried what?

"Triad. I live with a man and a woman. We're a triad. Throuple. Whatever. We all live together."

John's mind reeled for a moment.

"You what?" he said before he could stop himself.

"What's wrong?" Blue asked, and now he looked really worried.

"My son is in a triad," he said, stunned. "He's with…. With two people."

Blue grinned. "Really? How cool is that?"

"A man and a woman?" he somehow asked Alistair and reported to Blue at the same time.

"Yeah, Dad. I'm bi, and I live with a man and a woman, and fuck, I'm the happiest I've ever been in my life."

And looking at Blue, quite suddenly being hit—for the millionth time—with how happy *he* was now, he grinned.

Alistair is the happiest he's ever been!

"Alistair. G-God. That's wonderful." And he meant it. It was pretty wild. A man and a woman? How tough must that be?

"It is?" Alistair said.

"Yes," John said. "If you're happy, I'm happy!"

"Really?" Alistair asked, his voice hitching. "Really?"

"Fuck, yes!" John said and laughed, and then Alistair laughed.

"Oh God, Dad!" He laughed again. "Jesus. You just said fuck. I can't believe it!"

"What can I say?"

"Oh, Dad, You just don't know the relief I'm feeling right now." His voice sounded a little rough. Was he crying? "I knew I was attracted to guys for years, and I just knew if you ever found out you wouldn't want anything to do with me. So I...."

Oh shit. "So you ran off to Santa Fe and stopped having anything to do with me?"

Long pause. Then, "Yeah." Another pause. "Shit. I'm so sorry, Dad."

"N-no, Alistair." And now he was starting to cry. "I'm sorry. I am *so* sorry. I never meant to be cold. But...." But what? Then before he could think about it too much, he said, "I guess I was cold. I mean.... The world seemed so cold. And I... I wasn't...."

"Happy?" Alistair offered.

John nodded. Looked at Blue. Felt the sun rise inside his heart. "Yes," he said softly.

"And this guy makes you happy?"

"Yes," John replied. And then quickly added, "Not that there is anything wrong with your mother. I love your mother. It's just that...."

"She doesn't have a dick?" came the reply.

John blushed furiously. "Well... I.... Ah...."

"It's okay, old man. No, wait. You hate it when I call you that! Sorry. *Dad*. I understand."

"I didn't know that was what I needed. A man." Not just a dick.

"Yes! Dad, I *do* understand. You didn't know. Wow. Cool. And imagine my surprise when I found out I liked girls. Or at least this one. Meadow."

"Meadow?" What was he saying?

"That's her name!" Alistair laughed. "Really it is. Not just 'cause she's an artist living here in wacky artsy Santa Fe. That *really* is her name. Parents were some kind of hippies."

Meadow. He liked it. "I like it," he said. His heart got even warmer. And.... "And the man?"

"Barry."

"Barry?"

Now Alistair was really laughing. "*Right*? Barry? The most *un*-artist name there could be. Well... no. There's Barry Gibb...."

"And Barry White."

"And Barry Levinson."

Thank God for Blue. *He trained me for this.* "Barry Manilow."

"Well, not him so much," Alistair said.

"Hey! You don't like the Copacabana song?"

"Not even a little bit, Dad."

Now they were both laughing. And what were they laughing over? His son's lover's name. One of his *two* lovers. *I am sitting here hardly blinking over the fact that my son has two lovers!*

"God, Dad. You don't know how happy I am right now!"

"Me too, Son." John reached out and took Blue's hand, and Blue's smile was radiant.

"I want you to meet them, Dad. And I want to meet my new stepmom!"

"Stepmom? Who?"

"Your boyfriend."

"Step*dad*, Alistair." John looked at Blue. *All man.* "He might be young, but he is all man."

"Whew!" Alistair whistled again.

"Then let's plan on it," John said impulsively. Not boring.

"Soon?"

John grinned. "Really soon."

"We've got room, if you want to stay."

"We'll work it out." John's heart was skipping merrily.

"I am so fucking glad Mom told me about you," Alistair said then.

"Me too," John said. And meant it with his whole being.

"I want to tell you all about them. How we met. *Every*thing!"

"I want to hear. And tell you about Blue."

"But I got to go now. Can I call back in a few days? We got a show going on."

"Of course. Show?"

"My ceramics. I have a show. Starts tomorrow."

Now John's heart was leaping. His son had a show? "God, Alistair, that's wonderful!"

"I'm getting to be a big thing around here, Dad. You won't believe how much people will pay for one of my pieces. Still takes my breath away."

John couldn't believe his ears. "Son, I...."

"And you said an artist couldn't make it!"

And amid the happiness, a bolt of shame. "Oh God, Alistair. I am so sorry. I was so wrong...."

"Fuck that shit, Dad! In a way, I owe it all to you. You set the challenge. And if you could go from that shithole your parents came from to where you are now? I could do it too. My way."

In an instant any shame was gone. "Can we make seeing you sooner rather than later? I mean, I know you must be stressing out, but I want to see your show!"

"Fuck, Dad. That would be awesome."

They said a bit more and agreed to talk within a day or two at most and got off the phone, and then John couldn't help it. He jumped up, pulled Blue to his feet, swept him up in his arms, and carried him upstairs.

Where he made sweet love to the man he loved.

Because how could life get much better than this?

AFTER, AS they cuddled, John began to speak.

"My father had no idea who I was. Not a clue. He was an awful man. Dark and mean and cruel, and he made life horrible for me and my mom. But I escaped, and I promised myself I would never do that to my own child."

Blue snuggled closer, listening. He didn't know what else to do.

"I made sure never to be cruel to Alistair. To do things with him. Shoot the hoops, you know? The things sons want their fathers to do with them."

Blue gave a half nod. He'd never really been interested in sports, and if his father had lived, he wasn't sure if shooting hoops was something he would have wanted. But then.... Blue smiled. He and Indigo had played H-O-R-S-E with Mom and Dad, hadn't they? That had been fun.

"But Alistair had no interest in sports. Since he was a kid it was clay and pots and sculptures. He was remarkable. He did this... sort of woven sculpture when he was in high school. It was a bust. At first I didn't realize it, but then it hit me. It was a bust of me. Woven out of strips of clay.

"I couldn't believe it. I couldn't figure out how he had done it. And that was when I began to think I could never understand him...."

Blue shifted onto his back and looked up into John's eyes. Expecting tears. But instead it was a very faraway expression he saw on his lover's face.

"But God, Blue." He shook his head. "He was just following my example. He was being himself. I just couldn't see it."

To Blue's surprise, John was smiling. It was a small smile, but a smile nonetheless.

"And now?" Blue asked.

"I totally see it. I played football to please my father. But I soon found out I loved numbers. That's what made me. Gave me this home and everything in it. Boring to some people, maybe, but I love them! Numbers." His smile turned into a grin. "I love the way they fit like puzzle pieces. The way they line up. The way there is always, always an answer."

John's eyes widened. "But you know what? Life doesn't always line up. But...."

"But?" Blue asked.

"But that doesn't mean we can't find a way to fit the puzzle pieces together. And that's what I am going to do with Alistair. Oh, Blue!" John pulled him tight. "I tried to get Alistair to play ball because that is what I thought fathers were supposed to do, despite the fact that is what my asshole father did! I didn't just let him be himself. So he had to run away. And good for him!"

Blue's eyes widened. "Good?"

John nodded. "Because he found himself, and he found love, and Blue, I couldn't be happier!"

CHAPTER TWENTY-FIVE

BLUE COULD hardly believe they were here. That *they* were here.

Because getting John downstairs in his underwear had been one thing. Getting him to make love in rooms outside the bedroom thrilling. Why, they'd made love on the patio!

But to get John to come to a camp known for its pagan campers and clothing optional policies? That was something else again!

And yet that wasn't what happened. Blue hadn't gotten John to come. John had gotten *him* to come.

They'd been sitting on the couch, about to watch the newest *Star Wars* movie, which John had missed somehow. He'd been excited. And then out of nowhere, John had asked him about Men's Festival.

"I really think it would be best for me to just skip it this year," Blue had said.

John had given him one of those looks of his. The kind that seemed to see inside him. Then he said, "But I thought this festival of yours, I thought you said that it was one of the only places on earth that you feel safe."

Blue had looked away then, unable to meet John's eyes. Which was bad because he, *John*, was the one place Blue really truly felt safe.

So tell him.

"It *was* one of the only places I've *ever* felt safe." He trembled. "Until *him*...."

"Him?" John had asked, and when Blue turned back to him, when they locked eyes, he saw John *getting* it. "*Him*." This time it wasn't a question.

"Camp is where it happened. And I'm scared to go back."

John reached out. Took his hand. Pulled him against him. And to his surprise, said, "What if I go with you? To your camp? It's not time for that festival of yours. Let's go, just you and me...."

Blue had looked at him, speechless. *John? Go to Camp Sanctuary?* "I'm not sure it would be your thing, John."

"Well, if it's important to you, shouldn't I find out?"

And that's just what they did.

THEY SET up a big blanket on the sandy beach by the lake Blue loved so much, along with a picnic basket and a bottle of wine, and had a very nice lunch. It was weird sitting here with his clothes on. It wasn't something Blue was used to here. But, then, Camp wasn't the sanctuary it used to be, and he found himself a little afraid to shed his clothes, even though there were only a few other people around.

They did take off their shirts and slathered sunscreen all over each other's exposed skin, a high SPF for Blue with his pale skin. And then they lay back and cuddled, and Blue felt an old, familiar feeling try to sneak back into his bones.

Safety.

Then after a while, they took a large air mattress that someone had left under the big tree by the water's edge and climbed aboard. It was big enough for two, although they had to get close. That hadn't been a problem. And when John stepped out of his shorts and walked naked into the water with Blue, had gotten on the mattress with him right out there in the sun where anyone could see him, Blue's heart had swelled to near bursting. He knew what a big deal this was for John. At least skinny-dipping, people would have only seen him naked for the time it took him to get in the water. But now he was on display. Of course, he was lying on his stomach, and it was his ass people might see instead of his front. But still a big deal for John.

It got Blue's mind to working.

He looked south, along the length of Serenity Lake and the long grassy area that bordered it and on to the woods beyond. And he could see in his head what lay *in* those woods.

And he trembled.

John saw it. Blue knew he did. His trembling. But John didn't say anything. He laid a big hand on Blue's shoulder and gave a little squeeze, then took his hand and told Blue he loved him. As they lay on the raft hand in hand, a lovely breeze floating over their bare skin, keeping them from getting too hot under the early July sky, Blue made a decision.

And told John he was ready.

John didn't ask what he was ready for. He nodded, and they paddled with their hands to get the mattress to the beach. John put his shorts back on, and they held hands and traveled along the grassy shore to where the woods began, Chewie running just ahead of them.

Blue led the way through an opening so narrow they had to let go of each other to proceed. The path took them along a corridor through the trees. Blue never tired of this special place. It had been a place of peace and beauty for him for the last few years. Above them, the branches tangled together, green and cool, gentle shafts of sunlight coming down between them and adding their golden splendor.

The path widened as they went along, enough that they could once again hold hands. John's big hand holding Blue's helped with the apprehension that niggled and gnawed at the corners of his mind. About what was coming closer and closer with each step they took.

Birds sang, and cicadas made their metallic whirring noises in the branches above them as they walked along the twisting path, and soon Blue saw ahead of them one of the most magical places at camp.

"WE'RE COMING to something very special," Blue said, and before John could ask what, he saw it. First it was just a twinkle of light, a flash of red and blue and gold. They came around a turn, and there it was, and John let out a long sighing gasp.

Branches and thick vines had been turned and twisted and bound into some kind of archway. Strings and necklaces, beads, medallions, and crystals of every description hung from the branches. Among them were dreamcatchers and wind chimes, scarves, ribbons, Mardi Gras beads, and more. John could only stand and try to take it all in. Why, *there* was a wedding ring tied to a branch. Toys and dolls and small statues and plaques as well, and the ground was a virtual treasure trove of more of the same: polished stones, smooth pieces of glass, shells, a stone Buddha and other statues, figurines, a dancing Pan, fairies, Christmas ornaments, coins, more jewelry, bracelets.

"It's all for the fairies," Blue said quietly.

John gave him a curious look. "For the Radical Faeries?"

Blue shook his head and smiled. "The magick kind, John. People leave things to thank them. Or things that they want to let go of. Put behind them." He took a deep breath, and John saw tears come to his eyes.

Things they wanted to put behind them.

"It's called the Magick Gate."

John nodded. "I can see why." It was magical. It took his breath away. You could almost believe that fairies lived here. Who knew? Maybe they did.

Blue stepped under the arch. Closed his eyes and tilted his head back. Took a deep breath. Naked. Stunning. Impossibly beautiful. And not an angel. A fairy. Of course. The sight nearly took John's breath away. He joined his lover.

Lover.

Blue opened his eyes, looked at him. Such a deep and beautiful brown. But there was sadness too. Should they be doing this? Should they turn back?

Neither said a word.

Blue stepped up to him, and John wrapped him in his arms, then closed his own eyes, tilted *his* head back.

Felt something.

A stirring.

A slight… *thrumming.*

It was in his veins. His heart. His head. Weaving through his body. He gasped. Opened his eyes.

"Did I really feel that?" he asked.

Blue smiled, though his eyes still held sadness.

"Yes," Blue said. "I felt it. Strong today. Maybe this is the right time."

"Whatever you want, baby."

Blue smiled. Once more it was dazzling. Enchanting. How could this be? How could he be so lucky? His lover was an angel.

A fairy.
Now he smiled.
A Faerie.
Then Blue said he was ready.

A SMALLER path broke off from the main one after they went through the Magick Gate. Chewie dashed ahead as if he already knew that was where they were going. It was a tiny ray of sunshine in this dark walk—because Chewie could run. It was a blessing Blue could count. Blue took John along the side path after Chewie. His heart was pounding. Sweat broke out across his forehead. His pits went wet. Stones sat in the bottom of his stomach. With each step, he grew heavier. Or it felt like it.

The last time he'd walked down this path, there was a big man in front of him. A bigger one behind him. They were calling him slut and faggot and cocksucker. He was going along with it. They were playing a game. At least that's what Blue thought.

I'm not with them. I'm with John. John would never call me names. Not even for a game. Not names like that.

This path was narrower and wound its way this way and that until it suddenly opened up into a wide circular grassy area. Tall sunflowers bordered about half the circle in a large C shape before the trees began again, adding their sunny gold to the cool green. There were white daisies and deep purple coneflowers as well.

Beautiful.

And so special. A place of healing. A place of nature. There were times he thought he could almost hear the voice of nature talking to him. Almost-words spun from the cardinal's gorgeous, cheering song, the sweet *tee-yee, tee-yee, tee-yee* of the finches, the trilling *oh-ka-reeee* of the red-winged blackbird, and the *ooo-eee-ooo-eee* of the cicadas. Chewie was sitting under a tree, gnawing on a big stick, and he looked up and gave a little *wooah-rrr-ruff!* of his own, adding his voice to the chorus. The wind through the trees and the rustling leaves and the soft ringing of wind chimes. He'd always come to this special magickal (magic*kal*, of course, because that was how his Faerie brothers spelled it, many of them pagan or witches, and he'd come to love the word) place when he needed to connect with something greater than himself, and even when he came here all alone, he felt more a part of… everything. Of life and woods and the world and the universe. Yet today that beauty was marred.

Before them was a twelve-foot ring of stones stacked about knee high. And inside, at the other side, was the altar, made of slabs of stone and garnished with candles and little statues and more coins and several more abandoned rings. A sacred space. Or it had been.

Now?

Blue began to shake. "This is where it happened," he whispered, fighting to keep his teeth from chattering.

"I don't know what's worse," John said suddenly, just as quietly. "That it happened. Or that it happened here."

Yes, Blue thought, looking up at John, eyes filling with tears. "Yes," he said aloud. "Exactly. This place is special to so many people. Sacred, John. *Sacred*. And now it's not. Now it only has an ugly memory. For me anyway. Ugly images. I want it back, John!"

He began to shake, and tears filled his eyes, and he was hurting, and sad and mad too. Furious! Because it wasn't fair. "I want it to be sacred again," he cried. "I want it to be about love and kindness and nature and beauty. How can it be that ever again? I come here and what I see is a vision of *me*, what I must have looked like, *held* down on that table! Oh God, John!"

He burst into tears.

John stepped up to him, and Blue threw himself into his arms.

John rocked him.

Kissed the top of his head.

Told him he loved him.

And after a while, it wasn't quite as bad.

THEY SETTLED on a carpet of soft cool moss before the stone altar. John held him, pulled him into his lap, kissed the top of his head again, told him that he loved him.

Blue settled his head against John's chest. Listened to the heartbeat beneath those muscles. It was a comfort.

And surprisingly, he felt safe.

He opened his eyes and then slowly pulled back a little, just enough. Saw the branches and green leaves above him, the border of flowers—yellow and white and purple. The calling of the cicadas reasserted itself. And was that crickets? Now? In the afternoon?

Singing maybe for him?

For them?

For them both?

Blue took a long, deep shuddering breath. Let it out slowly.

Safe. He felt safe. He actually felt safe. He was at peace. At least for a moment.

He looked at John, who was studying him with love-filled eyes. Such beautiful hazel eyes. Looking at him. The love in those eyes was for *him*.

Blue sat up in John's arms. Found that he was straddling the big man. He pressed himself against John, feeling all that hard body against his skin. John's bare chest was against his, but there was fabric between their groins and thighs. Keeping them from touching skin to skin everywhere.

He pulled himself into those arms again and found he was looking at the altar over John's shoulder. The place where the bad thing happened.

He shuddered. Then turned his eyes from those slabs of stone and looked at John again.

"Does it make any sense that I can feel so safe and scared at the same time?" he whispered.

John gave a single nod. "Perfectly," he said, so quietly Blue barely heard him. "That's exactly how I feel right now."

Blue started. What?

"You're scared?"

"And I feel safe at the same time. I feel safe with you. I trust you. But I'm afraid I will do something wrong. Especially right now. In this place. And that I will only make things worse."

Worse? How could they be worse? "You can't make it worse," he said.

And then he kissed John. Lightly at first, and then, somehow, wondrously, inexplicably, the passion came. He kissed John harder. Felt John grow harder through those fucking shorts.

John pulled back. "B-Blue. Wait."

Blue shook his head. "No," he replied.

"I... Blue... I don't want to hurt...."

"I don't think you *could* hurt me," Blue said and felt the miracle of it growing in his chest and heart and body. More. He felt himself getting hard. Miracle. Here.

Now.

"John, make love to me," he said, and tears stung his eyes. "Make this place sacred again."

John's eyes were huge. Filled with questions. Fear too? But yes, beneath it all more wonders. There was love. John loved him.

"My friends that worship nature. They say that all acts of love and pleasure are sacred to the spirits of nature. All acts of love and pleasure are the rituals. Worship with me, John. Please."

There was an eternal pause.

Then John kissed him.

Kissed him and held him and touched him and loved him.

The shorts were gone in less than an instant, and they pressed their hard cocks together as they kissed. They kissed each other everywhere. Mouths and eyes and cheeks and ears. Down necks and Adam's apples. Chests and nipples. Fingers and palms. The insides of elbows. Stomachs. Navels. Cocks. Knees. The backs of knees. The cleft of each other's asses. Feet and toes.

And when Blue asked John to fuck him, to his surprise, John said, "No."

No?

"No. Fuck *me*, Blue. Please."

Blue did.

With one last shiver, Blue made love with John over the altar. The bigger man beneath the smaller, looking deep into each other's eyes. Worshiped. Made sacred love. Acts of love and pleasure their ritual.

Eyes filled with love.

They came together with loud cries. But cries of pleasure and joy.

Not fear.

No pain.

No hurt.

Only love.

With love, they made the spot sacred again.

AFTER, THEY made their way together back to the beach, and to Blue's surprise, John made no move to put his clothes on. They walked naked, and oh, it wasn't scary. It was pure and wonderful, like it had been before.

They settled on their blanket, poured the last of the wine, and drank as they looked out over the lake. Blue had never been so happy in his entire life.

It was John who broke the silence. "The book I was reading…," he said. "The one about leaping?"

Blue gave a slight nod, wanting to hear more.

"That book says the Universe is unfolding just as it should. And it says we should leap."

"Leap?" Blue asked.

John nodded. "And trust that the net will appear. Alistair did it. Left and leapt and now he's apparently making money as an artist. And I thought no one could make it as an artist. I am so fucking proud of him!"

Blue laughed. John, Saying fuck.

Then John's eyes went wide. "Blue?"

"Yes?" he replied.

"Leap with me? I'm ready. I'm finally ready. Leap with me?"

Blue's heart swelled. That sounded wonderful.

"Yes," he said. "All the way."

B.G. THOMAS lives in Kansas City with his husband of more than a decade and their fabulous dogs Sarah Jane and Oliver. He is blessed to have a lovely daughter as well as many extraordinary friends. He has a great passion for life.

B.G. loves romance, comedies, fantasy, science fiction, and even horror—as far as he is concerned, as long as the stories are character driven and entertaining, it doesn't matter the genre. He has gone to literature conventions his entire adult life where he's been lucky enough to meet many of his favorite writers. He has made up stories since he was a child; it is where he finds his joy.

In the nineties, he wrote for gay adult magazines but stopped because the editors wanted all sex without plot. "The sex is never as important as the characters," he says. "Who cares what they are doing if we don't care about them?" Excited about the growing male/male romance market, he began writing again. He submitted a novella and was thrilled when it was accepted in four days. Since then the romantic tales have poured out of him. "It's like I'm somehow making up for a lifetime's worth of story-telling!"

"Leap, and the net will appear" is his personal philosophy and his message. "It is never too late," he testifies. "Pursue your dreams. They will come true!"

Website/blog: bthomaswriter.wordpress.com

BLACK BEAR GUEST RANCH

Do You Trust Me?

B.G. Thomas

The path to happiness starts with acceptance, and sometimes the chance for a bright, loving future means letting go of the past.

All his life, Neil Baxter has buried a large part of himself—the part that's attracted to other men. He married a woman and denied that side of him existed. And he plans to keep right on pretending to be straight after his beloved wife has passed away.

To help him deal with his grief, Neil's sister-in-law convinces him to vacation at a dude ranch. There, Neil meets Cole Thompson, a young, gorgeous, unabashedly gay wrangler—who is unabashedly attracted to Neil. And try as he might, Neil cannot deny he feels the same way. But desire soon becomes something more profound as the two men get to know each other. Cole is much more than a sexy cowboy: he's kind, spiritual, and intelligent. In fact, he's perfect for Neil… except he's a man, and Neil isn't ready to let go of a lifetime of denial. If he cannot find the courage to be true to himself, he might let something wonderful slip through his fingers.

www.dreamspinnerpress.com

B.G. Thomas
J. Scott Coatsworth
Jamie Fessenden
Michael Murphy

A MORE
PERFECT
UNION

On June 26, 2015, the Supreme Court of the United States made a monumental decision, and at long last, marriage equality became the law of the land. That ruling made history, and now gay and lesbian Americans will grow up in a country where they will never be denied the right to marry the person they love.

But what about the gay men who waited and wondered all of their lives if the day would ever come when they could stand beside the person they love and say "I do"?

Here, four accomplished authors—married gay men—offer their take on that question as they explore same-sex relationships, love, and matrimony. Men who thought legal marriage was a right they would never have. Men who, unbelievably, now stand legally joined with the men they love. With this book, they share the magic and excitement of dreams that came true—in tales of fantasy and romance with a dose of their personal experiences in the mix.

To commemorate the anniversary of full marriage equality in the US, this anthology celebrates the idea of marriage itself--and the universal truth of it that applies to us all, gay or straight.

www.dreamspinnerpress.com

NEW
LEASE

B.G. THOMAS

Wade Porter spent his whole life in the shadow of a lover who doled out snippets of love and time as he saw fit—and who insisted that love stay deep in the closet. But now that man is gone, and Wade finds the oceanside cottage where they spent so many weekends together in the Florida Keys cold and empty. He has come one last time, not even sure he wants to keep living.

To his surprise, the house next door is occupied by another bereaved and lonely man. Kent Walker is an artist of romantic gay paintings who is open to the future—and determinedly interested in Wade. Kent wants to show Wade the beauty in being an openly gay man and the possibilities for a real relationship.

Maybe Kent can help Wade let go of the past and discover a better way to live—and love.

www.dreamspinnerpress.com

THE REAL THING

B.G. THOMAS

Bryan Mills has fantasized about cowboys all his life. Real cowboys, that is. He even dresses in what his roommate calls "cowboy drag" when he visits his favorite bar, in the hope of attracting the attentions of a genuine cowboy. But all he usually finds are posers and guys his own age.

Then one night, to his surprise, Curtis Hansen buys him a beer, and Bryan has no doubt this is the real thing. Curtis is a rugged, gorgeous man who is every bit a cowboy. He even owns his own ranch. What follows is about the most amazing night of Bryan's young life.

But can they move beyond a night of incredible sex when Bryan admits to Curtis that the only horse he's ever ridden was a birthday party pony? And that he's nothing but a poser himself? Maybe, just maybe, Curtis can find the real cowboy inside Bryan, and they can ride off into the sunset together!

www.dreamspinnerpress.com

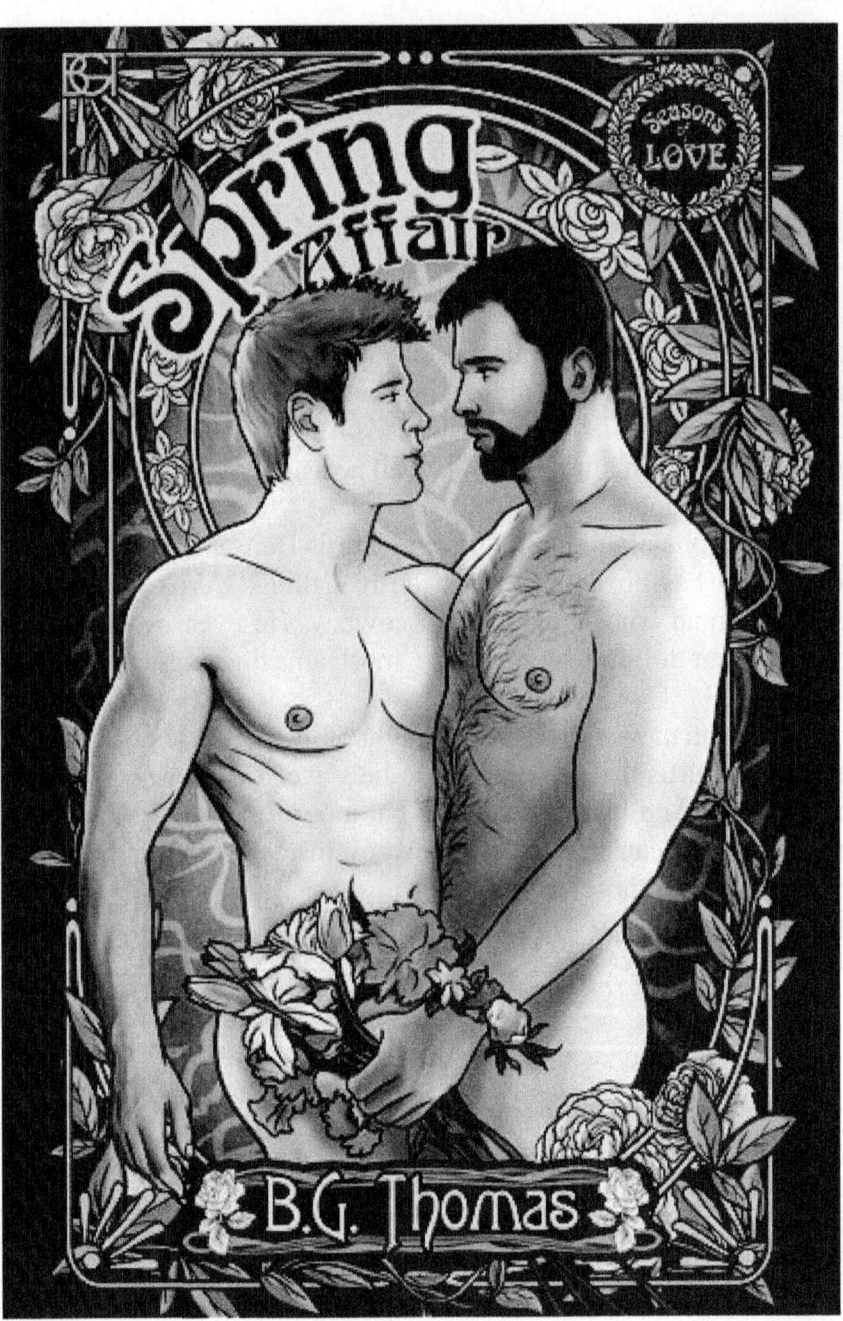

Seasons of Love: Book One

Sloan McKenna is going through a tough time. His beloved mother has recently passed away, leaving him her house and beautiful garden. But should he keep the house? Sell it? To make matters worse, he's in love with one of his best friends, Asher, a man who can't (or won't) love him back.

Sloan's neighbor, Max Turner, is married to an ambitious woman with far-reaching dreams, including moving the family to France. But Max is happy teaching at the local college and living in their nice, quiet town. Then he discovers his fourteen-year-old son is not only gay, but out and proud as well. That throws him into complete disarray, for more than one reason....

When Max's wife leaves on a two-month business trip to Paris, circumstances throw the two men together. As they become friends, Sloan finds himself falling in love with Max, who is completely unavailable... just like Asher. As for Max, he is discovering that both his son's coming out and his new friendship with Sloan are stirring up feelings he thought buried long ago. Spring is a time for rebirth—Is there any way the two men can find happiness and a new beginning?

www.dreamspinnerpress.com

Seasons of Love: Book Two

Scott Aberdeen doesn't believe in Santa Claus, the Easter Bunny, or God. Or love—at least, he knows no one will ever love him. After all, he has carried a torch for his best friend Sloan for a decade, hoping his feelings will be returned one day. But when Sloan finds springtime love with another man, Scott's fantasies are crushed and his skepticism confirmed.

Cedar Carrington, raised by rock star parents, leads a free-spirited, nomadic life, never staying in one place for long. Due to a dark past he refuses to share or even think about, he is willing to let men into his bed for sex, but never for the night.

When Scott finds himself camping in the middle of nowhere with over a hundred men who all believe in love—and faeries and a magickal gay brotherhood—he's pretty sure he's in the wrong place. And when Cedar connects with cynical, critical Scott, he wonders how he could be falling in for this man of all men. But hearts and lives have been transformed at the Heartland Men's Festival before, and it might be just the place where two very different men can release their pain and find true love at last.

www.dreamspinnerpress.com

CPSIA information can be obtained
at www.ICGtesting.com
Printed in the USA
LVOW03s0850260517
535793LV00014B/577/P